# Training Wheels

By Michael Stringer

Martin Sisters Publishing

Published by

Ivy House Books, a division of Martin Sisters Publishing, LLC

www. martinsisterspublishing. com

ISBN: 978-1-937273-61-3
Fiction
Printed in the United States of America
Martin Sisters Publishing, LLC

Cover photo by Max Kosydar

*For my girls, Laura, Cadence, and Emma*

*With fond appreciation for the love and support*
*of my parents and siblings*

An imprint of Martin Sisters Publishing, LLC

*"In each family a story is playing itself out, and each family's story embodies its hope and despair."*

~ Auguste Napier

# Chapter One

*I'm three weeks away from starting high school, and I still* haven't kissed a girl all summer. It just doesn't seem right. I'll be fifteen soon, and I can count on one hand the number of females I've kissed on the lips. Unfortunately, that number includes my mother and two overly affectionate aunts; gross, I know, but true. The only steamy moment of my life happened last year. Her name was Dana, an older, lanky girl with straight, golden hair down to her waist and braces on her teeth. She lived around the block about five houses down. One slow, summer day we climbed into our rundown powerboat on the side of our house, huddled underneath the bow, and several minutes later started making out. She taught me how to French kiss. It was a little sloppy, and my lips and tongue kept bumping against her jagged braces, but I started to get the hang of it. My mother pulled her car into the driveway before anything more interesting could happen, anyway. I was bummed out when she told me that her family was moving away. I thought she might be the one, I mean, the one who'd finally end all the mystery about sex for me.

Instead, another year has slipped away and I sit here, playing a game of cards with my older brother, Jay, and his best friend, bored senseless and trying to escape the smothering heat outside. I can't even call my own best friend to do something. He left yesterday with his family to visit his favorite uncle in Colorado. He gets to hike and fish and swim on a ranch for the rest of August, while I'm stuck in good, old, ordinary Rossmoor. That's where my family lives, in Rossmoor, California, about fifteen miles northeast of downtown Los Angeles. I shouldn't complain, really, or even call it ordinary. We have just about everything a kid could want here. We're situated roughly an hour in either direction from some awesome ski resorts, lakes, and beaches. And what luck that Walt Disney decided to build his amazing theme park only thirty miles away.

Our stucco, four bedroom house sits within the far southeastern corner of the city, in what I've heard the adults describe as a 'white collar, middle class' neighborhood. I guess that means the families are doing just fine and all the fathers either have steady work or office jobs. The boundaries of Rossmoor extend all the way up into the foothills of the enormous San Gabriel Mountains. Mostly it's a decent town, and I like living here, except sometimes the smog pushes up against that towering wall of earth and gets trapped, hovering like a dirty blanket over our heads. Smoggy days like this one have become far more common in recent years, putting a chokehold on my lungs and making me think twice before going outside to play ball during the mid-day hours. Personally, I put the blame squarely on all the gas-guzzling family wagons and big sedans that chug through our streets, blasting out black exhaust into the air. On really awful days, without the Santa Ana winds to sweep away the smog, I can barely make out the familiar ridgeline of our mountains, which always astonishes me.

My street is called Lyncrest Road, a cul-de-sac comprised of eleven houses that curves around in a bent L-shape before it forks into two separate streets, both funneling into the main access roads. I can't imagine growing up on a better street, because it expands into a wide circle at the enclosed end and another one at the open-ended turn, offering tons of space for games and sports. I've skinned my knees or fell off my bike or bloodied an elbow on my street more times than I cared to remember. But there was one thing my parents never had to worry about: speeding cars. Drivers were forced to slow down around the corner turn, and besides that, not many visitors or unknown cars ventured into our quiet neighborhood.

Despite no girlfriend prospects and my best friend in another state, these next few days did offer something kind of special. My parents, John and Audrey Copeland, left this morning for a short vacation to San Francisco. My sixteen-year-old sister Rachel and I were excited to have the house to ourselves, unsupervised for the first time. Riding a wave of support from Jay, who's twenty-three, and my oldest sister, Sarah, who's twenty, we convinced our parents that we could stay away from trouble. It wasn't so hard to do. My siblings and I are well aware that our parents favor any activity that empowers their children with responsibility and independence. And they practice what they preach. They've spent a small fortune on self-improvement seminars, getting in touch with your inner-child classes, or any other personal growth activities they could track down. I suppose they were trying to break the monotony of routine family life. Some days can get pretty dull around here, especially during the summer. I guess all those seminars helped balance the daily grind. It was interesting to observe my parents whenever they returned from a weekend session—they floated through the air on a magic carpet of high self-esteem and self-love. The euphoria never lasted more than a few days, though, which I assumed was the reason they kept returning for more.

So, while Jay and Sarah were told to keep their eyes on us, for all intents and purposes, Rachel and I were alone. Jay had established a track record for appearing and disappearing without forewarning, and Sarah often stayed with friends while searching for a cheap apartment closer to her job. I never knew who was coming and going, and certainly not why. But I did know that both of them were flat broke, often returning home as refuge and respite, doing laundry and filling up their stomachs on free food. Our house had become their crash pad.

The same could be said for some of Jay's friends. On any given day they'd plow through the front door and just melt right into the furniture. It didn't even matter whether Jay was around. I often walked through rolling clouds of smoke, carrying the aroma of tobacco or grass from room to room. I've never tried weed, although I soon became familiar with the smell. Any time my parents skipped town, there was an endless parade of visitors who drank and smoked, cranking the rock and roll music to ear-throbbing levels. Even when my parents were home, some of my brother's best friends were given a pass to stay for a few days, sometimes weeks, in exchange for good behavior. They had a pretty sweet deal going here, free room and board. I often wondered if they had anywhere else to go. Would they be homeless without the Copeland residence? Somehow, my house became a regular stop along the freeloader highway. On some days, it was comforting to have them around, and on others, they were as suffocating as the heat and smog outside.

"Sucked up that trick, just like a black hole," said Warren Gaffney, sweeping in the cards from the living room coffee table.

I always enjoyed playing the game of Hearts with my brother and his friends. When Jay needed a third player to start the game, he called me in from the bullpen. I'd improved as a player, although I needed some lucky cards to beat my brother and his buddies, all nearly a decade older than me.

"A black hole?" I inquired.

"Yeah, some guy found evidence of black holes in the universe, these huge voids in space that just gobble up anything that comes near them," said Warren, whom everyone called the 'Doctor' for reasons still unclear to me. The Doctor had a loose, offbeat way about him; nothing like my older brother. He often strutted around the house without a shirt, wearing only denim jeans that flared with bell bottoms. Lately he'd been sporting a twisted rope gold chain around his neck, which stood out against his tan, bare chest. For a guy in his early twenties, he had very little hair on his chest or arms, except for a small patch of curly black strands between his pecs. He and Jay attended college together up north at Cal Berkeley, but neither graduated. Maybe this was how their friendship bonded, through the misery of lost chances. I heard that Jay failed to graduate because he argued with his professor over the subject of his thesis paper and told him to shove it. Now that took big balls, or just stubborn stupidity; I haven't decided yet, though I'm leaning towards stubborn stupidity.

"You've been watching too much *Star Trek*, man," said Jay. "That's why they call it science fiction."

"No, it's real. I read it in a magazine," countered the Doctor. "This dude is some kind of genius. He's strapped to this big wheelchair, looks like he's barely alive."

"So where does it all go, the stuff that falls into this black hole?" asked Jay, his intense, dark brown eyes glued to his cards.

"Nobody knows, man. It's a scientific mystery," said the Doctor. "Just vanishes into space; maybe into another dimension."

"Wish I could push a few girls I know in there," said Jay, making the Doctor unleash his rapid, shotgun laugh, which drew attention to his large, sharp nose that flared, "maybe a sister now and then."

Jay led a ten of spades, and I only had one extra spade remaining in my hand. I was in deep trouble, since I was holding the queen. Jay stood and carefully flipped over the record on the turntable, returning the needle to the outside edge.

"I don't know, I think your sisters are pretty cool," chimed in the Doctor, tossing the jack of spades onto the table. Jay returned to the table, firing a penetrating gaze at his best friend. "As far as sisters go, I mean," the Doctor backtracked.

"Believe me, she's not your type," said Jay, annoyed by the topic of conversation.

"Who, Sarah?"

"Who else would I be talking about?" said Jay.

"Hey man, she has all the right body parts, that's the only type I need."

The Doctor chuckled and backhanded me on the shoulder, but clearly Jay was bothered. We all avoided eye contact for a few moments. For the first time in a long while I felt included in a discussion between Jay and his friend that actually went beyond small talk or sports. In recent months I'd become more attuned to the verbal exchanges between Jay's friends and Sarah, and until this instant, I never considered how they affected him. Maybe Jay was trying to protect Sarah from his hound dog friends. From what I'd seen, they passed around girlfriends like they were trading baseball cards. Jay led the five of spades, and I was forced to play the queen and eat the points.

"Damn," I said, dumping the queen on the table and sweeping the cards into my pile.

"Brutal game, isn't it?" teased the Doctor.

"Not if you don't take the queen," I said.

"Argh, a stone-cold bitch, she is," said the Doctor in a gruff pirate's voice.

"Yeah, and I think she's attracted to Kevin," Jay added.

"She likes younger, better looking men," I joked.

The Doctor laughed and tossed an examining glance over at Jay, who broke into a wide grin. It wasn't much, but a grin was enough for all of us to feel like the bumpy moment about Sarah had passed.

"The queen of spades is the real black hole," said the Doctor, clearing his throat. "She sucks up points like a vacuum cleaner."

"Two," said Jay.

"Six," said the Doctor.

"And that must mean you have eighteen, big guy," teased Jay.

"I can count," I said.

Jay recorded the points on the score sheet while I began to shuffle the cards. The Doctor snatched the last cigarette from his Marlboro pack and began to light up. I couldn't imagine why anyone would want to smoke during such a hot and smoggy day.

"When do your parents get back from that marriage counseling deal?" the Doctor asked innocently, drawing deeply from his smoke. My hands faltered, and the cards fluttered all over the table. Jay froze from recording the points, fixing his gaze to the table.

"Yeah, Jay, when do they get back from marriage counseling?" I asked with an accusatory tone.

I rarely saw my brother flustered and susceptible in the same instant. His composure during hard moments and the way he tactfully removed himself from almost any difficult situation were talents I admired and hoped to emulate someday. Except hearing the news about our parents, I had no intention of letting him slip away from the table without some answers.

"Did I say counseling?" stammered the Doctor. "Shit, I must be thinking of my parents, they're so messed up," he said with an ironic huff, taking a nervous drag from his cigarette.

"Your parents are awesome, Kevin, strong and dedicated. It's a vacation, right? San Francisco. What a bitchin' place. Berkeley baby, Cal Bears, Haight Ashbury? Come on, am I right, huh?"

The Doctor enthusiastically held up his hand for a high five. Jay just gulped hard and glanced away, annoyed that he fell into this trap.

"Jay, what's he talking about?" I asked.

"The game's over," said Jay, averting his eyes from me.

"Yeah, right, game's over," repeated the Doctor. They sprang from the sofa and started to exit the living room like criminals escaping the scene of the crime.

"Jay," I said. They paused.

"I have to split," said the Doctor. "I'll check you later."

Just before exiting the Doctor mouthed the word "sorry" to Jay and made a fast getaway out the front door.

"I *knew* something was going on around here. What's wrong with Mom and Dad?" I asked.

"Oh you don't know jack, and neither does the Doctor," said Jay. "He's always throwing stuff around, like that black hole thing. What a load of crap."

"I can tell, you're hiding something from me," I asserted.

"Just get off my back, okay?" he said, bolting for the hallway.

As the youngest, no one ever told me anything important. Still, I was no longer a child and had the right to know; I needed to know. Lately I'd noticed a hint of sadness in my mother's vibrant brown eyes, and despite my subtle attempts, I couldn't determine the reasons. The usual affection between my parents, the brief hugs and kisses and playful gestures in front of their children, had all but vanished in recent months. On some level, I suppose I knew something fundamental had changed between my parents, a necessary ingredient to a healthy relationship. I just didn't know what and why.

⚛︎

I paused at Jay's bedroom doorway, the tension filling my chest. I peered up the steps and caught him turning at the top and fading around the side wall. Jay made it quite clear that his room was a private place where he could be at peace with his music. If someone wanted to talk to him, they did so from the base of the stairs.

Making that first step was gut-check time. The uncarpeted board creaked. Moments later Jay blasted some music on his stereo, which gave me the courage to keep moving. I ascended the stairs while the haunting voice of Jim Morrison reverberated against the walls. When I reached the top, Jay stood in the middle of his room with his back turned. I had nothing ready to say. I felt in the wrong place at the wrong time. Standing there, he somehow loomed so much taller than me, and observing him alone with his thoughts reminded me of my father. It was the way he rested heavily on his right foot and casually stretched out his left leg. His thin, dark brown hair curled at the ends and had grown to his shoulders, and he was holding something in front of his waist, looking down.

The afternoon sun poured through his windows, and a layer of dust floated in the shafts of light. The room smelled musty, and I was short of breath. Inadvertently I coughed. Jay turned, and his surprise quickly evaporated. I noticed a photo in his hand. He casually shoved it into his pocket. I knew by his forced blank expression that the photo held meaning for him, and in this case, probably for me, too.

"What do you want?" Jay asked.

"I wanna know what's going on around here," I said.

"Nothing, go away."

"What'd you hide in your pocket?"

"Do you come up here and snoop around when I'm not home?

That's not cool, man," said Jay.

"No, I don't. But sometimes…"

"Sometimes what?"

"Well, I do come up here…"

"I knew it. I should keep a damn lock on my door."

"No, it's not like that. I just like looking out the window and into the other yards. Everything seems different. I can see why you like being alone up here."

Jay didn't respond, but I'd learned to read his subtle expressions. My words had connected in some way and made sense, but I'll never know how. He kept his emotions in check, private, safely locked away from predators seeking entry into his heart. I'm always trying to read the expressions of my family, since no one tells me anything of real significance. Many of my conclusions are based purely on nonverbal interpretation.

"I may not be around as much anymore, but this is still my room," he said. "And I don't like everybody hangin' out up here."

Just as he finished shouting his last word over "Break On Through," the song ended. We both agonized through several seconds of awkward silence. Then as soon as it came, the silence left us, similar to a sudden breeze that rises and falls. Another song piped into the room, and I felt as though something had been lost. There have been many of these lost moments with my brother, floating away and popping like soap bubbles. Then he said something I couldn't hear over the music.

"What?" I said.

"Leave me alone," he shouted. His desperate tone was alarming. Leaving me no choice, I turned for the stairs. As I made my way down the steps, I sadly concluded that I'd never once left his room knowing anything more than before I entered it. I was hoping that someday that record would change.

# Chapter Two

*It was hours later, and I couldn't stop thinking about the way Jay* reacted so nervously to my questions. I was aching with unbearable curiosity. The tension and bickering between my parents had escalated in recent months, but I had no evidence or understanding about the reasons. I just figured that all married couples went through these phases. What I learned today was my first real clue and I felt a strong pull in my gut to pursue more, to find the truth. I don't like being in the dark about things, especially when they happen under my own roof. Rachel was talking on the phone in my parents' bedroom, while her best friend, Jamie, sat on the bed nearby and painted her nails. The coast was clear.

At the top of the stairs I flipped on the light. It was a dim and dreary room in the lamplight. Jay's frameless bed was unmade and album covers were strewn all over the beige, shag-carpeted floor. The carpet had several cigarette burns and liquid stains. I pulled out the desk drawer expecting to find it stuffed with junk. It held only a few pens and pencils, some music store receipts, and two old issues of *Sports Illustrated*. I rummaged through the rest of the desk but found little else besides some old 45s, a few beaten paperbacks covered with a film of sand, and some letters. I was tempted to read the letters and learn more about my brother until I concluded I didn't come upstairs to pry into his personal life. I suppose that was a contradiction, considering my mission.

I searched through his closet, which only turned up some dirty clothes and smelly basketball shoes. I stood in the center of the room and made a full visual sweep along all four off-white walls. Then I realized he probably didn't hide the photo at all. He'd probably forgotten all about our brief exchange this afternoon. I wheeled back around to the closet and searched for the shorts he was wearing. Digging through a pile of clothes I found them— brown corduroy shorts with baggy pockets. I plunged my hand into the right front pocket and felt the sharp edges of a photograph. I withdrew the photo and hurried to the lamp. I slid the photo under the light and saw the image of my father standing with his arms around an unknown woman, their heads angled together, both beaming with joy. The woman had short, cropped, auburn hair framing her angular, lightly freckled face, and to my limited knowledge my father had never appeared happier or more content in his entire life. I was fairly certain this was no one in my family tree, and he didn't socialize with people from his office. Someone had scribbled the date May 21, 1974 on the back side, which was only about three months ago. If this photo had no significance, and if this woman wasn't suspicious in some manner, I had to wonder why Jay tried to hide it from me.

I descended the stairs, just about to enter the hallway when I heard, "Find anything interesting up there?" Startled, I turned and found Jamie standing in the open doorframe that leads to our backyard. Her fiery gaze at me was piercing. She took a drag from her cigarette and exhaled a puffy ball of smoke into the still night air, our silence only interrupted by the rhythmic chirps of crickets. It was a vision to behold, the sexy way she smoked. A cigarette, for Jamie, seemed like a natural extension of her right hand. She checked into our hotel now and then, more as an escape shelter than from any real desire to be here. She and Rachel met in continuation school, a place where the school district sent students with severe behavioral or academic issues. In Rachel's case, she had the smarts, but absolutely no interest in attending classes or learning through textbooks. I wasn't aware of Jamie's issues, but I knew that except for her hygiene skills, she was captivating on every conceivable level. She often came over in a frazzled state of disarray, with tangled, oily hair, greasy skin, and ragged clothes that, while colorful and interesting, appeared no better than thrift store quality. She dragged along a noticeable shadow of disappointment, as though the world was torturing her soul and wouldn't leave her in peace. But none of that bothered me. I was attracted to her like a moth to a flame, a sad little flame that barely flickered and needed reinforcement. I wanted to heal her, and yet I knew this was improbable. I would've settled for an endless night of necking and rubbing our sweaty bodies together, though I knew this, too, was a miracle not likely to happen.

"When you gonna get yourself a girlfriend?" she said with a twinkle in her sparkling blue eyes that seemed to flicker, as if a light was rotating inside them.

"I don't know, I'll get around to it," I replied.

"I bet I know what you want."

Her tone left me thinking that maybe I was about to receive it. Miracles did happen, after all. I've read about them.

"You want a perky little cheerleader with long legs and big tits," she said, flipping her light brown curls that fell just below her shoulder. "That's what every boy your age wants."

She wrapped her full lips around the cigarette again and inhaled in a suggestive way. She probably knew there was power in that visual, made somehow more alluring by the paleness of her malnourished complexion. She tapped the base of her high-heeled platform shoe twice against the wood floor, like a nervous tick, which caused her torpedo-shaped breasts to jiggle inside her blouse. Then she lowered her hand from her mouth to her side and the pounds of silver bracelets on her wrist clinked together. Jamie was a moving piece of art with the most intriguing features.

"I really don't have a type, I guess," I said.

"What about me, am I your type?" she said. While I fumbled for the response to that remarkable question, she erupted into laughter. Then she thrust the cigarette toward my face. "Here, you ever tried it?"

Without hesitation I took the cigarette and brought it to my mouth. I've tried cigarettes before, but never have I inhaled so deeply. When the smoke filled my chest, I coughed.

Jamie giggled and said, "You don't inhale if you're not used to it, dum-dum. You let it soak into your mouth… tickle your insides. Then little by little you let it slide down into your lungs. It's easy, watch."

She snatched the cigarette from my hand and demonstrated her point, inhaling and stretching out her long, porcelain neck. Most of the smoke hovered in and around her mouth, suspended like a small cloud. I felt the blood rush to my dick, so I snuck my hands inside my pockets and pushed out with my fingers. God made pockets for young men, I was certain.

"See?" she said, tipping the ashes onto the porch, "real smooth."

I thought she noticed something below my waist, and then she turned away and gazed at the stars, resting her head against the doorframe. She sifted her fingers through her long hair and drifted somewhere else with her thoughts. I'd seen her tune out like this before, the byproduct of a troubled mind, I'd always figured.

"A lot of boys like me. They buzz around me like bees around a hive," she said with a slight southern drawl that came out of nowhere. "They always tell me I'm beautiful, but I don't believe 'em much."

"You should, I mean, I think you are," I said, taking a swing for the fence.

I felt myself blush. She didn't respond for the longest time and with a peculiar, lost expression, she tried to focus on me, as if she couldn't recall the topic of conversation.

"Will you promise me something, Kevin?"

"Yeah, sure."

"When you get a girlfriend, treat her nice. There's no reason why a person can't be nice."

She inhaled another long drag from her cigarette and then leaned out the doorway and flicked the butt onto the grass with her thumb and index finger. She flashed a soothing smile and then stepped back inside and brushed right by and into the hallway.

I watched her stroll down the hallway with slow and thoughtful strides into my parents' bedroom, her swiveling hips causing her skirt to swing side to side. I tried to imagine her body naked, except the image slipped away.

Remembering my mission, I entered my bedroom and hid the photo inside a book on my shelf. I had to hope Jay wouldn't notice it was missing, because I'd be forced into a confrontation. If I wanted the truth behind the mysterious woman, it was entirely possible that I'd have to confront him anyway.

🚲

Later that night, I had the disturbing dream again, the one I've often dreamt since the age of eight. A bulging, one-eyed, half-man, half-monster crawls over our back fence with an axe and tries to break into my room and hack me to a bloody death. Then I wake up, startled and clammy, his disgusting and distorted face still vivid in my mind. I've heard it's impossible to die in the middle of your own dream, otherwise you'd really be dead. I didn't fully understand the concept. In any case, I didn't intend to give the crazy half-man, half-monster, half a chance.

# Chapter Three

*The next day I remembered the photo and the image popped into* my head. I pulled the book down from the shelf and withdrew the photo from between pages fifty and fifty-one. The mystery woman dared me to learn of her identity and the reasons for snuggling into my father.

I didn't think I could trust Rachel with the knowledge of my theft. She humored me, but she adored Jay with a kind of religious devotion. They were rebellious in ways Sarah and I—even if we tried—could never match. Rachel might use the information against me the next time I crossed or angered her. Still, it was possible that she hadn't seen the photo before nor even knew it existed. I elected to see what she knew.

The door to Rachel's room was open as I walked down the hall to find her. I heard another door open behind me and turned to find her exiting the bathroom, wrapped in a light blue terry-cloth towel, her hair twisted up in another towel, and steam floating into the hallway. Rachel could tie a towel around her chest and make it hold just right. She has what most guys would consider a knockout figure, and her smile—when she displays it—is sweet and playful. Her serious eyes measure you, and when she feels like exposing you for a mistake or insincerity, her eyes become mirrors that clearly reflect your own guilt.

"Take a picture, it lasts longer," Rachel said passing me, walking with her erect, fluid stride, like a model on the runway.

"I wouldn't wanna break the camera. You're not looking your best right now," I said.

"Best you'll ever see."

"Then I might have to kill myself."

She snorted and entered her room and then slammed the door in my face. This had been the extent of our communication recently, a series of snappy and sarcastic remarks that were meaningless and meant to keep the other at a distance. Not so long ago, we were actually quite fond of each other; best buddies even. We were the first to start games outside with our neighborhood friends and the last to retreat inside for supper. I didn't know why we'd embarked upon this new, unpleasant phase in our relationship. Everything was changing in my house and moving in directions I couldn't follow. I knocked on the door.

"What do you want?" shouted Rachel.

"I need to talk to you," I said.

"About what?"

"Something important, can I come in?"

"What…ever," she said.

I opened the door half expecting to catch a glimpse of her naked. But she'd already thrown on a pair of white underwear and a bra. In a way I was relieved, and in another way, mildly disappointed. I don't get many chances to see a real, live naked girl, even if that girl is my sister.

My room is mostly composed of dark, earthy colors, whereas Rachel's is an explosion of color. The shag carpet is a bright blend of orange and yellow, and her dresser drawer is painted white with yellow knobs. Along the back wall she constructed a sort of coffee table, which consisted of two pinewood boards propped up on either side by gray cinder blocks. On these boards she kept her multi-colored candles and burned enough different types of incense that they blended into one, heavy perfume scent. Her closet, which is directly underneath Jay's stairs, has accordion style doors, painted white. When our dog, Amber, an energetic Golden Retriever, was nowhere to be found, we'd often find her gnawing on a shoe in the back corner of Rachel's closet. The most distinctive trait to her room is a huge poster of Elvis Presley above her bed, wearing his white jumpsuit and performing his Aloha in Hawaii concert. Recently, and for reasons perplexing to us, Elvis had become Rachel's one and only true savior. I, on the other hand, have two saviors: Barbara Eden of *I Dream of Jeannie*, and the movie actress, Raquel Welch. I have a pull-out poster of Barbara posing in her skin-tight red and pink Jeannie costume, and right next to her a magazine cut-out picture of Raquel in a tight, white tank top, holding a sparkling stick of dynamite like a big firecracker. If I was stranded on a desert island and could have only one blonde or one brunette to join me—in the biblical way—those two would represent their hair color group just fine.

"What do you think of this top?" asked Rachel. She held up a cream-colored cotton top against her chest that plunged in a semicircle at the neckline and had lace patterns at the ends of the short sleeves.

"You want my opinion on fashion?" I replied, surprised.

"I'm desperate."

"Well, it's hard to tell when it's not on you."

She grimaced and draped the top over her upper body.

"There, God forbid you should have to use your imagination."

"You want my opinion or not?"

"What...ever."

"Looks fine." She rolled her eyes and clicked her tongue, annoyed with me.

"Do you think it'll make my boobs look too big?" said Rachel, twisting side to side in the full-length mirror.

"Uh... I don't really see that as a problem."

She rolled her hazel-blue eyes again. One day, I thought, her eyes would stick like that.

"Who cares about guys, anyway? All they do is crack lame jokes about my chest. They treat you like dirt sometimes, but I know they'd all drop their pants in a heartbeat if I gave them the green light. They're so immature."

I felt my face turn warm. As much as I wanted to think otherwise, I still wasn't quite ready to graduate to these kinds of conversations with my siblings. I always felt a little strange inside, as if I'd crossed a sacred boundary from which I could never return. Rachel checked herself again, and while she didn't seem satisfied, she left the top on and searched for another item.

"Where you goin'?" I asked.

"That's really none of your business, is it?"

"Sorry if I take an interest in my sister's life."

"Why should you start now?"

"Because you've always been pretty boring up until now. Now things are getting interesting."

"What do you mean?" she asked sincerely.

"You're getting into a lot more trouble with Mom and Dad, and you're starting to bring home some real hot friends. That's always a bonus."

Initially she was puzzled by my comment and then her eyes lit up knowingly.

"So who is it?" she asked.

"Huh?" I grunted.

"I know, it's Jamie. You have a thing for Jamie, don't you?" asked Rachel.

"She's okay."

"She's a woman, you're a boy-child. Get real. She's dated guys twice your age."

"Does she have a boyfriend?"

Rachel paused from fixing her hair in the mirror and shot me a disapproving look. "She doesn't date virgins. Take off your training wheels and she might notice you're even alive. Besides, you don't wanna get mixed up with a girl like Jamie. She has..." Rachel paused for quite some time, checking her hair again in the mirror and said, "oh, why don't you just find a girl your own age?"

"We talked a little last night," I said.

"What'd she say?"

"She wanted to know if I had a girlfriend, and I said no. I think she was happy to hear that."

Rachel pushed out her distinctive, explosive, high-pitched laugh, which seemed oddly misplaced considering her caustic attitude every time she set foot inside this house. Yet on those rare occasions when she let one fly, I was reminded of the playful sister I once knew and all the good times we had.

"And then you woke up, right?" she said, applying some blue eyeliner.

"Whatever happened to that loser you were dating, the motocross rider. What was his name?"

"Chad. It didn't work out."

"Smelled like a dirty car engine, huh?"

"We just didn't click, no great loss. He was just like all the rest. Thought with his prick. I need a little more mystery, you know? Somebody who can appreciate me for who I am, wants to have fun, and someone who can keep me entertained," said Rachel, primping her clothing and twisting to view her entire reflection in the mirror.

"By entertained, you mean they should have lots of weed," I said with sarcasm.

"Shut up, Kevy," she snapped. She knew I despised that name. She strapped on her leather shoulder bag. "Everybody gets high. You will too, when you grow up," she said leaning into my face, starting to pass me on the way out.

"Wait," I said.

"What now?"

"Do you know who this woman is?"

I extended the photo to Rachel, and she examined it with an acute interest, though nothing registered. I sensed, however, that she was wrestling with the same question I was: Who was this suspicious woman, and why did my typically reserved father look so jubilant next to her? She jabbed the photo back at me.

"Never seen her before. Could be a relative, we have a ton of relatives. Where'd you get it?"

I wasn't prepared to answer that question, and I was certain it showed in my apprehensive reaction.

"I found it…on the floor in Mom and Dad's room," I said, not so convincingly.

The answer pacified Rachel but only to a degree. "It could be anyone… anyone at all. Maybe it's someone from work, a friend of mom's, who knows?" she said.

"I was just curious."

"Don't make any trouble," she said, starting to leave again.

"That's your department."

She flipped a dismissive hand at me without turning around and just before leaving her room, blew a quick kiss to Elvis on the wall. It was obvious she knew nothing of the mysterious woman in the picture and for the most part, could care less. Rachel was a dead end. I stood and stared at Elvis, trying to figure out what all the big fuss was about.

# Chapter Four

*I went for a bike ride to clear my head and devise a plan.*
Cruising through the streets of Rossmoor with the air rushing
against my face somehow made everything come into focus. Most
of our streets were wide and well-paved, which made my town
ideal for cycling. I have a blistering fast Peugeot ten-speed bike that
really cooks on smooth, open roads. I pumped the pedals at high
speed, leaning up and forward like a jockey on a thoroughbred
horse. I always keep two primary views in constantly shifting focus:
the stretch of road about thirty yards ahead and the path directly in
front of my tires.

I rode by the property that backs up against our house. The
man who lives there often works and digs in his backyard garden
and generally keeps to himself. Actually, we've never uttered a
single word to each other. I've never seen a woman in his yard, nor
heard a female's voice from within the house. He has jet-black hair,

and his shoulders are always hunched over, his eyes surveying the soil like a beachcomber with a metal detector. I've never once captured a full frontal shot of his face, and no longer tried to. My dream image of the half-man, half-monster probably originates with him, from the sheer mystery of his persona. Of course, my dream could stem from Mr. Resnik next door. He bangs and clinks and clanks his tools in his work shed right outside my window every evening, while shouting profanities at his two sons, Matt, who was thirteen, and Ronnie, eleven. Those boys are constantly infuriating their short-tempered father. It made matters even worse that I didn't have curtains on my windows, so my imagination ran wild with frightening images and evil doings. I guess it's not so unusual to have uncovered windows, although I'm certain my nightmares are aided by the black of night, which makes my room a ghostly shadow dance of tree limbs and leaves. I never ride by the monster man's house without searching for a woman or any other signs of life. Once again, I didn't see evidence of either.

I peddled up the main boulevard and underneath the huge eucalyptus trees that tunnel over and give the street an ominous slant. I decided to stop by the liquor store for some Jolly Rancher apple sticks and Now or Later watermelon chew candies. As I exited the store with my candy and began to unlock my bike, I heard two men chattering nearby.

"All right, I'll bet you a clean, crisp twenty that I can sell that car for five hundred bucks," said one man, pointing to a parked Ford Pinto that had chipped paint and rusted tires.

"Who are you, Cal Worthington?" said the other man, a short, gruffly character with a beer belly. "You'll never see anything more than two-fifty for that piece of junk. You know those cars blow up, don't you?"

"What's the matter, don't have the stomach for a little wager?"

"Oh hell yes, I have the stomach," he said, holding his big belly and laughing.

They shook hands on the deal as I hopped on my bike and rode away. Then like a sparkplug that ignites an engine, an idea fired in my brain.

I was shooting baskets later in the day when my brother rumbled up in his custom Gran Torino car. It's not a newer model, but it's an awesome piece of machinery. It has thin blue and red lines that run the length of the white sides and custom-made mag wheels that reek of sportiness. He started to walk up the driveway, lost in his thoughts.

"Wanna play a game of OUT?" I asked. I zipped a chest pass that hit him square in the numbers. As though receiving a pass from a teammate, he immediately launched a shot from the corner of our driveway. His jump shot form is impeccable. He stretches his lanky six-foot-two frame to the extremes so that his fingertips extend to their highest points above his head, and his toes point almost straight at the ground. As the ball made its high arc toward the basket, I wondered again why he didn't continue with the sport in college. As a guard, he made first team all-league in high school for a team that advanced to the state semifinals. Then, for some reason, he gave up competitive basketball and turned to music. Looking back, it was probably a wise career choice, since he had no shot at the NBA. After all, he was a Copeland man. We have strong hand-eye coordination and agility, but my parents forgot to pass down some speedy feet and high jumping ability. The ball swished softly through the net and spun down to the cement.

"Not right now," he said.

"I'll make you a bet you can't refuse."

"You? What do you have to offer me? You barely have a nickel to your name, and I know you don't get much of an allowance."

"I'll wash your car three times, whenever you need it. You name the time and I'll do it."

He glanced at his filthy car, and I knew immediately that he liked the offer.

"And what do you want?" he asked.

"An answer to a question. The truth and nothing but."

"What question?"

"You'll hear it if you lose. Are we on?"

He thought it over, and by his expression I don't think he made any connection whatsoever to the photo or our previous conversation. Jay is a bright individual, but when it comes to my sisters and me he never retains many details. That's my ace in the hole.

"All right, let's go," he said. "But no crossing T's. We could be out here all day."

For the next ten minutes we battled for driveway supremacy. In the hour before his arrival, I'd brilliantly mapped out my strategy. He was the more accurate shooter, but by playing the shorter version of HORSE I figured that I might catch him while he was still cold and steal the victory. I was only half right. He didn't sink many of his own shot-calls, which he took from long range, but he matched mine almost shot for shot. I wanted to apply the pressure by making a series of easy shots and forcing him to follow my lead. Once he started firing those long-range missiles and getting hot, there was no chance in hell for me.

With the game tied at OU, I decided to pull out all the stops. I used my patented fall-away bank-shot from the lawn, about fifteen feet out.

"Fall-away bank," I said.

I lined up the shot, turned and jumped away, and let the American Basketball Association round ball fly. It banked high and softly off the backboard, rattled in a circle around the rim, and dropped through the nylon net.

"Is it your birthday already?" said Jay sarcastically.

"I make that shot all the time," I said.

"Maybe, but not under pressure."

"I live for pressure, dude."

Jay faked at chest pass at my head and caught the ball in mid-air, making me flinch. He grunted a chuckle and barely thought twice about the shot, planting his foot to the spot, falling away and launching a rainbow arc. His height was an effective weapon as a shooter, and he rarely needed to fall away from his defender, especially against me. The ball rotated in parallel lines of red, white, and blue, and from the angle I had, it looked good. Then, as if Lady Luck smiled upon me, the ball hit the backboard and clanked hard against the front rim, bounced off and fell to the cement. Jay had put too much backspin on the ball, so when it made contact with the backboard, it shot like a rocket to the rim, and the rim couldn't hold it.

"You're out, big guy," I said.

Jay just stared at the hoop and shook his head in disbelief.

"Shit. That should've gone in."

"Yeah, well it didn't, bro," I said, rubbing it in.

"All right, let's get this over with. What's your big question? I'm sure it'll be fascinating."

I debated whether to pull out the photo from my shorts, but then it dawned on me that he'd know I took the picture once I asked the question. So I withdrew the photo and thrust it in front of his impatient face, my hands trembling.

"Who's the woman in this photo?"

In a remarkably clear transition of expressions, Jay turned from surprise to confusion to contempt, all in the span of about three seconds.

"You took that from my room?" he asked resentfully.

"Yes, I did." I held firm. My only hope was to speak with a tone of strength and determination. I felt like David going against Goliath, only David had a rock and slingshot.

"What the hell were you doing nosin' around my room?" he asked. "You told me you never did that. Now you're a thief *and* a liar?"

"That was the truth. But this one time, I had to."

"Why?"

"Because you wouldn't tell me who she was."

"Big fucking deal. You still had no right to go sneaking around in my room."

"You lost, so who is she?"

"Forget it. You stole that from my room, so you forfeit the win."

Jay turned to leave, taking the answer to my question with him.

"Come on, man, just tell me," I pleaded, realizing my plan

backfired and resorting to my usual tactic, begging.

"No."

"If you don't tell me I'll—"

He pivoted and stood his ground in defiance. "You'll what?"

I had absolutely no idea. I had nothing behind my idle threat. He turned into the dim hallway and faded from my view. I listened to his heavy steps take him farther away. Out of sheer desperation I shouted, "I have the right to know, Goddamn it!" His steps paused. Then my heart stopped. Much to my surprise he shouted back from the hallway, "You really wanna know that badly, huh?"

"Yes," I shouted.

"Bad enough to wash my car five times?"

"Five?" I shouted, annoyed.

"Start complaining and I'll make it ten," he said.

"Okay, fine, five, I'll do five," I said reluctantly.

He made me wait and sweat, my heart doing a da-thump, da-thump. Or maybe he was gathering courage, I don't know.

"That's the woman that dad is sleeping around with."

Those agonizing, unforgettable words filtered down the hall, around the doorway, and into the entry hall, smacking me right in the face like a sucker-punch. A waterfall of conflicted emotions flooded me all at once. Prickly needles of tingling pain erupted in my chest. Deep down I had my suspicions about the woman, although I wasn't ready to fully acknowledge them. I'd always been a curious child and as the youngest, had to fight and scratch my way to the truth, even when it knocked me down sometimes. I moved to the doorway leading into the hall and saw Jay leaning despondently against the wall, his head lowered. He'd probably dealt with this truth long before I had.

"I found the picture underneath the front seat in the station wagon," he started, his voice slow and defeated. "Damn," he said shaking his head, "things are getting so screwed up around here."

"How'd you know who she was?"

Without looking up he replied, "I didn't, until I asked him."

"You asked him, just like that?"

"I had my suspicions for a long time. Something wasn't right. When I asked him, he was totally uptight. I saw the truth in his eyes. He couldn't hide it from me anymore."

"He told you everything?"

"No, not everything. But I know she lives somewhere in town."

"How long has this been—"

"He wouldn't say, a while, I know that. Several months maybe."

I was stunned. I was angry, too, that so much truth was circulating around this house and none of it was reaching me.

"Why's he doing this?"

"Look, we're the only ones who know about this. Dad practically begged me to keep it quiet. You have to promise to keep your trap shut. They have enough problems as it is."

"Does he love her?" I said, still dazed.

He appeared reluctant to answer that question.

"I don't know. All I know is that it's still going on."

"What about Mom?"

"She knows everything."

"What?" I blurted out, stunned.

"Listen, let Mom and Dad deal with this in their own way. It's their relationship. They don't need you messing around in their personal space, like you did in mine."

"So this vacation, it's not really a vacation?"

"No, it's an experiment. They're doing some sort of group marriage counseling session. All I know is that they're trying to save the marriage…what's left of it, anyway." Jay waited for my reaction, although I think he knew I'd gone completely numb. "You wanted to know the truth, well, welcome to the real world," said Jay. "Maybe you'll think twice next time before you go sticking your nose where it doesn't belong."

Jay sighed and headed for his room, his steps heavy and slow, like an athlete who'd just lost the championship game. I stood there for the longest time. I was unable to move my limbs and my chest felt funny.

# Chapter Five

*I watched a lot of television during the next couple of days in a* blank, foggy haze. Strangely, I found myself drawn to the Watergate hearings. Those people all looked miserable, too. Even at the highest levels of government people were hiding valuable information and lying. The truth was unraveling, and the nation was finding out that our political leader was a thief and liar (ironically the same words my brother used to describe me). Before, Watergate was nothing more than a circus sideshow. The adults took it seriously but I never did, until today. Now I saw the world in an entirely different light; a gloomy, dull light. Nothing was black or white anymore; nothing could be taken at face value. I began to think that everything and everyone was connected in some way, that despite what people said and did, there was always something more revealing or truthful lurking beneath the murky surface. There were layers to the truth just like layers to a cake.

They broke to a silly commercial showing kids and adults prancing and singing in the park about Coke, something about teaching the world to sing. It all seemed totally ridiculous. Why would anyone who drank Coke actually break out into song? Meanwhile, in the capitol, they were deciding the fate of men who'd risen to the highest levels of achievement in their field. It made you wonder, really wonder, how they got there.

"Why are you watching that boring stuff?" asked Sarah, standing there in her peach-colored, two-piece bathing suit, just home from a day at the beach. "Doesn't seem like your thing."

"I like to see people squirm in front of the cameras," I said.

"Okay, whatever you say. Where's Rachel?"

"Beats me, probably goofing around with Jamie."

"I don't like Jamie. She's a little creepy, don't you think?" said Sarah.

"No, not really… why?"

"She stares at me funny sometimes, like she's sizing me up. I don't like it."

"She doesn't bother me. Besides, we don't talk all that much."

"But you'd like to, huh?" Sarah nudged me with her toes. "Have you heard from Mom and Dad?"

"They called yesterday."

"God I'd love to be on vacation right now. I'm sick of my job. Are they having a great time?"

"How the hell should I know?"

"Jeez, you're in a mood today. Hey, I'm gonna be spending the night here tonight, maybe have a few friends over, make some drinks. You cool with that?"

"Sure, join the party," I said with a bit of disdain.

"What do you mean?"

"There's Rachel's friends, Jay's friends, it's just one, big, non-stop party around here."

"I like it that way. Those people who live in a commune have the right idea."

"Doesn't feel like a home anymore. Feels like a Holiday Inn. And I don't think Jay and Rachel really like it when I hang around their friends."

"Well you can hang with us. My friends like you." This was by far the best news I'd heard in weeks, even though the information was virtually useless. "You used to sing songs with them. Remember…'It's my party and I'll cry if I want to, cry if I want to, cry if I want to.' Come on, sing," she said in between lyrics. "'You would cry too if it happened to you.'"

As I watched Sarah belt out the tune, bobbing slightly as she sung, I wondered—as I had before—if she was adopted. Even though I knew she wasn't, she was far too gregarious and excitable for this family. She spoke with a rapid-fire tongue that steamed like a runaway train through a conversation, and she reacted suddenly and with great bursts of energy to situations where most others would pause and measure their thoughts. It occurred to me, while she kept blasting out the song, that Sarah didn't seem to mind what others thought of her. Whether she was too loud, overly exuberant, or willing to stand out where others might retreat, she intended to let it all hang loose. I decided this was an acceptable way to live, even if I couldn't bring myself to live it.

Sarah entered the kitchen while the Doctor emerged from around the corner, also showing signs of a long beach day—windblown hair, sandy feet, and a wrinkled bathing suit.

"Hey Sarah, a bunch of us are going out to Hollywood tomorrow night. You wanna go?" said the Doctor.

"Yeah, sounds great. Where to?"

"Don't know exactly, maybe The Rainbow or the Roxy. We'll hit as many as we can. Bring some girlfriends if you want to. The more the merrier."

Sarah emerged from the kitchen, not so enthused anymore. I could read her as clearly as a football playbook, unlike everyone else in my family. She handed him a glass with ice that cracked and popped.

"Oh, okay," she said. "Are we going together or not?"

"Yeah, sure, but if the crowd gets too big, we may end up driving separate cars. Who knows where we'll end up."

Sarah never could hide her feelings, and she was definitely disappointed it wasn't a date.

"Hey, Kevy, can't you find something better than this shit?" he said. Again, my blood boiled when someone called me Kevy. For some reason, the name jolted me with a peculiar, childish feeling. "Watch whatever you want," I said, rising dejectedly from the sofa.

"Hey man, cheer up," said the Doctor. "It's summer, you're not working, the world's your playground. You can do whatever the hell you want."

I shot him a cold look, and he uneasily cleared his throat, returning his gaze to the TV. I wanted to talk to someone but felt as though Jay had confided in me, and I couldn't jeopardize our new bond; the only one we really had.

�⚲

I went outside to the front lawn, hearing the hiss of the leaves brushing together in the breeze. Down the street, I noticed Kyle Bollinger doing something in his garage. I needed a distraction from my troubled thoughts, so I meandered toward Kyle's house at the open end of the cul-de-sac.

I found him carving a thick block of wood about four feet long and five inches deep. He ran a large blade along the block that removed long strips of the wood, which fell to the floor in a pile. Some of the light wood shavings had attached themselves to the sparse blond hair on his long legs. Standing at the worktable in his shorts and no shirt, I noticed his strong and lean build, his large hands and feet, and I thought his build would be perfect for a competitive swimmer.

"What are you making?" I asked.

"Baseball bat," he replied. "I'm gonna use it for games...burn my name into and give it cool name, like the Rossmoor Raider or somethin'."

"Awesome, but what if it breaks?"

Befuddled, Kyle paused and turned to me.

"Then I'll make another one."

"Seems like a lot of work for something you can buy at the sporting goods store for a few bucks. Besides, those metal bats have a lot more power."

"I got plenty of power in these arms," he said, flexing his right bicep.

As he flexed, I was flooded with the memory of the moment I thought I was going to die from those arms. I was ten years old and Kyle had just turned twelve. In the backyard my father had erected one of those above-ground pools called a Doughboy, and Kyle,

Matt, Ronnie, and I were swimming. This was long before the pool rusted and began caving in around the sides and formed enough algae to support an entire ecosystem of sea life. The pool lasted all of three summers, but the first summer was pure joy.

We were engaged in a heated game of Marco Polo, when Kyle and I began to argue over whether he tagged me. When backed into a corner, he often resorted to cheating. This time, I just couldn't tolerate it. I turned my head momentarily to Matt, and Kyle pounced on top of me, pushing me down and dunking my head under the water. I thought he'd release me after a few moments, so I tried to remain calm. After several seconds nothing changed, so I started to panic, trying to fight my way loose from his grip. I couldn't break his hold, my chest starting to tighten and my head feeling woozy. It was after about thirty seconds, which is an eternity under water, especially when you're struggling, that I thought I was going to black out and die. I heard some yelling and commotion above the water, and moments later he released his hands from atop my head. I ejected from the bottom with all the power in my legs and flapped my upper body over the side of the pool, gasping for air and choking violently. I was so traumatized by the moment that I didn't invite Kyle over for a swim the rest of that summer. And I had bad dreams, as if I were drowning, for weeks.

I watched Kyle continue to strip away sheets of wood from the block. The ends had begun to round off and I could visualize the beginnings of a baseball bat. Nowadays, I always tried to approach Kyle with the utmost caution and care, because I could never be certain of his mood. It didn't take much to set him off, as I'd discovered from the pool incident and other moments in our turbulent friendship. He'd never punched me in the face, but I took some heavy-handed shots to the stomach and arms on more occasions than I cared to remember.

"Are your parent's home?" I asked.

"Nope."

"Let's play some hoops," I said.

"Nah, I already played some today. Hey, check this out," he said, suddenly excited. Kyle set down the blade and leaned to the side of the workbench table. He lifted what resembled a small shotgun. My heart skipped a beat.

"Where'd you get that?" I asked.

"My dad bought it for me a few weeks ago. Bitchin', huh?"

I'd never seen a rifle before, and it was the last item I expected him to show me. In the hands of anyone else, the gun would've only intrigued me. In the hands of Kyle Bollinger, it made my pulse quicken.

"It's a BB gun, fires accurately up to a hundred feet," he said in a proud tone. "It won't kill anybody, but it'll sting like a motherfucker. I know a guy who got hit from one, and they had to take him to the hospital. It was close range, about ten feet. Dumbshit, huh?"

"Yeah," I said, swallowing hard. "What happened to him?"

"He didn't die or nothin', but he had a big welt on his arms for weeks. You wanna try it out?"

"Okay."

I answered too fast and without forethought. I followed Kyle around the side of the house where they kept their trash barrels. Mr. Bollinger had laid a path of small white rocks between the sidewall and garage wall so that when a person treaded on the path, it made a crunching sound. I always enjoyed hearing my feet crunch on the rocks, although today the sound set my nerves on edge.

Kyle carried the gun like a briefcase, and then abruptly stopped and knelt down low. He cocked his BB gun and brought it to eye level. I peered ahead in the distance, trying to follow the direction of his aim. I found an apple tree in the backyard about ten paces straight ahead. At first his true target didn't register to me, and then the noise filtered into my head and grew louder, until it practically shouted at me. Several small chirping sparrows occupied the tree. Before I could say anything, the gun snapped like a belt-whip, and Kyle's upper body kicked backwards. It wasn't a deafening loud crack, but it was piercing enough to feel the pressure in my ears. He quickly lowered the gun, hopeful and excited that he hit his target.

"Damn it," he said. "Those little shits are tough to hit. Here, you try."

He extended the gun to me, and I clutched it with both of my hands, one at the barrel and one at the handle. Only a few birds scattered from the tree after the shot, leaving four or five poor fools behind. I enjoyed the feeling of the gun in my hands—the barrel's warm metal and the extra weight that toy guns didn't have. I brought the gun to eye level and took aim at a happy little sparrow perched on a branch. A part of me wanted to beat Kyle and prove that I was the better shot. Secretly, I resented Kyle for all the years of abuse, both physical and verbal, despite the fact that he'd left me alone recently. I was nearing his size in both height and weight, and it was already evident that my shoulders were wider than his. I found myself aiming with far more intent than I really wanted to.

"Go on, shoot the damn thing," he urged.

The kickback was stronger than I expected. Again a few birds scattered on the blast, and I was positive that I'd missed everything. A moment later I heard a ruffling feather noise, and I caught a glimpse of something small and brown falling in a blur from the tree.

"You got one!" Kyle shouted.

Kyle hustled over to the ivy growth underneath the tree and searched for the fallen victim. My body shivered and my hands were clammy. I didn't think it was possible to hit such a small target from ten full paces away, at least not by me.

"Come here," he said, searching through the growth.

I gently laid down the weapon on the rocks and approached Kyle. I didn't know where it came from, maybe out of anger for those stupid birds, but I swiped real hard at the tree's branches and the remaining birds fluttered away.

"Look," he said. He raised the small creature in his hands, its head bent back wobbly and bloodstains all over its belly. "Bull's eye, dude."

A gush of guilt and shame overcame me. I shivered again, and I could feel the sweat oozing from my skin. I stared at the bird with a morbid fascination, and I began to feel sick to my stomach. Kyle flipped the dead bird into the thick ivy growth and it sank into the deep forest green, just another chunk of the soil now. Its life was over, and I had ended it.

"Okay, it's my turn. You can go again after me," said Kyle.

"Uh… I have to go," I said.

"Why, this is fun. Look at all the birds back here. We could have a shooting contest."

The chirping of birds was ringing in my ear, and it sounded like a dire warning from Mother Nature.

"I'll see you later."

"Ah come on, man, don't flake out on me!" Kyle shouted.

I took my first step onto the rocks from the grass, and in my mind, the crunch noise made a rapid-fire submachine gun sound. I lunged forward, as if someone had lit a match under my ass, and I started to run. But then I realized I didn't want Kyle to see me running away so I downshifted into a hurried walk. It didn't matter, since he quickly drew his own conclusion.

"Go home and play with your sissy dolls!" shouted Kyle in the most humiliating tone possible.

At the moment I didn't care what Kyle thought of me. I only knew that I had to escape this deathly scene. I hustled through the front door of my house, and went directly to my room and closed the door behind me. What had become of me? I'd turned into a snooper and even worse, a killer. I wanted to throw something to release my rage, but I couldn't find the right item. I wondered where all this was heading and what would become of me next.

# Chapter Six

*I must've drifted into a late afternoon nap because when I awoke,*
my room was pitch black, and loud music blared from other parts
of the house. I staggered to my feet and entered the hallway,
catching a whiff of the sweet smoke drifting through the hallway
from the front part of the house.

Several people were hanging out in the living room, most of
whom I recognized as girlfriends of Sarah's and guy friends of
Jay's. Sarah was trying to pull the Doctor to the dance floor while
she balanced a cocktail in her hand. She'd always been fond of
dancing, anywhere, anytime, to almost any kind of music.

"Hey, look who's here!" said the Doctor. He often made a small
production out of my appearance, which baffled me. "We thought
you'd never come outta that room."

"Must be something real interesting in there," said Nelson, a
friend of Jay's, making a jerky motion with his hand near his

crotch. Everyone laughed, and by the sudden flush of warmth in my face I probably turned bloodshot red.

"Come on, let's dance," said Sarah, tugging my body into the room.

I was constantly being hog-tied by Sarah to dance since I could move relatively well, and sometimes no one else would oblige her. I was embarrassed to dance with my sister, although I was quite certain that no one cared, at least in this room. The Doctor smiled and whispered something to Nelson, and they busted into a loud guffaw. I couldn't spot Jay anywhere, which was certainly not unusual.

I found myself swirling and twirling in the middle of a party and listening to people laugh and watching them smoke and drink, and for a moment I thought I was still asleep and dreaming. Actually, I wished the last couple of days *had* been a dream. I wanted to wipe away the truth, like Mr. Clean wipes away germs with one power-swipe of his sponge. Then the music stopped, and Sarah shouted a hoot, kicking up her leg and spilling her drink on the carpet. I stood in the center and glanced around the room at the many drunk and stoned faces, content to fry their brains, and I knew this was no dream. I knew the knowledge I had was real and permanent.

Before anyone could notice, I slipped away from the living room and into the formal room. I wasn't in the mood for a party. I couldn't shake the feelings of restlessness and bitterness and wasn't sure how to cope with them. I plopped down on the sofa, kicked up my legs, and stared out the window into the night's soft moonlight, when moments later I heard something bang into the entryway wall followed by some giggling. I saw the Doctor and Sarah emerge from the hallway, kissing and stumbling. The Doctor tried to maneuver Sarah into the dark formal room until I coughed as a courtesy, or maybe more as a warning.

"Oh, Kevin, that you?" said the Doctor.

"Shit," I heard Sarah say under her breath.

I turned on the lamplight.

"What are you doing sitting in the dark all alone?" asked Sarah.

"I like the dark."

"I like the dark too, but not alone," said the Doctor. They giggled together, and Sarah poked at his midsection.

"Come on, let's go boogie on down, baby," said Sarah, trying to drag the Doctor away.

"I'll catch up with you in a few minutes," he said.

"You're gonna stay here?" asked Sarah, disappointed.

"Yeah, just for a while."

"Fine, suit yourself."

Irked, Sarah left the room, and the Doctor sank into the sofa chair. I didn't know why he decided to join me when my sister obviously wanted to spend time with him. As I observed the Doctor running his fingers through his rings of long, curly, black hair, it finally dawned on me why Jay avoided these nights. It stirred a strange feeling inside me, something that could only be described as mild contempt, watching my sister make out with the Doctor. And he wasn't my best friend; he wasn't even one of my good friends.

"You started football practice yet?"

"Not yet."

"You dig the pigskin, don't you?" I nodded. Everyone close to me knew it was my sport of choice and that the football field was where I intended to make my mark as an athlete. Jay made his mark in basketball. "You guys gonna kick some ass this year?"

"We have a couple of good guys. I think we could win the league," I said.

"You're gonna love high school, man. All those new girls come in from the other junior highs, you've just tripled your selection. You psyched up for that?"

"Yeah, real psyched," I deadpanned.

No words were spoken for several seconds, and I think he sensed my introspection.

"Hey, you ever seen this before?" he asked, trying to lift my mood.

The Doctor glanced at the entry hall, and then withdrew something from his pocket. He held up a quarter, like a magician about to perform a trick, and broke into wide grin. I had no idea what he was up to until he brought the coin to his nose, flared his nostrils, and slowly shoved the quarter inside his nose. He completely submerged the coin.

"Ta da," he said, extending his arms. I must not have supplied the reaction he was expecting since his big smile abruptly flattened out. "You haven't seen someone else do that, have you?"

I shook my head. He pinched the edge of the quarter inside his nostril and tried to remove it, but the coin was stuck. He muttered words of pain until finally the coin slipped out and he sighed in relief. He wiped the coin on his t-shirt and shoved it back into his pocket.

"Easier going in than coming out, which is not true of most things in life," he said with a chuckle. I'm not sure why, but I always got the impression the Doctor was trying to win my approval and that he was far more comfortable with younger people.

"What are you doing in here?" I asked.

"I needed the break, man. Those girls are dancing maniacs in there, and I get tired of it. You ever get tired of doing something?"

"I get tired of being in this family."

He arched his eyebrows, and I became aware of how resentful that sounded.

"Uh-oh, warning Will Robinson, warning Will Robinson," he said in a monotone voice, ejecting his arms straight out like the robot in the show *Lost in Space*. "Something's up, talk to the Doc, I be cool."

I just shrugged half-heartedly.

"I know, it's that deal about your parents. Sorry you had to find out about that. Hey, don't sweat it, man. Parents sometimes just need a little push to get them back on track."

"It's not only that."

"Chick problems? I can help, loads of experience there." He winked and grinned.

"I really don't wanna talk about it."

"Hey, there's a lot of crap I don't like to talk about either, but if you keep those negative vibes inside, man, it's bad news. They'll eat you alive like a gopher diggin' through dirt. People need to get all those feelings off their chest. My old man got an ulcer because he kept everything inside. It's gnarly shit."

"That ever happen to you?" I asked.

"Not the ulcer. But yeah, sure, I've held things in. Then I realized, hey, this isn't helping me. I don't feel any better keeping it in. So I decided to attack the problem instead of letting it attack me. A lot of people just sit around and let things boil up inside them until they get sick or something. Most physical illnesses are mentally induced, you know."

"I don't see how that's possible."

"Your body and your mind all work together, like a Swiss watch. If one's not healthy it screws up the other. You have to make things right, one way or another."

"What if you don't know where to start?"

"Just dive in, man, take the big plunge. It may be a little cold at first, but you'll get used to it."

"I guess you're right."

"You better believe I'm right."

I gave him a grateful smile and I think he felt better because of it. "It's easy to talk to you. You should be a psychologist or something," I said.

He chortled ironically. "That's what I was studying to be in college."

"Really? What happened?"

He glanced aside, and for the first time since I'd known him, he was burdened by a weighty sadness. He'd always been the guy who balanced my brother's more prickly moods with a perpetual grin and positive nature. He repositioned himself in the sofa chair, as if trying to rub off the extra weight from his body.

"I keep wondering that myself. I had everything, man, right there. I was so close to getting what I always wanted. Then, I don't know, it didn't seem to matter all that much anymore."

"You can still go back, can't you?"

"Maybe… someday. I'd like to help people, but I'm not ready just yet. I have to figure myself out first before I can help anyone else."

"Well hurry up, because there are a few people in this house who could use your expertise." He released his rapid, clown-like laugh.

"Why do you think I'm so drawn to your family?" he said. "Hey, I'm just joshing you. I dig your family. They accept me, and that's totally righteous, man."

He rubbed the top of my head and ejected from the sofa chair. "Come join the party, man. Bouncin' titties galore."

I nodded weakly, and he left the room. I was still feeling restless, but at least I figured out why his friends called him the Doctor, even though he never really earned that title. Later that night in bed, I thought about his advice. It made good sense, sharing one's thoughts and feelings with another person, which in my case had always been my mother. How could I talk to her now? What would I say?

I could still hear shouts and laughter from the other rooms, the occasional loud thumps on the floor, the music's heavy, pounding bass, and I felt comforted and protected. I guess I'd grown accustom to having the house filled with voices and sounds. The problem was, I wasn't accustomed to the heavy and peculiar feelings that had taken residence in my own body.

🚲

Later in the evening I was awakened by some banging and shouting noises from a nearby room. I thought it must be the party still in full swing, but I couldn't hear any music. I glanced at my clock radio, which read 1:47 a.m. I stumbled out of bed, scratched my ass, and realized I needed to empty my tanks. Still hearing the noises, standing in the hallway, I noticed the door to my parents' room was ajar. As I moved curiously closer I heard the creaking sounds of steel bed hinges, along with rhythmic grunts and groans. On some instinctual level I knew what these sounds meant, but I was not very alert, so I casually peered inside. I really wish I hadn't, because I was shocked by the visual. Sarah was bouncing up and down on top of the Doctor, riding him like a jockey, moonlight illuminating their naked bodies, and making raw, animalistic sounds that didn't seem natural for any woman, let alone my sister. I immediately shut my eyes and whipped around, pounding my back flat against the wall, horrified and shaken to high alert. Thankfully, they were oblivious to me, while they just kept grunting and groaning in unison.

Repulsed and okay, if the truth be told, a little enthralled, I shook my head, sighed deeply, and tried to understand how they could possibly arrive at the peculiar decision to have sex in my parents' bed. I mean, come on, are you kidding me? Humping like dogs in heat is one thing; I'm all in favor of it. But man, doing it in the bed where my parents slept together? Now that decision just seemed so completely out of whack to me. My next thought was how in the hell would I get back to sleep after witnessing that spectacle? I decided to take that leak I intended to, but still being able to hear the squeaking bed hinges and the occasional vocal outburst by my sister, it was the longest and most unpleasant piss of my life.

# Chapter Seven

*The next morning I was struck by an idea. Even though I* couldn't entirely eliminate the scarring image of Sarah and the Doctor in bed last night, I had no time to dwell on that now. And really, why would I want to? I removed the photo from the book, pulled out some scissors from my desk drawer, and then started to cut around the image of my father. A strange stir of satisfaction tingled in my body while I carefully guided the scissors around my beaming father. He dropped to the floor, and I picked him up and dumped him into my Los Angeles Rams trashcan. I was left with just the redhead and some pointed curves around her upper body.

Jay said that she lived somewhere in town. As I rode my bike through the streets, I rehearsed in my head what I'd say. Nothing sounded right or appropriate, though. But it didn't matter. I was compelled to try something, anything, to find out more details and the truth. I didn't want to believe my father could be guilty of such behavior, that he could commit this heinous crime against my mother. In a place where only hope exists, somewhere in between my gut and throat, I wanted desperately to stumble upon a fact that proved his innocence and revealed Jay had it all wrong. The alternative was unthinkable. I'd always believed my father was a man of quiet dignity and humble honor. He was a man of virtues, and yet I sensed—like most men—that he battled his own internal demons and contradictions. Nevertheless, he always came home from work, joined us at the dinner table, and asked questions about our day. He proudly taught me how to throw the football, hit a baseball, bait a fishing line, and ride an ocean wave on the raft. When I struck out, he consoled me, and when I scored a touchdown, he cheered me. He never laid a hostile hand on my body and rarely raised his voice in anger. And when he did shout, the intent never seemed malicious, and I always deserved more punishment than I received.

All the anguish of hearing something so contrary about my father was eating a hole inside me. I envisioned the gopher just munching away at my flesh and bones, and I could hear the Doctor's voice, 'Negative vibes, man, they're bad news.' I had to see this woman with my own eyes. If I was unable to make this woman and mystery more real, the doubt and secrecy would just linger in the air around me, hanging over my every step, every thought, and every breath. With only a couple of weeks left of summer, I had to confront and resolve this situation before the start of school and football season. Maybe I could bring some kind of resolution to it, if not for my parents, then at least for myself.

&#x6bb;

I maneuvered my bike into the Market Basket grocery store, the largest store in town. Since it was mid-morning, only a few customers were scattered about, and a couple of the check-out ladies were just shooting the breeze while flipping through magazines. I approached the first woman, her hair pulled up neatly in a bun and chewing on a wad of gum the size of a ping-pong ball. She blew a huge bubble that snapped in her face, and she expertly licked the film of gum around her bright red lips. I waited for the right moment to interrupt their conversation.

"I hear he's the real brains of the operation," said the gum-chewing checker. "Cher has the talent, but Sonny's got the brains."

"I think he's kind of cute, in a goofy sort of way, don't you?" said the other checker, a heavy-set woman with puffy cheeks.

"He's all right. I mean, shoot, I wouldn't turn the man away. He's probably worth a million bucks, you know? But if he was just Joe Blow on the street, I probably wouldn't give him the time of day."

"Excuse me," I interrupted.

"What can we do for you, hon?" said the gum chewer.

"I was wondering if you've seen this woman. Maybe she's a customer."

I extended the photo. The gum chewer clutched it, a puzzled expression on her face.

"Where's the rest of it?"

"I don't know. Somebody must've cut it out."

"That's a bit odd, don't you think?" The other checker smiled and nodded while the gum chewer examined the photo. I saw no hints of recognition, and I thought, strike one.

"Don't know the woman. Why's it so important?"

Darn, another question for which I was totally unprepared. I made a silent promise that from now on I would think these matters through more carefully.

"I think she has my dog. See, I lost my dog at the park the other day, and I think this lady has her." It didn't sound half bad, and I stood a little straighter for having thought of it. The gum chewer handed the photo to the heavy woman, but nothing registered with her, either. Strike two.

"We get a lot of customers through here, and a lot of different checkers work different shifts," said the heavy checker. "You might try the banks or the post office. They keep more regular hours, and the staff is usually the same. If anyone's seen her, it's probably someone there."

⤳

The day was searing hot with barely a whisper of a breeze. I rode my bike all over town, from the bank to the post office to several of the larger retail stores on Walnut Street, the largest and busiest boulevard in town. No one knew her. One man in the post office said he recognized her although he couldn't come up with a name. After a couple of hours, my stomach rumbled from hunger. I rolled into Thrifty since they had the best deal in town, a double scoop of ice cream for ten cents. A cone would fill my stomach until I got home and raided the cupboards.

At the plate glass freezer cases I feasted my eyes on all the colorful flavors while the employee helped another customer. The counter clerk was a lanky young man with a severe case of acne and limp eyelids that gave the impression of someone slow-thinking. I felt sorry for the guy, not only for his pimpled face but also for having to wear a girly white apron and a ridiculous paper hat. The customer before me left, and I sidestepped closer to him.

"Two scoops of Rocky Road on a sugar cone, please," I said.

He didn't reply and simply went about his job. His forearm was strong, and the muscles rippled when he reached down and scooped out the ice cream. As he stuffed the ice cream onto the cone it occurred to me that he probably came across a hoard of women every day. I paid him for the ice cream and then reached into my pocket and withdrew the photo. I extended the photo over the plate glass and asked the all-important question.

"Sorry, man, don't know her," he said. "Next."

He seemed in a hurry to dispose of me and help the next customer. When he returned the photo it dropped, slicing a path to the floor behind me. I sneered, though it didn't catch his focus, and bent over to retrieve the photo. I was tired of failing at this mission, and this numb nut was the last straw. I suppose I was even feeling a little sorry for myself, too. My search was going nowhere fast.

While bent over, I noticed a pair of bright white Vans sneakers attached to a pair of tan, shapely, and more importantly, hairless calves. Gradually, I lifted my head and upper body while trying to balance my ice cream. I didn't want to hurry this. My view followed the calves and toned legs up to a pair of skin-tight, cut-off denim jeans, to a flat, tan stomach that slimmed down nicely into the shorts, to a tight, pink halter top that bubbled out perfectly in the chest, to a sparkling gold chain with a shiny gold heart dangling from the end, finally resting upon a face that sent shockwaves of joy pulsating though my veins. This was a vision of pure delight, head to toe, and then the pure delight spoke to me.

"Can I see that picture?" the girl said, holding out her hand. My eyes locked on her in awe, and I had no power in my throat to speak. I raised the photo to her hand and she snatched it from me. Where in the world did this incredible creature come from?

"That's my mother," she said. "What are you doing with a picture of my mother?"

The words never clicked in my head nor made any sense. They were just words that dripped from her lips—her sweet, inviting lips that swirled and puffed in the middle and then tapered off thin and long at the corners. Her radiant green eyes were set against the whitest of eyeballs. Her thick, strawberry-blonde hair was curled and flipped back at the sides, and her skin, oh Lord, her skin, was silky smooth and evenly tanned, covered by a mist of sweat that glistened every time she moved.

"Are you deaf?" she asked. "I said what are you doing with a picture of my mother?"

"Yeah, dude, that's like… seriously disturbed. Why would you have that?" said the ice cream boy, trying to impress her.

"I, uh…I…this is your mother?"

"I just said that, didn't I?" she said with disdain.

"I, um…I found it, on the floor…in the store. I thought maybe she lost it." I certainly found myself telling a lot of lies lately, which wasn't a trend I wanted to continue.

"My mother would never cut up a picture like that. It must be somebody else's."

"Yeah, must be," I said.

She stepped around me and up to the counter. "I'll have two scoops of rainbow sherbet on a sugar cone, please," she said.

From behind her I permitted my eyes take a slow and enjoyable journey up and down her body. I had her pegged for about sixteen, possibly seventeen. The ice cream boy kept flashing a goofball smile at her to draw her attention, the little punk.

"What's happening?" he said.

"Not much," said the girl. "What's it like being out of high school?"

"It's okay, except you have to work. I never had to do that in high school."

"Yeah, work's a total drag."

He finished serving her, accepted her coins, and she flashed a goodbye wave of her hand before turning and brushing right by me.

"Later," he said, with a big, dopey grin. Man, this guy was a dipshit if he thought a girl like her would date a guy who wore a paper hat and apron. As for me, I was planted to the floor like a statue. She didn't even notice I was still standing there. I watched her in wonder and disbelief while she exited the store.

"Hey, shit for brains," the ice cream boy said.

"Huh?" I mumbled, coming out of my trance.

He pointed at my hand. I glanced down and the top scoop of my Rocky Road had slid way over the side and just as I lunged to devour it, the ball of cream swiped the side of my mouth and fell to the floor, splat.

He leveled his limp eyes at me while I yanked some napkins from of the metal dispenser and cleaned the mess. I high-tailed it out of there, trying to cram the remaining scoop of ice cream into my mouth. I dashed out to the parking lot and scanned the area. She'd already made her way a fair distance up the street, about to turn a corner. I took one last bite of my cone, reluctantly dumped the remainder in the trash, then unlocked my bike and peddled hard out of the parking lot. I made a wide, sweeping turn around the corner of the street and found her straight ahead.

Before I had the chance to slow down she abruptly pivoted. Reacting purely on instinct, which felt like a mixture of fear and embarrassment, I slammed on the brakes and tried to turn. The bike dovetailed and the back wheel sprang up in mid-air. I rolled forward and went airborne over the handlebars. I was in the air for what felt like forever when my right side pounded the pavement with a thud, and I tried to tuck and roll to keep my head from cracking open. When I finally came to a stop and realized my head had survived with no more than a moderate bump, I just lied there, trying to focus on a lone, small cloud in the sky, and waited, and waited, and waited. Then it came, like the inevitable and unstoppable emergence of a sneeze. An intense throbbing pain shot right through my arm and up to my shoulder.

"Ah shit!" I yelled. My forearm was bleeding where a chunk of skin had been scraped away from the flesh. That would be a real nasty cherry in the morning.

"Are you okay?" I heard someone call out in the distance.

I'd almost forgotten about the girl. I leaned up too fast, and a dizzy spell bobbled my head. I tried to zoom in on a blurry image moving fast in my direction. Something told me this was an image I wanted to see as clearly as possible. Finally she came into focus like a fuzzy Polaroid picture coming to life. Everything else in my view just faded away. It was only her, running with that blonde hair flaming out against the air, her muscles throbbing from one bronze leg to another, and her miraculous breasts bouncing in the most extreme and enticing way imaginable. I hadn't noticed this fact in the store, but I was quite certain of it now: she wasn't wearing a bra. For a few moments I was the luckiest young man in the world, minus the fall and injuries, of course.

"Hey, say something," she said, hovering over me, alerted by her hair draped near my face and the herbal scent from her shampoo. I was afraid that the sound of my own voice would shatter this fantasy, so I hesitated to speak. "Can you hear me?"

"Yeah," I said.

"That was a radical fall. You could've really hurt yourself. What were you trying to do?"

"Uh, pull a new wheelie."

"That didn't look like any wheelie I've ever seen."

"It's new, a back-wheel... front stop sort of thing. Not many guys can do it yet. I'm trying to perfect it."

"Yeah, well, it's not going so well."

I forced a smile, then hopped to my feet and brushed the tiny pebbles of hot asphalt from my body. It was a nasty tumble, and my body hurt in several parts, but I didn't want this beautiful girl to think I was a wimp.

"You're bleeding," she said, noticing the blood dripping from my arm to the asphalt. "My house is right up the street. We should get something on that."

"Uh... no, that's okay. I'll be fine."

"Don't be one of those hard-ass jerks who can't accept help from a girl. I hate those guys. They're such Neanderthals. Are you a Neanderthal?"

"Uh...no, I'm not even sure what they are."

She smiled softly. "Good. Then you're coming home with me."

She turned and walked away while I hoisted my bike from the road. The chain had fallen off the gears, and my front brake pad had bent a little, although these kinds of problems held no concern now. I had to quickly figure out a game plan. I was about to enter enemy territory, a place I never expected to be. This was an astounding turn of events, a chance encounter of epic proportions. My feet kept moving even though inside, I was screaming with fear. I had to think of how I would handle this, although there was an unbelievably seductive distraction moving just ahead of me.

The house was dark and cool, the air-conditioning on full blast. Everything inside this house felt sterile, quiet, and tidy, unlike our house. The magazines were fanned out evenly on the oak wood coffee table, and the decorative pillows were placed as bookends in both corners of the leather, brown sofa. I was detecting a theme. I knew nothing about interior design, but the house definitely had a Southwestern flavor. Anything metal was wrought-iron style that looked antique. There was a wicker-rattan chair next to the sofa and the wall paintings depicted landscape scenes from the desert and mountains, perhaps somewhere in New Mexico or Arizona. Nothing in particular was modern in this house except for the television, which was state of the art in a polished cherry wood cabinet. I rarely stepped inside a home that actually had some cohesive theme to the decor. I liked it, and I didn't want to like anything in this house. On a tall bookshelf near the television I noticed several framed photographs. As I started to move toward them the girl returned with a damp towel.

"This might sting a little," she said. She wrapped the towel around my arm, and I released a gasp of pain before I smothered it with macho cool. "I sprayed some Bactine into the towel with the water, so it would disinfect the wound."

"Cool, thanks."

"Once we soak up most of the blood we'll wrap this in some gauze and Band-Aids. That should take care of it. Then you have to leave."

She said this in such a dry and factual tone that it almost slipped by me.

"Leave…why?"

"My mother gets really mad when I let strange boys into the house when no one's home. She throws a hissy-fit."

"I'm not strange."

"I don't mean strange strange, I mean strangers. She doesn't know you." It was silent while she dabbed the towel against my skin. "I don't mind helping you this one time, but I don't want you following me again, all right?"

Gulp. This girl had some nerve while mine had escaped me.

"I was riding home."

"What's your name anyway?

"Kevin," I said.

"I'm Shelly. Not Shelly-belly, not Shell-bell, not Smelly-Shelly, or any other variation of the name. It's Shelly, okay?

"Yeah, sure."

"You wanna know how I knew you were following me? I added up all the clues. You had a picture of my mother, cut in half, which in a court of law would probably be enough right there for a guilty verdict. You ordered an ice cream, but you didn't spend the time to

71

eat it. Not many guys would do that. Then you came flying around my corner and flipped over your bike because you were so shocked that I turned around. See? Easy as pie. I read all the Nancy Drew mystery books by the time I was eleven. Come on, you're ready for the gauze."

We entered the bathroom where for the next, few glorious minutes we stood inches apart while she attended to my wounds. I would gladly fall off my bike every day if it meant being this close to her. A jolt of electricity raced up my spine whenever she touched me. I started to feel guilty about my real reason for being here. I didn't know how I'd start the conversation about my father, and I was quite certain that it would ruin any chance I had with her, if I had any at all. I inwardly berated myself for falling into enemy territory and letting my attraction for Shelly derail my master plan. Then it occurred to me that I really had no master plan at all, other than to somehow, in some way that I had not yet conceived, stop Shelly's mother from seeing my father.

"Damn it!" she blurted out, startling me from all my thoughts.

"What?" I said.

"I didn't wrap it tight enough."

"Oh... no, look, it's fine."

I twisted my arm back and forth to demonstrate that it would hold tight, although it could've been tighter. I was basking in the glow of this girl's attention, and then we heard a door open and shut.

"Shell-bell, are you home?" a woman called out.

"Shit, my mother's home," Shelly said in a panic. "You have to hide. Quick, get in here."

She pulled me into her bedroom and shoved me into her closet, then slid the door shut. I never even got the chance to see what her bedroom looked like.

"What are you doing in there?" her mother yelled.

"Umm, nothing," shouted Shelly.

I was engulfed by darkness, accompanied only by the musty aroma of perfume entrenched on Shelly's clothing. A dress hung down in my face and tickled my nose. My heart was pumping out of control and I could barely move a muscle. I eavesdropped on the conversation in the other rooms.

"You're home early," said Shelly.

"One of my patients canceled," her mother said. "I should start charging them for that. It's not courteous. Why do you look so frazzled?"

"Me, frazzled? I'm not frazzled."

"Whose bike is that in the driveway?" I heard no response from Shelly. "Is there someone in this house? Well? Is there a boy in this house?"

I heard the shuffling of feet come closer as I huddled down low. The heel of a shoe pricked my butt.

"I don't know where that bike came from," said Shelly.

"Shelly, don't lie to me. You know we don't tolerate lying in this house."

"It must be one of the neighbor's."

They were moving through the house and doors were opening and shutting.

"Mom, would you just stop that!" shouted Shelly in a desperate plea. "Don't treat me like a child."

"I wouldn't have to treat you like a child if you didn't act like one," said her mother. "For goodness sake, Shelly, when are you going to shape up and starting acting like a young woman? In two years you'll be going away to college."

"I bet you just can't *wait* for that moment, can you Mom?" said Shelly.

I heard nothing from Shelly's mother. Then, as if she had a radar sensor, the footsteps grew heavier and led right to the closet. A hand forcefully slid back the door, and there I was, crouching at the back of the closet, looking up timidly at the mystery woman who was having an affair with my father.

"Come on, get outta there," she said.

I rose before Shelly and her mother, brushing a dress away from my face, and stepped outside the closet. Shelly's mother looked pretty much like the photo, except her hair was longer and styled differently. She was taller than I'd expected, trim and fit, with high, chiseled cheekbones and caramel brown eyes. I somehow imagined her as this mythical, radiant creature who could cast a wicked spell over every man she met. Yet, as she stood before me, tense in her shoulders and stiff in her posture, somewhere in her early forties, my first impression was nowhere near that description. She was a mother, albeit a professional mother, a little heavy in the make-up to hide the lines of worry and tension around her eyes.

"Well, at least you still have clothes on," the mother said.

"Mother!" shouted Shelly, offended.

"Okay, so what's your name and why were you hiding in my daughter's closet?"

"Uh… Roger, that's my name," I said, panicking. The only name that flashed in my mind was Roger Staubach's, the quarterback of the Dallas Cowboys. His nickname was Roger the Dodger, known for his scrambling skills and ability to escape pressure in the pocket. I could certainly use some of that right now.

"But you—" started Shelly, completely confused.

"—Uh you should be very proud of your daughter, ma'am. I fell off my bike and she took me in and fixed me up," I offered.

I held up my arm as evidence and a peace offering. While her mother studied my arm, with my eyes I implored Shelly to keep my secret. Miraculously, her mother's expression softened from an angry scowl to something more similar to compassion. My line worked.

"Maybe we should call your parents so they can take you to the hospital."

"No!" I said much too emphatically. "Really, it's just a scrape."

She focused hard on me as though she were trying to access a memory to match the image. I suppose it was possible that she'd seen a picture of me, and I was petrified that my true identity would soon be revealed.

"Do I know you from somewhere?" she said.

I wanted to reply, 'Yeah, you home-wrecking tramp, you're balling my dad!' Inside I was vacillating between rage and anger for the mother, to lust and infatuation for the daughter. At that moment, lust and infatuation had taken a slim lead.

"I don't think so," I said.

She pondered deeply and then turned to her daughter. "Why did you feel the need to hide this young man in your closet?"

"Because you always yell at me when I have a strange boy in the house… not strange strange," said Shelly, again clarifying for me.

The mother was embarrassed and glanced my way with an uneasy shame.

"He was hurt, and you took care of him. I don't see any harm in that," said Shelly's mother.

Then she turned her head to address me. "I try not to raise my voice to my children. I don't think it's a productive way to communicate. But sometimes they don't listen. Besides, I know my daughter tends to exaggerate."

"Mom," said Shelly, annoyed.

"Well it's true. She has an active imagination. I guess there's nothing wrong with that, except when she makes a mountain out of a molehill."

"She's a real good nurse. She knew just what to do," I said.

"Well, as long as you're okay, that's the important thing," said Shelly's mother.

I couldn't do it. I searched all over town and sacrificed an entire day, not to mention risked an already precarious bond with my brother, but I couldn't bring myself to confront her mother in front of Shelly. I didn't have the courage, and I didn't know what to say that would make any difference. Besides, meeting Shelly had changed everything.

"Well, guess I should be going now," I said.

"I'll see you out… Roger," said Shelly with a smirk.

"Keep that arm clean, wouldn't want it to get infected," said her mother.

Shelly and I quietly made our way to the front door. She joined me outside and shut the door behind her. I felt quite proud of myself. I'd rescued Shelly with my quick thinking and managed to slide into the good graces of her mother. I was in a great position to end this day on a positive note and regroup for another ambush at a later date.

"You didn't have to do that, you know," said Shelly with a tone of resentment.

"Huh?" I asked, caught off guard.

"That kiss-up routine with my mom. God, that was humiliating."

"Hey, fine, I was just trying to keep you outta trouble."

"It wasn't that big of a deal. I've had boys in the house before. It's not like you're something special."

"You're the one who dragged me into the closet."

"Yeah, well if you were any kind of a man you would've just come out and faced her," she said, folding her arms. "In fact, I was testing you, and you failed. You chickened out. And what was all that Roger stuff, anyway? You're so chicken of my mom you can't even use your real name?"

I struggled for the right words or comeback, something that would really sting, except I was paralyzed by anger. I just turned and stomped away toward my bike. Just before she turned and entered the house I found my reply, and I knew it would strike with a vengeance, and I knew I had more artillery stocked away, if necessary.

"You know what, you're just like your mother," I said.

"What's that supposed to mean?"

I wasn't entirely sure, but I marched right up to her and withdrew the photo from my pocket. I held the photo mere inches from her face.

"You know who I cut out of this picture?"

"Yeah, probably me. I bet you have some sort of sick, perverted fantasy about me."

"Uunnhh," I made a game show buzzer sound, which sounded a little childish, "wrong. I cut out my father. I rode my bike all over town trying to find the woman in this picture because she's destroying my family."

"And just how is she doing that?"

"She's messing around with my father, my happily married father. At least he was before *your* mom came into the picture."

Horror and disbelief washed over her face. "You're lying, just like all the other lies you told," she snapped.

"I'm not lying about this."

I flipped the photo into her chest and turned away. With each tortuous step away from the house, I regretted my statement and felt as though my body was shrinking. But the words were gone now, forever etched in time.

"I should've let you rot in the street!" she yelled, slamming the door behind her.

I hoisted my bike by the handlebars and straddled the seat, riding away under a black cloud of gloom. How did everything turn so abruptly? I went from hero to zero in almost nothing flat. I rode home as fast as my aching legs would take me and wished that I could somehow turn back the clock five minutes. I would've done or said something to charm her and win her admiration. I would've found the right words to make her think better of me. Instead, I loaded up my verbal cannon and fired the most damaging and spiteful sentence I could, quite certain that I had crippled her. I knew now that she'd have nothing to do with me.

# Chapter Eight

*I pushed our gasoline-powered mower over the thick front lawn,* lost in thought about the encounter with Shelly and her mom. I needed something simple and mundane to process through everything. Plus, I promised my father I'd mow the lawn before he got home.

Next door I noticed Helen tending to her garden, keeping a roving eye on the neighborhood. Helen was every neighbor's best friend and worst enemy all bundled into one. She could turn on you in a heartbeat and then let everyone know why she did. Her young family moved next door about three years ago, the newest additions to the street. She had beady little eyes that darted around the area, searching for suspicious behavior while keeping her small, oval-shaped head almost perfectly still. Helen was never as interested in her own yard as she was with the activities happening in other yards. She would dig ferociously for a few moments and then pause to look around with a keen eye, like a squirrel that stops eating a peanut to check its surroundings for danger. Sometimes she laughed hard and at nothing in particular, maybe from nervousness. Although pleasant and mostly harmless, I tried to keep out of earshot. My brother and father did likewise. If you moved within Helen's range of voice, a comfortable range where she didn't have to shout, you ran the risk of being snagged and eaten by her desire to make conversation.

Unfortunately, we had a stretch of lawn about ten feet wide on the far side of our driveway that bordered her lawn. When she was outside, I usually waited as long as possible to mow that side. But today, I had no time or patience. I mowed the last strip of lawn, turned off the engine, and began to rake the chopped blades of grass.

"Don't you hear that over there?" Helen said to me.

"Hear what?"

"The shouting, for heaven's sake. It's clear as a bell to me."

My ears were probably numb from the mower. I stood still and allowed my ears to tune. Then I heard the noise from the house across the street. The woman who lived there was yelling at the top of her lungs.

"Sounds like a doozy," said Helen.

"Yeah, that's a pretty big one."

I continued to rake the grass.

"That's the second fight I've heard this week. She's totally lost her mind over there," said Helen.

"I don't think she ever had it," I said.

"It's not her I'm worried about, it's that little boy. He suffers through too much. Nobody should have to grow up in a house of horrors like that one."

Just then a loud crash blasted from the house. It sounded as if a glass bottle had been tossed against the wall with a fury.

"Oh my God, that poor child," said Helen with a gasp. "For all we know she could be hitting him."

"I don't think she'd do that."

"Don't put it past her. She's a mean woman. I know what it is, too. It's her daughter, that no-good louse of a mother. Mrs. Morgan practically raises that grandchild all by herself. That's no excuse for her tantrums, though."

"She's been like that for years, even before the kid was born," I said.

"Are you kidding me?" said Helen, dumbfounded.

"She's always fighting with somebody, usually her husband. But ever since the daughter came back around, it's been her and not him. I don't see him around much anymore. Probably split town."

The shouting escalated, and now another woman's voice barked louder, probably the daughter's. I never talked to anyone in that family, and from what I knew, everyone else kept their distance as well.

"Why hasn't anyone reported her?" asked Helen.

"To the police?"

"Yes, of course, the police."

"I don't know. I guess no one's ever thought about doing that."

"Well, she'd better watch her step or I'll turn her in faster than you can say 'guilty as charged.' Have you ever noticed that she always has a cigarette in her mouth? And those eyes, they have droopy bags under 'em the size of my purse. I think she's…" Helen made a motion with her hand as though she were tipping a bottle to her mouth.

"A drunk?"

"Bingo. All I know is that since I've been here, it's gotten worse and worse in that house."

She was right. It had been worse, and for that matter I couldn't remember a long spell in my life when that house was peaceful. The fights and baby wailing had become so commonplace that I'd learned to hear them without really listening, and certainly without any concern. They'd become background noise, like the trains that rumbled on the Southern Pacific tracks just a quarter-mile north of my house, making my windows rattle when the really big ones rolled through. I hardly noticed them anymore. And these fights, as disturbing as they were, had become an extension of a neighborhood that simply accepted them at face value. I suddenly realized that my family had accepted them, too. Was it possible that a child was being abused inside that house and no one was doing anything about it? How could the entire street turn a blind eye to such despicable behavior? That is, everyone except Helen, the queen of all gossip.

She went back to digging in her garden while taking an occasional hostile glance at the house, and I became aware of a newly found appreciation for her. I observed her again, digging and pruning her flowers with total, single-minded concentration. Then she looked up and smiled at me, a light, breezy smile that didn't demonstrate a care in the world.

"You should tell your father to trim that ivy on the fence. It's growing too high and coming over into our side," she said, standing up.

"Sure," I replied, perplexed by her sudden shift in mood.

"Don't worry, I won't tell them about all the parties and people you had stay over. It'll be our little secret. I keep lots of secrets," she laughed and winked, the humor of the moment escaping me.

"It's no big secret. They're okay with it."

By the way she furrowed her eyebrows, this fact was well beyond her range of comprehension.

"Oh. Well, bye-bye now."

It was rare when Helen peeled away first from a conversation, and I felt relieved. She waddled toward her front door with her short, choppy steps, and I had to grin at her mannerisms and her way. Then it crossed my mind that she'd gone inside to call the police, to put an end to that lunatic bitch of a woman before she hurt someone. Helen had done very little in her garden except dig up the dirt and pulled some dead petals from the flowers. Then I looked closer. She sprinkled some seeds here and there and loosened the hard soil so that it was dark and rich, ready for fertilization. I would imagine there was a woman like Helen on every street in America, and every street needed one, if not to spin the web of gossip, then to plant the seeds of action.

I was broken from my thoughts when a horn honked in the near distance. I turned to find our big, clunky, lime-green station wagon rounding the corner. Jay steered the wagon to a stop in the driveway, and my parents exited the car with their luggage.

"You timed it just right, huh man?" said Jay knowingly.

"No, I love mowing the lawn in the middle of a hot summer day."

For the first time in my life, I felt very awkward and nervous around my parents. It was an odd feeling, as if I'd detached from the mother ship and was now floating around in orbit, observing them from a distance and seeing objects I never had before. Not wanting to address my father, I suddenly lunged at my mother and tightly embraced her.

"Oh, Kevin, wow, missed you, too," she said, kissing me on the cheek.

"Good to be home," my father said, stretching out his arms. "Hello, Kevin," he said, wrapping his arm around me briefly and receiving no warmth or enthusiasm in return.

"I see you survived without us okay," my mother said.

"Yeah, but the cupboards are cleaned out, and the refrigerator is empty."

"First thing we'll do is make a run to the market and get those stocked up right away. We have to beef you up for football."

"Have you been watering the lawn every night? Looks a little on the dry side," said my father while he carried the luggage up the front steps. I was festering a deep resentment, but I couldn't afford to show my emotions and tip my hand. Not yet, anyway.

"It's been really hot. It could probably use some more."

"We'll give it a good soaking tonight. Everything okay while we were gone?" he asked. "No disasters, no breakage, anything like that?"

Jay and I exchanged uneasy looks.

"Everything's fine. Did you have a good time on your vacation?" I colored the word 'vacation' with just enough cynicism to elicit some type of reaction from them. I caught a darting, apprehensive glance between my parents that indicated that one was hoping the other would answer the question.

"Yes, we did, wonderful weather… great scenery, too," said my mother. "We had a good time, didn't we, John?"

"Oh yeah, it was nice, very nice. Love that Golden Gate Bridge and the harbor… just beautiful. But we're glad to be home," said my father. Amber bolted from the hallway, her toenails screeching against the slick, hard floor, and jumped up against my father's legs, her tail slashing side to side. When she got that tail going she could knock over a small child.

"I have to split," said Jay.

"So soon?" said my mother.

"I'm recording this afternoon at the studio. It's gonna be an all-nighter."

Jay had been working as a recording engineer for rock music groups, trying to land his biggest job yet, Steely Dan's next album. He'd been edgy and quiet lately, and despite everything that was happening with the family, I just assumed his restlessness was related to the impending studio deal. Until now his jobs had consisted primarily of no-name bands with deals at small record labels, and he knew that a job with Steely Dan would propel his career into a higher stratosphere.

"You'll be around for Kevin's birthday party, won't you?" said my mother.

"Yeah, but I really have to go," he said. He was out the door in a flash.

"I'll go finish the lawn," I declared.

While I pushed out the screen door, my parents exchanged befuddled expressions, which probably stemmed from my unusual commitment to the yard. I caught up with Jay outside just as he opened his car door and sat inside.

"Jay, wait up," I said.

"You can play my records, just don't scratch 'em."

"It's not that. I did something crazy, something really crazy."

"You? It's not your style. You like to go with your strong hand."

When Jay and I played basketball in the driveway, he always overplayed my right hand since he knew I had trouble going to my left. He constantly needled me about this weakness, always challenging me to drive left: "Go to your left, man, come on," he would taunt. We'd sometimes play late into the cool summer nights, beaming my father's car headlights against the garage. One time, we played so long that we burned all the power in the battery, and my father couldn't start the wagon the next day. He was furious and told us the next time we'd have to pay him for a new battery. It never happened again.

"Well, this time I drove to my left," I said.

"So what happened, get stuffed as usual?"

"I–I—"

"Come on, I'm waiting, blow my mind."

"I went to that woman's house."

"What woman?"

"Dad's woman."

There was a long pause as Jay weighed the significance of my admission. I anticipated his outrage, at least some anger, but nothing came. I think he was stunned, as if the words never registered with his Spock-like logic.

"You mean the woman in the picture?"

"Yeah, I went to her house. I've seen the inside."

"Wow, that's way out there, man, totally gone. I didn't think you could pull it off, but you blew my mind. Okay, well, good luck with that."

He pushed a silver key into the ignition and the motor kicked over and rumbled. He grabbed his sunglasses from the dashboard and slipped them over his eyes. Once again we were talking over noise other than our own voices.

"Did you hear me?" I said louder. "I went to her house. I've talked to her."

"Yeah, I know. Listen, I'm running late and I have a lot to do. Check you later."

"What's wrong with you, don't you care?"

"Can't worry about something I can't control. I have my own shit to worry about. There's a lot going down right now."

"But what about Mom and Dad?"

"My car's getting real dirty. Next time I come by, I'm cashing in on that promise you made."

"Don't worry, I'll wash your damn car," I said angrily, ramming his door shut.

He leaned his head out the door window while I started to walk away. "Hey, I tried to keep you outta this, but you pushed your way in."

"So?"

"So now you're in the real world, playing in the big leagues. Believe me, it's not all fun and games. Sometimes the only way to win is not to play."

He shifted the transmission into drive and punched the gas pedal. The car lifted and blasted away. He burned rubber at the end of our cul-de-sac before racing back the other way and out of sight. Despite our exchange and his indifference, his ongoing disinterest,

I wanted so much to be in the passenger seat near him, to go wherever he was going. It didn't matter where. The thought of going back inside the house and facing my parents alone made my stomach queasy. Then I remembered I could waste a few more minutes on raking the rest of the grass, and I was actually glad to have a chore to finish. I took my time and considered my next moves. As usual, nothing brilliant or even worthwhile came to me, although perhaps it was just as well.

# Chapter Nine

*The next couple of days I kept a close eye on my parents to pick* up any clues as to whether their relationship had improved. I was hoping the counseling session had actually done some good. I found nothing to support my hopes and in fact, I thought the opposite was true. On the other hand, knowing the truth about something must automatically broaden a person's field of vision to realities not seen before. It was possible they were no different than before they'd left, and I'd chosen to interpret their interactions in new and more analytical ways. I'd never really analyzed anything before at such a profound level, and I found it intriguing. I knew something deeply personal about my parents, and without really wanting or trying to, I measured every word they said and judged every action they took. I was certain that even the most simple of gestures between them had meaning. My only problem was trying to figure out what those meanings were.

"Come here, Kevin, I wanna show you something," my father

said, leaning under the hood of our station wagon. "Look at this."

The night before I made a conscious decision to carry on with my father as usual, to pretend everything was normal. Although the burden of my knowledge was heavy to bear, I kept thinking about Shelly, her family, and my brother, wondering how this would all play out. I was determined to set aside my heavy resentment, at least temporarily, while I sniffed around for more facts and information. Mostly, I was just hoping for something to change for the better.

I leaned in under the hood, and the familiar engine odors of dried oil and dusty metal filled my nostrils. My father withdrew the oil stick from a small hole and raised it to his eyesight. My father was born into a large, poor family from South Fallbrook, about fifteen miles from Rossmoor, after the fallout from the Great Depression. He was one of fourteen brothers and sisters, ten boys and four girls, which probably explained why they were so poor. Just about every year we heard the same line about how the brothers had to share the one, snazzy pair of dress shoes for their dates. My father started working when he was thirteen, mostly painting houses and doing odd jobs where he could find them. He and his brothers excelled at painting homes, so years later they decided to open a family business. He finally opted against manual labor and went into the numbers game, becoming the budget director for the city of Los Angeles. I didn't really understand what he did for his paycheck, although I knew that he came home just after six every night, a briefcase dangling from his hand, his shoulders slumped, his walk slow, and his expression defeated, as though someone had dropped some bad news on him. It took him a while before he could unwind and find humor in something. He rarely talked about his job, so I assumed he didn't care much for it. Perhaps he should've joined his brothers in the home painting business; at least they got to wear overalls, splash paint around, and work in the California sunshine.

"See that line?" he said, pointing to a thin indentation that crossed the long silver stick. "Oil should measure all the way up to that line, or at least be close. What does that tell you?"

"Could use another quart of oil, I guess."

"The worst thing you can do to your engine is let the oil run dry. Regular oil changes, that's the way to keep your car running smoothly."

"So how come it doesn't help this engine?" I joked.

"There's nothing wrong with this car, it just runs a little heavy."

"Like an army tank, you mean."

"Hey, this wagon got us all the way to Lake Powell and back, hitching a heavy boat to its tail. I'd say that's pretty good for a car this old."

"Dad, the engine overheated in Utah, through the National Park. We were stuck there for hours."

"Well sure, those high grades were murder on the engine. But if you remember, I got her running again. Believe me, this car will run forever if you treat her right. That's true of most cars. Regular maintenance is the key. You'll have to remember that when you get your own car."

"Are you gonna buy me some wheels when I get my license, Dad?" I asked, already knowing the answer.

"Can't promise anything. Money's a little tight. We'll have to see how things go."

I swore under my breath that 'we'll have to see how things go' was my father's family motto.

I went inside the house to wash my hands. The putrid scent pressed against my face. It would eventually circulate throughout the entire house and stick to the walls and furniture. It smelled like iodine mixed in with insect repellent. My mother was dyeing her hair, a practice she'd maintained several times a year. The house stunk for at least an hour after she worked her magic. She tried to keep her hair deep auburn and bouncy, and lately I think she'd begun to see evidence of graying, which multiplied the hair dyeing days by two.

She stood in front of her bathroom mirror, clear plastic gloves over her hands, an assortment of spray cans and jars of creams and plastic tubes and cotton balls strategically laid out on the white tiled counter, and an old bath towel wrapped around her shoulders. She had this activity down to an art form. She'd divide her hair into little sections and then dip a cotton ball into the solution. Then she'd dampen her sectioned piece of hair with the cotton ball and roll it with a brush roller, securing the entire section with a plastic pin that had a tiny bulb at the end. She'd hold these pins between her teeth, then move to another section.

"Why do you dye your hair, Mom?" I asked.

"I'm not dyeing today, I'm perming it," she said.

"But sometimes you dye it. What's wrong with the color you have?"

She cranked her head around and smiled and then returned to the mirror and applied more perming solution. My mother had a warm, genuine smile that made people feel appreciated, and long, finely buffed fingernails she used to scratch me to sleep when I was a boy. When her hair was fixed just the way she liked it, it sat on her head in a swirling helmet ball of reddish brown, and stayed perfectly in place when she moved. Like my father's family, her family was dirt poor, except her parents only had two other mouths to feed, instead of fourteen. My mother's younger sister, Mary, a beautiful woman who always reminded me of Elizabeth Taylor, once attended an Elvis Presley concert and watched him perform from the front rows. Apparently the King was smitten with my aunt and instructed one of his sidekicks to invite her back to his room after the show. As legend would have it, Aunt Mary was escorted to his hotel room but at the last second, just moments before stepping inside the door, for some inexplicable reason she chickened out and made a hasty exit. What a shame. Spending some private time with the king of rock and roll would've definitely made for a great story or at least an interesting memory.

"I'm not ready for gray hair just yet," my mother said. "Looks pretty horrible right now, doesn't it?" I nodded as she carefully pinned back a section of hair and worked on another. "In a few hours you'll think I went to the salon and got the full work-up."

"I thought it looked fine the way it was."

"That's nice to say, but you look at me and see your mom, and I look in the mirror and see a mother of four, putting on a few years and pounds, trying to look…" She paused and examined herself in the mirror, dogged by a visible doubt and regret. "Well it all must seem pretty silly, huh?" I just shrugged. "I can feel some solution trickling down the back of my neck. Could you dab that for me?"

I reached out and ripped a few sheets of paper from the toilet roll. A trail of solution streamed down her neck, so I wiped it dry. My mother could've easily wiped the liquid herself except I think she knew this was a special privilege for me, to help in a more personal way. As I finished wiping, I listened to her sigh heavily and noticed her shoulders sag a notch. Moments later my father entered from the bedroom door, and she perked up, her shoulders straightening, her expression more alert. It was then I figured out the real reason she crafted her hair so neatly: to look nice for my father. Maybe she considered this a competition between women, and she was falling behind in the race. I couldn't fathom her reasons for sharing a bed with my father or even standing near him and making lighthearted jokes and conversation. How could she carry on as if nothing had happened? How could a marriage survive infidelity? I was confused, and yet I realized that I was standing on the outside, looking in. I could also rationalize that she just wanted to keep up appearances and sustain the marriage and family, at least temporarily. Once she removed her finger from the leak and the dam busted wide open, our family—and her life— would never be the same. I've seen huge momentum shifts in sports, teams and athletes that made stunning comebacks to snatch the victory at the last second. Perhaps my mother was hoping and praying for a comeback, for the tide to swing in her favor. In any case, her words and actions, all her mannerisms and routines, suggested she wasn't prepared to raise the white flag. My father reached for something in a drawer.

"Lovely smell, huh, Kevin?" said my father.

"I don't know how she puts up with it," I said.

"Never underestimate the power of vanity, especially in women," said my father.

"Oh, John, you don't like gray hair, either," said my mother.

"But Dad doesn't have gray hair," I said.

"He most certainly…" my mother started, and then caught herself and glanced at my father for his reaction.

"Thanks a lot, Audrey," said my father. "I use something on my hair too, Kevin."

"What, that Grecian Formula they're always advertising on TV?" I said excitedly, as if discovering another secret about my father.

"Well the stuff works," he said.

"There, don't you feel better about telling someone?" said my mother. "Now you don't have to hide it anymore. Your father didn't think he should have gray hair yet, not at age forty-four. But I told him that most men start to gray by then, and some men are all the way by the time they hit forty." Turning to my father she added, "Your father was gray by your age, almost completely."

"You'd be gray too, if you had fourteen children," said my father.

While he spoke I studied my father's physical features. He had bushy eyebrows like two black caterpillars and a forehead that hung more than normal over the rest of his face. His thick sideburns extended almost two inches down around his jaw, and in my opinion, could've used a trim. At a solid six feet with broad shoulders and sleepy blue eyes, I suppose women might consider him handsome. He was no Paul Newman, though, the actor in *Cool Hand Luke*; more like George Kennedy, Luke's best friend in prison. Of the two, my mother inherited the good-looks gene. My father snapped up my mother not long after he started college, getting hitched before they even turned twenty years of age. Less than two years later Jay was born, and they were off to the parental races, for better or worse.

"Kevin, by the way, that's not something you share with your friends, that your parents are dyeing their hair," said my father.

"How much is it worth to keep it quiet?" I said, holding out my hand.

"How about a roof over your head and food on your plate," my father countered.

"Got that already," I said.

"How about no roof over your head and no food on your plate?"

"I'll stick with the roof and food."

My father smirked and left the bathroom. The fact that he colored his hair seemed in direct contradiction with his portfolio of character traits. I mean, a few years ago he took the family to a place called Venice Beach. I'd never seen anything so bizarre and yet fascinating. The people were mostly young, long-haired hipsters who wore tie-dye shirts and gobs of bright costume jewelry. Many were navigating the boardwalk on roller skates, skateboards, or bicycles, wearing only skimpy bathing suits. The peace symbol was ever-present on clothing, necklaces, posters, and even headbands. Some people were holding signs that denounced the war in Vietnam. And while a great many were smoking, I noticed an enclosed workout area where hulking bodybuilder dudes were pumping massive amounts of free weights.

While we stood together at the end of the street that funneled into the boardwalk, absorbing the full flavor of the colorful scene, my father looked down and said, "Kevin, this is where the *real* people live." At first I was mildly charmed by his words. My own father, who rarely made such declarations, wanted to communicate something meaningful to his son. Moments later I started to wonder about that meaning. Did he mean to imply that our more conventional family lifestyle was somehow fake or unreal? Or maybe he just found the freedom and peace-loving attitude that radiated from the people on that strange strip of humanity far more appealing. In any case, there was nothing real about coloring his hair.

"I hope I never go gray, but if I do, I'm just gonna let it happen," I said. "I couldn't put myself through that torture." My mother smiled gently with the wisdom of knowing differently.

"People don't like seeing themselves turning older, including your father. His Christian Scientist upbringing can't conquer the great Copeland male ego. He talks about vanity, but ego is a much more powerful emotion. The Copeland men have that in spades."

"What's a Christian Scientist?" I asked.

"They believe that God takes care of all His children, whether they're hurt, sick, or just growing old. Science and medicine have no real place in their lives."

"I've seen Dad take lots of medicine. Plus you always give us stuff for colds and fevers."

"He doesn't practice the religion, but his parents did, so it's in his blood. One time when he was a little bit younger than you, his school sent him home with an injured leg. He'd fallen during a football game. His parents sent him right back to school and said he was fine. Your dad complained of so much pain that the school finally sent him to the hospital. Know what they found?"

"What?"

"He'd broken it. They put a cast on his leg, and his parents came to the hospital to pick him up. The strangest part was, they weren't too happy that the doctor put a cast on their son's leg without their permission."

"Well anyone who has fourteen kids must be a little nuts," I said, making my mother laugh, which always made me feel warm inside.

"Yes, and they didn't believe in abortion or birth control."

There were a few moments of silence between us, since I was caught off guard by her last sentence. I decided to roll with it.

"Would you have an abortion, Mom?"

My mother paused from rolling another curler into place, trying to find the words. I don't think she expected her youngest to follow up with such a direct, hard-hitting question. I'd certainly become more inquisitive in recent days. I finally realized that no one in my family would offer me any interesting information unless I asked for it.

"I can't imagine my life without my children, if that answers your question," she said, then continued working on her hair.

"Why are so many women doing it?" I asked.

"I'm not sure, Kevin. Maybe some people are scared by the idea of being parents. My advice to those people would be to take the necessary precautions. It's mostly just laziness."

"Do you think it's wrong, I mean, morally?"

She stared at me with inquisitive eyes.

"Kevin, is there something you need to tell me?"

"No, no... I'm just wondering, because, well..."

"Well what?"

"Well Jay said I was a surprise to you and Dad. He said everyone was planned but me. I didn't know if... if he was telling the truth or just, you know, messin' with me." I nervously sputtered on my words. My mother sighed, then set down the cotton ball in her hand and leaned in closer to me, the smell of the solution now plastering my face and nose.

"Yes, you were a surprise and no," she emphasized, "we never once thought about not having you. Besides, as you grow older you'll find out that oftentimes the best gifts in life are unexpected, and you were certainly one of those." She smiled soothingly and planted a smooch kiss on my cheek. I cringed and pulled away, repelled by the strong aroma of solution.

# Chapter Ten

*I'd heard the phrase 'ignorance is bliss' before although the* meaning always rolled right over my head until now. I was a happier, carefree young man before I found out about my father. Yet, if given the choice, I'd find that picture all over again and bump into Shelly at the store. I was learning more about adults, too, why they seemed to carry an undertone of defeated awareness in everything they said and did; a kind of pessimistic caution that children rarely displayed. They simply knew too much.

Late one night I was awakened by the shuffling of feet down the hallway and some hushed voices. I was groggy but realized the voices were moving down the hallway and past my door. Bodies moved by in the soft light as the shadows stretched against the wall.

"What've you been doing all night?" said my father, agitated.

I heard Rachel moan something, but I couldn't understand the words.

"She looks real bad, John, maybe we should take her to the hospital," said my mother.

A few seconds later I heard a thud as if someone had fallen against the floor. I hurriedly threw back the sheet on my bed and hopped over to my door. At the end of the hallway my father was leaning over a collapsed Rachel, while my distressed mother stood nearby. I'd never seen my sister so utterly wasted before. I'd seen her drunk and stoned, but she'd always been capable of standing and talking to some adequate degree. This time her eyes had rolled back in their sockets and her face was drained of any color. She looked like a puppet whose strings had been cut, devoid of any animation.

"Rachel, what'd you take?" my father said, lightly slapping her face in attempt to revive her. "What'd they give you?"

She didn't awaken, and my father, a pacifist by nature, slapped her pretty hard on the meaty part of her cheek. The force surprised me, and I winced.

"Ow," Rachel mumbled angrily.

"Was it a pill of some kind?"

"We shouldn't take any chances, John. We should take her in right now," said my mother.

"Okay, you're right," my father agreed, though none too thrilled about it. "We have to keep her awake. Go get a cold towel."

Rachel began to convulse, gently at first. Her shoulders undulated with more speed, and her stomach bloated until a river of liquid chunks gushed out her mouth and splat right into my father's lap.

"Jesus," my father cried out, falling back on his hands. To my father's misfortune he'd chosen to deal with this trauma wearing

102

only his white Fruit of a Loom briefs, so the chunky barf dripped down his hairy legs and knees. "Better make it a big towel," he said despondently.

The violent heave revived Rachel somewhat. She actually straightened her wobbly head and opened her eyes enough to view her handy work. She tried to focus, and then oddly, she started to giggle like a little girl. My father wasn't the least bit amused.

"Oh shit, I puked on you," Rachel gurgled while pointing. My mother turned to me with the hope that I hadn't been emotionally traumatized.

"She'll be okay, Kevin, why don't you go back to bed," she said.

"I wanna help," I said.

"If you wanna help, don't ever come home looking like this," said my father.

Rachel giggled again while I watched this bizarre scene with an underlying fear. Was this what happened to a person when they turned sixteen? Would I ever look that blitzed? And damn, would I grow up to be a hairy beast like my father?

"Would you get the towels, please?" said my father, irked. My mother and I hurried to the bathroom. We pulled some towels from the cabinets and soaked them under the cold, running water.

"Did she get this way while we were gone?" asked my mother.

"She seemed all right to me."

"I don't know what we're doing wrong with her. She just keeps testing us."

While we soaked the towels together, I sensed that my mother was drifting deeper into herself and her thoughts. The cold water rushed over our hands and she paused to check herself in the mirror. She stared at her reflection in a grim way, and I was pretty certain that she disliked the view. Her eyes were bloodshot and drowsy, and she had the dreary face of someone who hadn't slept well in days. She appeared old to me, and by her defeated expression she was probably thinking the exact same thought. She'd never looked so old before.

We connected eyes in the mirror, and I did my best to offer her comfort in my expression. Her eyes became wet around the rims, and the corners of her mouth turned down and quivered. A tear trailed down her cheek. She lowered her head on her forearm and leaned against the sink, as if she had nothing left to hold her upright. I'd seen my mother cry before but only in private, stolen moments from a crack through her bedroom door. Never had she allowed me inside the circle of her grief, and I didn't know how to occupy that space with any real value. I only knew I wanted to fix her and wash away the pain, the way she'd always done for me. I turned off the water and gently laid my arm across her shoulders.

"It'll be okay, Mom," I said. "She'll get better."

She sniffled and lifted her head from the sink, trying to contain herself, wiping her tears. She even managed a listless smile that acknowledged my efforts. She wrapped her arms around me and hugged tightly, trying to communicate something important, perhaps something I already knew or sensed. I heard my father's voice from the hallway and bodies moving toward us. Moments later my father plowed through the bathroom door with Rachel dangling from his arms and shoulders, half struggling to break away.

"Just let me sleep, damn it," said Rachel. She appeared slightly more coherent than before. I think the old heave-ho cleaned out her system.

"John, what are you doing?"

"Forget the towels. She's getting a cold shower and right now," he said.

"No way!" shouted Rachel.

"What about the hospital?" asked my mother.

"I had some drinks, big fucking deal!"

My father twisted the knob on the shower and didn't waste a moment shoving Rachel inside, fully clothed. She shrieked at the first contact of cold water and shouted, "It's fuckin' freezing in here!"

My father grabbed one of the wet towels from the sink and wiped the vomit from his legs. I could tell my mother fiercely disapproved of the shower method, and being married as long as they had, my father picked up on the sign.

"It'll wake her up, and then we'll watch her," he said. "If she doesn't get better we'll take her in."

"You don't fool me, John. You just don't wanna take her to the hospital."

"She doesn't need a doctor. It would only be wasting their time and ours."

"It's not a waste of *my* time," my mother said in a hostile tone. "I can't watch you do this to her. I'm calling the hospital to find out what we should do."

"Fine, if that makes you feel better, go ahead, call 'em," my father said.

She scorched him with a penetrating glare and left the bathroom, crashing the door behind her. I'd heard too many slammed doors during the past few months in my house, and they always made me uncomfortable. Most of them occurred after blistering arguments between Rachel and my parents.

Rachel fell back against the shower wall and slid down gradually to the floor tiles, the stream of water pelting her body and clothes. My father rubbed his forehead, his eyes to the floor, which I'd learned was his reaction to anything that irritated him.

"You can turn it off now!" yelled Rachel.

"Are you waking up?" he said.

"I just want out!"

My father faced me. "Listen, Kevin, sometimes we do things because we have to, not because we want to. That's part of being a parent."

"Turn it off!" Rachel shouted again.

"Go back to your room now. I'll take care of your sister," he said.

My father reached in and shut off the water. Before I left the bathroom, I took one more lingering look at my sister. Sitting upright in a fetal position, her arms and legs tucked together and her forehead resting against her kneecaps, Rachel reminded me of a helpless young child. Then she gradually raised her head, and with thick, dark lines of make-up trickling down her cheeks, gazed up at my father with a genuine longing that I'd never seen before, a desperate wanting, perhaps pleading for my father to embrace her and never let go. My father extended one leg inside the shower and pulled Rachel to her feet, wrapping a dry towel around her shoulders. Then I left the bathroom and returned to my room.

I heard only sporadic noises later that night of my father putting his youngest daughter to bed. I suppose she was fine after the cold shower. I was fairly certain the same couldn't be said about my mother and father.

# Chapter Eleven

*The next day was unusually quiet in my house with many* curious, sideways glances and carefully crafted words. The tension was too thick for me, and I wanted nothing more than to escape it. Just before noon I was glad to get a phone call from Kyle Bollinger. His mom bought him a new board game called Stratego, and he invited me to play. I would've rather spent time with someone else, but Kyle was the only offer I had.

I knocked on the door of the Bollinger's house, and Kyle answered almost instantly. He was in a much better mood than usual, and I thought it must be the excitement of playing a new game. Maybe he knew he could beat me, and this thought cheered him. He'd probably been studying the game all morning to gain a competitive advantage.

"Come on in," he said as he turned from the door and ambled away. I followed him inside and we made our way through the living room and into his bedroom. As Kyle set up the game, I was struck by his room's simplicity. Except for some sports equipment dumped randomly throughout the room, and a poster of the Dodgers' first baseman Steve Garvey on the wall, it was pretty bare. He explained the game and the concept seemed fairly straightforward. The idea was to capture the opponent's flag by strategically killing off the opponent's army of pieces. We positioned our pieces, and I hid my flag in the far left corner of the board.

"School's coming up, bummer, huh?" said Kyle.

"Yeah, homework sucks."

"High school's a lot better than junior high, though. The chicks, they're up for anything. They have experience."

He killed one of my number eight pieces, a minor, which was important since they were the only pieces that could break through bombs, allowing other pieces to capture the flag contained within.

"You mean the seniors," I said.

"No, juniors and sophomores, too, if you meet the right ones."

"I never meet the right ones."

"Just start showin' up at parties and hangin' out after games and stuff. It'll happen."

"I don't think it's that easy," I said.

"Hey, if Timmy Baker can score, you can too."

"Who's Timmy Baker?"

"He's this total dipshit who wears glasses… the biggest klutz on the planet."

"He got laid?" I asked, disbelieving.

"Some senior girl asked him to the prom, and I heard his sister found 'em doing it in the living room. It was all over campus last year. The girl was a real bow-wow, though."

"Who cares, he got laid."

Kyle paused to make his next move, and I countered with a move that captured his Colonel, a key piece. He grimaced.

"What kind of chicks do you like?" he asked.

"I never really thought about a type. Blondes are nice. Brunettes are good, too. I'm not really picky."

"Know any hot ones? I mean, you've had almost all summer. You had to meet someone by now, right?"

"I know some girls from my classes, but most of 'em are either total nut jobs or already have boyfriends. Except I met—" I started to say excitedly. I caught myself, but not before Kyle noticed my enthusiasm.

"Met who?" he asked, far too assertively.

"Um, just some girl," I shrugged.

"Where?"

"In Thrifty's. We were both buying ice cream. No big deal, but I thought she was kind of hot."

"What'd she look like?"

"Hmm... I don't know. She had blonde hair, tan legs. But the best part was," I said, perking up, "she was hangin' loose underneath her shirt and, man, they were perfect."

"Damn, that should be a rule, no bras. Imagine how great life would be with no bras."

We both paused and considered the concept with a dreamy wonder in our eyes. A vision of Raquel Welch came to my mind, and then it vanished.

"Yeah, but so what? All the good ones go for older guys anyway. Besides, she's a grade higher than me."

"Ah come on, man. You never know what girls are thinkin'. Maybe she liked you."

"Not this girl. She was flirting with the guy who scoops ice cream. She was sort of uncool, anyway. Bit my head off for no good reason… probably not my type."

Then I heard, "Okay, that's enough," from an unseen source. I twisted to the voice behind me with a swelling tidal wave of fear. The closet door slid to one side, and to my horrific surprise, Shelly stepped out, crossing her arms, and trying to hide her guilt and shame with an uneasy half-grin.

"Uncool?" she said. "I may be a lot of things, but I am *not* uncool."

Kyle started laughing real hard. "Oh dude, we reamed your ass so bad. You didn't have a clue."

Kyle was reveling in his devious scheme, and instead of fear, the tidal wave turned into a raging sea of anger. I stood up and drilled a mean glare right into Shelly's guilt-ridden eyes. "Screw you both," I protested and then stomped out of the room.

I could hear Kyle rollicking, which sickened me, as he shouted, "Ah come on, man, we were just jokin' around. We have to finish the game."

"Kevin, wait!" I heard Shelly shout.

I walked hard and heavy through the living room. I was suffocating in this house, and the walls were breathing and beating against me. When I finally got outside I sucked in a big gasp of air and picked up my pace for home. After a few seconds, I heard her voice again.

"Kevin, wait up," Shelly shouted again. I kept walking. "Kevin, please, I'm really sorry." Now I paused and kept my back to her.

She'd have to keep going if she wanted to see my face. "That was a rotten thing to do, but it was his idea, not mine."

Of course it was his idea, I thought, but that doesn't absolve you of any guilt.

"I really just came here to see you." I could tell by her voice that she was moving closer, and I knew she was only a few steps behind me. I pivoted with all the high drama in my artistic soul (hoping that I actually had some art in my soul).

"Why'd you come to see me?" I asked.

She approached slowly, and for some strange reason, I backed up a step, as if she'd threatened my safety. It was an involuntary response.

"I felt bad about the way things ended," she said. "I said some pretty horrible things. I've been trying to find you the last few days."

"So how'd you find me?"

"I told you, I'm real good at figuring out mysteries." She smiled with so much sweet charm it nearly erased every ounce of resentment I had left. "When I found out you lived near Kyle, I called him. I know him from school. He said he wanted to do something fun, set up a surprise meeting. But I never thought he'd make you talk about girls, especially not me."

"You could've called me."

"I wanted to see you. And obviously I couldn't just knock on your door."

She had a good point, and beyond that, she looked damn fine today, super fine.

"It was hard to hear, everything you said, but I knew you were telling me the truth the day I met you."

111

"How'd you know?"

"My parents haven't been real... cozy lately. Something's not right about them. And my mom, she's been as jumpy as an alley cat."

"Are you gonna say something?" I said, silently praying that the answer would be no.

"I don't think so," she said. "It's too major to just to blurt out, you know?"

"Yeah, I'm not ready, either. I wouldn't know what to say, anyway."

There was a pocket of silence between us while she sighed and glanced away. Then she spoke these glorious, momentous words, "There's a party tonight at my friend's house." She extended a small piece of paper to me. "Would you like to come?"

I lunged at the paper, and then tried to stop my momentum before I embarrassed myself. She may have noticed my eager lean, though thankfully she let it slide. I regrouped and calmly took the piece of paper.

"Maybe," I replied.

"Well, I really hope you can make it. It should be a blast."

She left her gaze on me, curiously, then smiled and started to stroll up the street.

"You walked all the way over here?" I asked.

"Yeah... I like long walks. They give me time to think, plan things out."

She paused and turned after a few steps and back peddled as she spoke. "Do you really think I'm uncool?"

Somehow I was rendered speechless by the question and simply shrugged in tandem with a headshake. It must've seemed pretty indecisive. Neither satisfied nor dissatisfied with my reply, she pivoted and kept walking. I watched her stride away until she reached the end of our street and turned left, fading from my view. I glanced down at the precious paper in my hand and felt a surge of excitement. I suddenly thought of Charlie, the poor boy who found a dollar in the street and moments later, unwrapped a Willy Wonka chocolate bar to find the last golden ticket. Like Charlie, I sought entry into a mysterious and magical world of sweet delights, but my cravings would never be satisfied by feasting on pounds of candy and chocolate. I'd set my sights on something far more interesting.

# Chapter Twelve

*I was blow-drying my hair in the bathroom, a routine I recently* started, when Rachel turned into the doorframe and leaned against it. The skin on her face was pasty and tired, with thin rings of exhaustion under her eyes. She observed me with a distant caring.

"You're not doing it right," she said, reaching for the blow dryer. I didn't trust myself in matters of hairstyle and fashion, so I permitted her to take the blow dryer. "I'll give you hair like Donny Osmond's."

"Why would I want hair like his?" I inquired.

"He's got nice hair, and besides, you sort of look like him," said Rachel.

"A girl at school once said that, too."

"Just don't let it go to your head. You don't have his talent."

Rachel picked up a plastic brush and made long, smooth strokes at the sides of my straight and thick brown hair. She aimed the blow dryer at an angle and feathered back the sides so they had purpose. Her movements were slow and thoughtful. As I examined her face in the mirror, I noticed a rare contentment. She glanced every so often in the mirror to assess her efforts and then continued to stroke the brush through my hair. After a few minutes she powered down the blow dryer and added the finishing touches to her creation by pulling back the front so it made one, sweeping wave around the right side of my head. She focused on my image in the mirror, then paused, seemed content, and laid the brush down on the counter tiles.

"I was pretty fucked up last night, huh?" she said in slow and guilty tone.

"You coulda fooled me," I said, sharing a gentle grin.

"I guess I got a little carried away."

"Feeling better?" She just shrugged and tilted her head. "Maybe you should take it easy. Lay low for a while, you know?" She barely nodded.

"I met a really awesome family, a friend of Jamie's. They live a few blocks from here. They really talk to each other and have a good time. It's nothing like here."

"Is that where you go all the time?"

"Not always. Sometimes I just hang out with my friends. We all go riding on motorcycles. We found some great places up in the mountains. We go up there and make campfires, play some songs."

"And get loaded," I added, not sure why. She sighed deeply.

"I don't know why I bother talking to you, you're just a child." She turned into the hallway and left me. I felt remorse about my comment and went after her.

"Hey, I didn't mean that," I started, as she paused, waiting for more. "It's just that, you're never around anymore. Then when you are…I don't know, nothing seems the same around here."

"It's not like my life is one, big nonstop party, you know. It's more...interesting than that." She turned around, intent on convincing me of something, or maybe convincing herself. "I'm meeting lots of fascinating people. They aren't just satisfied with punching a clock every day or reading a book in class. They're living… they're finding themselves and what they want out of life. We get into these deep conversations about real things, and we help each other grow. They really care about me for who I am."

"But we're your family," I said. "Doesn't that count for something?"

"It's different in this house. I'm a different person with them. I don't know how to explain it, but I feel more myself with them."

I nodded softly, not knowing how to contribute to her comment or draw more conclusions. For a few moments, we were silent. I could sense she retreated into her mind, into the recent events of her life, a life I knew nothing about. I was beginning to believe that the people in my family had all changed identities, and now I was an unwitting accomplice in some sort of bizarre *Twilight Zone* episode. The only living creature in our house that I could still figure out and connect to was Amber, our dog.

"Hey, you wanna go in the backyard and wait for butterflies to land on our arms, like we used to?" I said, trying to raise her spirits. There's always an abundance of Morning Glory butterflies fluttering around our backyard, and sometimes, one will land onto my outstretched arm.

"They only land on you, not me. They don't like me for some reason."

"Okay, then you can take pictures. Nobody believed they landed on me until you got the idea to take pictures."

I noticed an uptick in her mood, as if she tapped into that happy, playful girl I once knew, more interested in spending time with her younger brother.

"I suppose tomorrow you'll wanna play kick the can in the street," she said, showing a trace of enthusiasm, though sarcastic. "And maybe the next day you'll wanna play hopscotch in the entry hall."

"Hey, I'm game for anything. Whatever you want, I'm there," I said.

Any shred of enthusiasm she had rapidly drifted into a more somber mood. I tried to imagine what could take her there, to that somber place, and why she'd decided to push aside the carefree girl that once occupied her mind and heart. The only conclusion I could draw was the influence of her new friends. She was experiencing too much, too soon, and while my parents encouraged us to broaden our horizons and try new things, in Rachel's case, she'd taken everything to the extreme.

"Why can't everything be simple, like it was back then?" she asked, wistfully.

"Things were simple because we were," I said, feeling proud of my response. Maybe I was gaining some wisdom about people and life.

"Can you keep a secret?" she asked. "I mean it, I'm not kiddin' around. I'll never tell you anything again if you spill your guts on this one."

"I'll lock it up and throw away the key."

She waited several seconds, inwardly debating whether or not to trust me, then uttered, "I don't wanna live here anymore."

"What—why not?"

"Mom and Dad always fight, and they don't care what we do. Well, let me rephrase that, they don't care what *I* do. Jay and Sarah aren't around very much. It's weird. I get bad vibes here. There's no positive energy."

"So what are you gonna do, just run away?"

"My friends want me to. They think I'd be happier."

"But what about Mom and Dad?"

"They won't stop me. Shit, they'll probably hold the door open for me. Bye-bye, have fun, send us a postcard now and then."

"They'll be crushed, and you know it."

"Maybe a little, at first, but they'll get over it. They always do. It's all about discovering who I am as a person, right?" she said, mocking my parents with her cynical tone.

"But you can't. That means I'll be the only one left in the house. You can't leave me alone with them, not now." My urgency puzzled her.

"Oh come on, they adore you, the little golden child. It's probably what they want anyway, to be home alone with their precious baby."

"Oh I see. You're just lookin' for any excuse you can to run away."

"I don't need excuses, just the truth. And it's about time we all faced it, even me," she said. "I'm the troublemaker in this family. I'm the one who can't do anything right. Mom and Dad are ashamed of me. I can feel it. I just can't stand to see that disappointed look in their eyes anymore."

She glanced away uneasily, and just before turning around,

caught my gaze, awaiting my reaction. I could tell she wanted some encouraging words or an inspirational message that could reel her in from the rushing river that was dragging her away from home. But I was locked in a conflicted state of mind, torn between telling her my own truth, as I saw it—to dump her new friends and stop doing drugs—and knowing she'd hate me once those words left my mouth. So I just stood there in a kind of silent agony, and it must've shown in my expression.

"Just like that," she said, turning and retreating into her room.

# Chapter Thirteen

*Daylight was fading when I rolled down our driveway.* There was always a sense of adventure whenever I hit the end of the driveway and my front tire bounced off the lip and onto the street. The party was only a few blocks from Shelly's house, in an upscale area of town. When the first gush of warm summer air brushed against my face, I realized how useless it was to perfectly blow dry my hair.

The front door was open when I set foot onto the porch and music blared from within. Inside the house, I was struck by the feeling of not belonging, and every step I took was plagued with doubt. I'd probably be the youngest person in the house, and except for Shelly, very few people would know me. I should've made plans to bring somebody older, maybe Kyle. Of course, if I'd had any balls at all I would've simply asked Shelly to join me, since she made the invitation in the first place. In fact, now that I thought about it, maybe she'd been waiting for me to ask, and I blew it. All these thoughts were ping-ponging inside my brain as I wandered like a lost puppy dog into the living room, and not a soul uttered a word in my direction.

The house was awash in deep shadows and silhouettes and multi-colored lights that streaked against the walls. Bright party streamers funneled from the brass ceiling fan out to every corner of the living room. With each step I could feel the carpeted floor vibrate from the music's heavy bass thumping. Someone had hung one of those mirrored spin balls from the ceiling fan, although it was idle at the moment. A few lava lamps were scattered about on counters, and a long snack table with various trays of food ran underneath the bar near the kitchen. I smelled some incense burning, though I couldn't see any trails of smoke. Small groups of people were huddled together in corners, near doorways, in hallways, talking with occasional outbursts of laughter. I saddled up next to the snack table and swept in a handful of cheese puffs, plowing them into my mouth. Doing something with my mouth always calmed my nerves.

"Hi, Kevin," said a sweet voice from behind, just as I crunched the puffs. I turned to find Shelly standing there, all dolled up in blue eyeliner that highlighted her green eyes and lips painted a rosy shade of red. I knew she was a natural beauty, but I never suspected she could transform herself into a sexy young woman.

"Hi," I said, trying to slowly and quietly munch the cheese puffs.

"I'm glad you could come," she said. "I thought you might…you know, be mad at me."

"I'm over it. I don't like to hold onto… negative vibes."

What did I just say, *negative vibes*? I wasn't sure how that comment escaped my mouth, but there it was, just twisting aimlessly in the air. She faintly smiled, and we averted our eyes from each other.

"Wanna dance?" she asked.

She'd injected a pure shot of fear into my nervous system, asking me to be the only guy dancing in front of people I didn't know. But I was in no position to refuse her. She clutched my hand and started to turn when we both realized that I had a thick residue of cheese dust on my hand. She released my hand and by her polite half-smile I knew she was annoyed. An odd comment and cheese dust hands; I was off to a lousy start.

We brushed off our hands and arrived separately at the center of the room. I wasn't paying much attention to the music because my mind had been so preoccupied by other thoughts. When I started to move my stiff limbs, I was repulsed to learn I was dancing to the Bay City Rollers. Spinning one of their records in my house was grounds for dismissal, permanent dismissal. Still, I was dancing with the sexiest girl at the party, and I knew this since I took a quick inventory the minute I entered the room. It was strange; there were two girls for every guy. I wasn't complaining, although I began to wonder if I was one of a select group of guys who'd been invited to the party, and if so, it most likely meant that Shelly invited only me.

I wanted to dance freely and without restriction except that far too many eyes had landed upon us, mostly male. I wanted to believe they were just curious, but it probably went deeper than that, to hostility. I tried my best to ignore them and concentrate on Shelly, except I could feel the daggers of hate piercing my back. They were bigger and older, and I was certain that one guy, standing in the corner, could've started at middle linebacker for the high school team. The other girls were flirting and trying to distract them, but there was no doubt that Shelly was the main attraction here, and I had the ringside seat.

"The Bay City Rollers are so awesome, aren't they?" said Shelly, contorting her body wondrously.

"Yeah, couldn't be awesome...er." I said awkwardly. I should just shut the hell up and dance, I thought.

"Why are you so uptight? Come on, loosen up, it's a party."

With her approval I felt myself relax, and my arms and legs start to fling in a more careless manner. I managed to forget everyone else in the room for just a few moments until I felt a strong arm brush me aside.

"Step aside, pal," said the middle linebacker in a stern voice. With his dull eyes he dared me to deny him, his sly grin an indication of his physical superiority. I think Shelly was hoping I would reject his macho move, although it was far too early to make a mistake and blow my lead. After all, she invited me. So, as any gentleman would, I motioned for him to step right in, and I moved aside.

Shelly was somewhat confused and I was concerned that I'd dropped the ball somehow. This big brute muscled his way in and danced like a dog in heat. I positioned myself near the snack table again since it always gave me something to do. I didn't want to stand there and gawk at Shelly, so I started for the sliding glass doors, which led to the backyard. I heard a loud commotion from the entry hall where a couple came barreling through like the king and queen of the prom. He was brutally handsome with a thick head of wavy black hair and tanned skin, and his smile showed off his glistening white teeth. He moved in graceful, cat-like strides, standing straight, tall, and supremely confident. The girl was a petite, energetic brunette with a healthy chest and a thin waist, and she couldn't have been more thrilled about being on his arm. They drew the lion's share of attention, and by Shelly's irritated expression, she didn't appreciate it. She stopped dancing, and much to my surprise, came directly over to me.

"Come on, let's go outside," she said with an agitated tone.

She grabbed my hand and led me to the backyard. The glassy water in the rectangular pool shimmered in the moonlight. We were alone. The yard was neatly landscaped with a rose garden and lighted palm trees, and just beyond the pool was a cabana room large enough to serve as a guest house.

"Make a wish," she said.

"Huh?"

"Starlight, star bright, first star I see tonight."

"Oh, right," I said.

I gazed up at the brightest star amidst the heavens and made my wish, that Shelly and I would soon press our lips together in a long, passionate kiss. Moments after making the wish I felt a twinge of guilt for not wishing that my father and Shelly's mother would go their separate ways.

"It's your turn," I said.

She tilted her head and her flowing, silky hair fell back. I wanted so much to run my fingers through it. The way she engulfed the sky with such desire and hope, I almost embraced her right then and there and made my wish come true.

"Okay, I'm done. But we can't tell each other. Then it won't come true," said Shelly.

We lapsed into a reflective, quiet period and I wondered why she invited me to this party. I didn't fit in here, not by age or popularity standards, anyway.

"What's your father like?" she said curiously, her eyes to the stars. While my father and her mother were never completely removed from my thoughts, I nevertheless tried to tuck them away whenever I was near Shelly. I didn't want anything to interfere with our progress, if there was any to be made.

"Uh... he's your typical dad. Likes sports, wears a suit to work, paints things."

"He's an artist?" she said excitedly.

"No, he paints walls, bedrooms, that sort of stuff. He comes from a family of house painters. It's sort of a family business."

"Oh." She sounded disappointed. I'm not certain why I chose to connect my father's personal interests to house painting, except that the visual of him mixing paint and the strong paint thinner aroma that always lingered in the garage reminded me of him.

"What's your dad like?" I asked.

"He's pretty cool. He's always reading old books by dead writers. I guess that's where I got my love for books. He's quieter than my mom, more mysterious. He doesn't get all huffy and mad too much, which is nice. But sometimes he'll snap when you least expect it."

"My dad's a little like that, too. It's all right except I never really know what he's thinking," I offered.

"I know. I guess that's the downside of it. I never know how he's going to react to something. It gets me into trouble sometimes. With my mom, I can usually tell you what she's gonna say before she says it."

She closed her eyes and breathed in deeply, as though trying to inhale the entire world. The loud noises pouring from inside the house kept the long, quiet moment from being noticeable.

"The parties here can get pretty wild," she said. "I wasn't here, but last summer some people went skinny-dipping in the pool. Would you do that, go skinny-dipping?"

"Sure, I do it all the time."

"You do?" she said, fascinated.

"Yeah, in the bathtub."

I thought it was funny, but she huffed and barely cracked a grin. She turned her gaze to the shimmering pool and the light from the water flickered and danced across her flawless face.

"Have you ever tried pot?" she said.

Before I had the chance to answer, a girl shouted from the house, "Shelly, come on, we're mixing pina coladas!"

"Ooh, those are really good, come get one," she said, quickly moving away from me. She left me in the dust, alone on the patio to ponder my situation with her and this party. It was as clear as the twinkling stars above that I'd have to make a break from Shelly and stand on my own two feet. My only chance to survive and earn Shelly's respect was to blend in, talk to people, and act as though I belonged. I accomplished this the only way I knew how, by saying 'yes' to everything that was directed my way.

"Want a beer?" asked some guy.

"Yes," I said.

"Who wants the last pina colada?" a girl shouted in the kitchen.

"I do!" I yelled.

"We're doing shots of tequila. You in, Kevin?"

"Hell yes," I shouted.

&#x1F6B2;

As the night wore on I became everyone's agreeable little brother in a great, big fraternity of obnoxious teenage drunks. I don't recall seeing much of Shelly during the course of my drinking binge, only blurry, golden-hair flashes moving back and forth in the swirling mirrored ball lights. I occasionally heard her voice escalate in between songs on the stereo.

I kept plowing food down my throat since the Doctor once told me that food kept a person from hurling. He never told me how to keep from getting light-headed, though. I was certain that another drink or two would put me over the edge, or over the porcelain god, and that I'd be incapable of functioning. Suddenly, Shelly yanked me into the hallway, laughing and giggling and pushing me into a dark bathroom. My heart raced and my mind sharpened to prepare for the moment about to unfold. I wasn't sure why she'd chosen the bathroom for our first romantic encounter when there were so many other rooms in this house. She started to move toward me and I licked my lips to receive her. I actually began to pucker when she reached behind and flipped on the light. There I was, under the bright, high wattage light, starting to pucker my lips and stretch my neck while some dude watched from his sitting position, leaning back against the toilet. He gushed with laughter and pointed at me, but I'd relaxed my face before Shelly could step back from the light switch.

"What's so funny?" asked Shelly.

"Oh man... nothing," said the dude, letting me off the hook. "You owe me one, dude."

"Owe you for what?" asked Shelly.

"Forget it," said the dude.

"Yeah, just forget it," I added.

"Okay, whatever. Craig, this is Kevin, Kevin... Craig," she said.

"What's up?" he said, and then he lifted a monstrous, plastic purple bong from the top of the toilet, holding it in both hands like a gift from above. "Your ticket to ride, my friends," he said proudly.

He'd plastered stickers of skeleton heads and Led Zeppelin emblems all over it. Within its cylinder walls the water was a murky, dull green. He held out the enormous bong, and I felt my chest twitch. Although I'd never seen one, I'd heard that using a bong was the ultimate way of getting high, and I feared for the safety of my mind, which had already drifted into uncharted territory.

"Loaded and ready to launch," he said with enthusiasm. "Who's going first?"

Shelly and I exchanged nervous glances before I spoke up.

"Girls first," I said.

"No, you go, I don't want that much. I'll finish what you can't."

"I don't wanna be rude, so girls first."

"What's the matter, Kevin, you scared?" said Shelly.

"Yeah, man, come on, you chicken shit or what?" said Craig.

Girls always had the option of bailing out whereas boys had no excuse, and when Craig called me a chicken shit, I became downright determined. I took the bong in my hands, which was heavier than I expected. Shelly observed with a fascinated gleam while Craig torched the end of the metal bowl with the flick of his thumb on the lighter. I took a reasonably large hit that I thought might make me cough, but I was pleased to find out the smoke was milder than tobacco. Of course, it might have been that my senses had been severely distorted by alcohol.

"Hold it down in your lungs, dude," said Craig. "You get a real good buzz that way."

I gradually let the smoke exhale into the bathroom and felt proud of myself for not coughing. With confidence I extended the bong over to Shelly, who seemed impressed by my ability to hold the smoke. By the way Craig beamed I think he was pleased that he initiated me, and soon Shelly, into his pot-smoking club. Shelly placed her mouth inside the round opening and began to suck in the air. The smoke filled up in the cylinder, then filtered into her mouth, the water gurgling at the bottom. Shortly after the smoke evaporated from the bong, Shelly began to cough, prompting Craig and me to exchange superior grins. The bathroom was flooded with a haze of smoke swirling around our heads.

"Rookie," said Craig.

"Yeah, some people can't handle their weed," I said, smiling at Craig, who enjoyed my smart-ass comment. Shelly finally stopped coughing and looked at me.

"Do you feel anything?" she said.

"Not a thing," I said.

I didn't know whether it was the weed or the alcohol or the fact I was standing in a room and doing something very personal and forbidden with Shelly, but I felt real grown-up. And I liked Craig, too, even though I knew he was just a stoner without a useful bone in his entire body.

"This shit has a way of creeping up on you," said Craig.

"Maybe I need another hit," I said confidently.

"Hey, hey, don't Bogart that bong, man, it's the master's turn," said Craig.

Craig loaded and smoked the bong with such smooth expertise that I was almost envious of him–almost.

"Craig's gonna be a senior next year," said Shelly.

"Yeah, king of the whole fuckin' school, man," pronounced Craig. He set down the bong and began to rummage through some of the drawers under the sink countertop, releasing the smoke in measured shifts from his thin, sunken chest.

"He's gonna get me into all the awesome senior parties."

"Abso-fuckin'-lutely. I know everybody, and everybody knows me. I'm like the Hugh Hefner of Rossmoor High."

While they talked I felt something strange come on, as though someone were slowly pumping air into my blood and my body was expanding. My head felt thicker and heavier and everything in the bathroom became slightly fuzzy and more abstract. I couldn't accurately assess the actions and words buzzing around me.

"Bitchin', found it," gushed Craig.

Craig held up a tube of lipstick and removed the cap. He started to write the letter H, then E on the mirror, in candy apple red.

"Are you crazy, this is somebody's house," said Shelly.

"Crazy like a bat outta hell," said Craig in a wicked tone, sticking out his tongue and laughing like a maniac.

"Well I'm not hanging around for this," said Shelly.

She darted out the door, and I intended to join her, except that something made me stay behind, maybe indecision brought on by the drugs. Craig lunged and shut the door behind me, trapping me inside. He continued his writing on the mirror, spelling out the words HELTER SKELTER. Damn, this smoky, bathroom scene was getting weird. I remember being totally freaked out about the Charles Manson murders. I certainly knew about wars and political assassinations, but at the oblivious age of nine, I didn't realize human beings were capable of such senseless butchery. Seeing his ugly mug and bugged out, beady eyes plastered on television and all over the newspapers and magazines, Manson had become the face of evil for me and countless Americans.

"Death to pigs, man," said Craig, raising his hand for a high-five. I slapped it without any enthusiasm as my brain started to go berserk with harrowing thoughts. Could Craig be one of those acid-trip Manson freaks? Was he planning to carve me up like a pig and splash my blood all over the bathroom? My mind started to run wild with the possibilities. Then he positioned himself over the toilet, lifted the seat, and began to unzip his shorts.

"Uh, I'll let you do your business," I said, moving for the door.

"What's the matter, man, never seen a dude piss before?" said Craig. I shrugged. "Just hang tight, we'll go out together."

He started to piss into the toilet, releasing a long groan of relief.

"Whoa," he said to himself, chuckling. "I just had a weird thought, man. You know when you're taking a leak and you feel those little splashes of liquid hit your legs?"

"Okay, yeah?"

"Is that the water from the toilet coming up to hit your legs, or is the piss hitting the toilet water and then bouncing back up and splashing your legs?"

He zipped up his shorts and flushed the toilet, turning and standing with his arms crossed, waiting for the answer. I was bewildered. I wasn't sure I heard the question right. Nothing in this bright and mirrored room was making any sense to me.

"I don't know," I said blankly.

"Well, who the fuck cares? It's just your legs. I've stepped in dog shit before, haven't you?

He launched into an air guitar version of a familiar rock song.

"*Smoke on the water, and fire in the sky,*" he sang and played. He didn't sing one note on key. "You like Deep Purple, man?"

"Yeah, it's my favorite color," I said, making him chuckle.

"Hilarious dude. Check this out, I'm gonna be the best damn guitar player on the planet, better than Page. Then I'll have all the babes I want. I'll be fighting 'em off like Elvis."

He glanced away with a soured expression—almost offended— and even in my altered state of mind I knew that he was the chump who probably brought the weed to every party so he could feel special and appreciated. His wiry, greasy hair was slicked back, and his face was broken out with acne; there was nothing attractive or athletic about him.

"Fuck the chicks at this party, man," he said. "They can suck my fat dick. Hey, I know this guy in Fairmont who's having a party, and the babes there aren't stuck-up prudes. I got some wheels, wanna come?"

"Nah, I'd better stick around," I said.

"Whatever," he said. "Oh shit, look at your eyes, dude. They're all red," he said, pointing at my face.

"So?"

"That's totally bogus, man. People can die from that shit." I quickly checked my eyes in the mirror, feeling the paranoia creep in.

"You could really get fucked up," he said.

"Pot can kill you?"

"If you get the wild red-eye, yeah."

"What should I do?"

"I don't know, dude. It's totally outta my hands now. Shit, it's getting redder and redder!"

"Can't you do something? Please, help me!" My voice had reached full-scale panic. Then Craig blasted into a loud guffaw.

"You can't die from red-eye, you moron." He slapped me hard on the back. "Man, you're a suck-uh."

Craig left the bathroom, shaking his head and still laughing at his prank. And that was my first experience with smoking pot.

The rest of the evening passed in a blurry rush. I could count on my hands the people who remained at the party. Somehow, I survived it all. I tested the limits of my body in every way imaginable and broke through the other side without a scratch. I was drowsy and listless and my brain was a fuzzy mess, and yet I could logically comprehend everything that was going on. I couldn't see Shelly anywhere so I assumed that she left without saying goodbye.

I pushed my sluggish body from the sofa and lumbered outside toward my bike. By the curb I noticed Shelly and another girl leaning inside a car and talking, and then backing away as the car accelerated down the road. I headed for my bike not expecting to spend another moment with Shelly.

"You leaving?" said Shelly. I nodded. She turned and made a comment to her friend and then approached me. Her friend continued toward the house. "Walk me home?"

"Sure," I replied.

I pushed my bike alongside while we strolled through the dark and empty streets of Shelly's neighborhood. The conversation had long spells of stillness except when Shelly would point out someone's house or tell me an interesting fact about the people who lived there. She was contained and thoughtful, her gaze mostly pulled upward to the sky, content to soak in the peaceful surroundings. I wondered how her mind could drift so easily when practically every moment I was near her my mind resided in Shellyville. We didn't speak of our parents or discuss anything significant, until we came upon her house. We stopped and faced each other at the end of her driveway. We paused, and I could sense she'd rather not go inside.

"Do you think your dad and my mom are really in love or just fooling around?" she asked in a soft voice, her head lowered. I was forced to drastically shift gears again, always trying to meet her speed and change of direction, like a defensive back trying to cover a speedy wide receiver.

"I don't really like to think about it too much," I said.

"But you went to all that trouble trying to find my mom, how come?"

"I guess I thought I could do something, maybe break them up or something. I don't know. It all seems pretty crazy now. Maybe I just overreacted."

"You don't wanna split them up anymore?"

"Maybe. I guess, yeah. I'm sort of mixed up about it all."

"Is it because of me?" I couldn't contain a bashful grin, and she noticed, even in the black of night. "Do you think it's weird, you and me being friends? I mean, with our parents and all?" she asked.

"Um, kind of. I never thought we'd be spending time together, that's for sure," I said.

"I think it's a good thing that we have each other, don't you?" she said.

"Yeah, I like talking to you. And we're both in the same boat. But I haven't told anybody about all this stuff, have you?"

"Oh no way. It's not something I wanna broadcast to the world, you know?"

"Right, me neither," I agreed.

"Well, it's pretty late, I guess I should go inside," she said.

She leaned forward for a hug, and I was stung with a compelling urge to kiss her. She leaned back, paused just a few inches in front of my face, presenting me the chance, but I hesitated, and she turned away. Shoot, that was my chance. She started up her driveway while a tight urgency squeezed my chest. I was overwhelmed by the sudden inspiration to toss my bike hard to the ground and fling my body to the street. I made loud moaning noises of fake pain.

"Kevin!" shouted Shelly. I could hear the tone of her footfalls change from the dull thud of grass to the sharper smack of asphalt. My ploy worked. I held my arm as if pained while she leaned over, her nose only inches from my face.

"Are you all right?" she gasped urgently.

I abruptly rose up and my momentum carried me a bit harder into her lips than planned. At first touch she flinched and I kept my lips forcefully to hers until she giggled and gave in. I put my arms around her while her body weight fell into my chest, a willing partner in my romantic scheme. Stretched out on the road, we kissed and held each other tight and showed no signs of stopping until a familiar voice cracked like lightening right between our lips.

"Shelly, you out there?" her mother shouted.

"Oh shit," hushed Shelly. She sprang to her feet and started to turn, then paused. "Come see me during the day."

"I want you in here right now!" her mother shouted again. She tried to walk with an air of composure but her legs were moving way too fast. I hustled onto my bike for fear of being recognized, and just as I was about to peddle away I heard them speak.

"What were you doing in the street?" her mother said.

"He fell again," said Shelly. "He falls a lot."

Riding away, I broke into a huge, giddy grin. The streets were empty, and I cranked up the bike to high speed as the adrenaline of that kiss electrified my system. I could've sworn that I was about to rise into the air and soar home above the trees. I could taste the sweet cherry flavor she wore on her lips, and her last words kept replaying in my head, "Come see me, come see me." I could see nothing else.

# Chapter Fourteen

*I was hunched over a plate of bacon and toast, drinking a tall* glass of Carnation chocolate instant breakfast, trying to revive myself after a poor night's sleep. I was too wired from the kiss and spent half the night wondering where it would lead. I watched my mother attend to her routine and noticed that her eyes had no connection to her movements. The bright colors of gold and yellow and beige in the kitchen irritated me for some reason; they never had before.

My mother paused from the dishes and sat down at the table. She stared blankly outside at our maple tree in the backyard. I recalled the days when she'd come home from teaching nursery school with a shoebox containing several caterpillars. She always claimed they were leftover from her class at school, although I had a hunch she simply swiped them for me. She knew how entertained I was by plucking leaves from our maple tree and feeding the hungry insects in the shoebox, then watching them spin their silky white cocoons and emerge days later as butterflies. I was captivated by this evolution of nature.

We sat quietly together, only the sounds of my teeth crunching on the crispy bacon and the sports section ruffling when I turned the page. I glanced at my mother every so often, enough to gauge any change in her mood.

"Can you stop reading for a minute?" she asked. I sighed with an exasperated edge and closed the paper to listen. I didn't feel like having a heavy conversation this morning, and by the tone of her voice, I could hear it coming. "I think you should know something. Rachel didn't come home last night, without our permission," she said.

"Oh... okay," I replied, with far too little grief in my tone.

"Okay? That's all you can say? It's not okay, Kevin, it's anything but okay." My mother rose from the table and continued to clean the kitchen and aimlessly fidget with sponges and dishtowels. My lukewarm reaction bothered her. "We just wanted you to know, so you wouldn't be worried, but apparently, that's not an issue for you."

"No, it is. It's just that, I guess I'm not that shocked that she didn't come home."

"Why, did she say something to you?"

"No, no, but come on, Mom, everybody knows she hasn't been real comfortable around here lately," I said, remembering that Rachel had sworn me to secrecy about her plans.

"Comfortable," my mother mumbled bitterly. "Rachel's *too* comfortable, if you ask me. I don't know, maybe if we'd been tougher on her, right from the start. It's so hard to know sometimes, the right thing to do, how to react in certain situations. Every child is so different."

She stared out the kitchen window and into the backyard with a solemn longing. She was probably recalling a time when all of us were in that backyard, laughing and playing, younger, content, and less involved with our own personal dramas.

"Mom," I said, bringing her back.

"Yes?" she said.

"What are you gonna do about it?" She thought for a few moments.

"We're not sure," she said. "The only good thing is, we know where she is and we're in contact with her."

"Well I have an idea," I said. "Why don't we get in the car right now, go get her and bring her home? You and me, Mom, we can do this. And if she won't budge, we'll just take her by force. You grab one arm and I'll grab the other. She can't take us both."

My mother released a gentle and appreciative grin. After I said it, I realized my plan sounded unrealistic and rash.

"That's sweet of you, Kevin, but it wouldn't solve a thing. We can't just lock up our children, especially Rachel. She's a free spirit. She'll just run off again."

"So, you're just gonna let her live somewhere else, no questions asked?"

"For right now, yes. We need to handle this carefully."

"What does Dad say?"

"He agrees with me. We've talked to the parents of the household and—"

"You've talked to the parents?" I blurted out.

"They don't want to push her, either. We're all very concerned that Rachel might take off and disappear if they force her to leave. At least this way she's close to home, and we know where she is."

"What if she never comes back, Mom?"

Her glassy brown eyes, on the verge of tears, were deeply troubled. The question probably crossed her mind long before I asked it.

"Then I guess she's on her own."

Her words were drenched in agony, and yet she said them with a purposeful clarity, as though trying to convince herself. She neatly folded the dishtowel, draped it over the sink, and entered the dining room. I heard a brief yelping sound and glanced below to find Amber sitting by my side, begging for food. Her tail slashed back and forth across the kitchen floor while she panted heavily. I gave her the rest of my toast and watched her devour it in about two chews. Then she lifted her head to me again with happy, hopeful eyes, and at that moment I wondered if being a dog wasn't such a bad deal; you were fed every day, you had no chores, and someone else cleaned up your crap.

When my mother left to run some errands it gave me the mental freedom to think more about Shelly. It was hard to concentrate on her when a storm of turmoil was enveloping this house and while my mother sulked around with a noticeable trail of gloom. When the clock finally struck one p.m., I couldn't wait any longer.

I parked my bike in the empty driveway and approached the front door. I stood there for too long before I rang because my father popped into my mind. No matter how hard I tried, I couldn't forget that this was the house where the other woman lived. This knowledge consumed me, ate away at my joy, even though I was on the brink of starting a relationship with Shelly. I tried to squash my contempt for Shelly's mother since I knew it would interfere with my feelings for her daughter. With the kiss last night, I'd begun something that might exceed my wildest expectations. My mission had changed direction, taken another path, and while I felt a pang of guilt for this, I no longer felt in control of the wheel.

I rang the doorbell. No one answered, so I rang again. Finally the door swung open and Shelly appeared, lethargic and dressed in only a long Mickey Mouse t-shirt.

"Oh, hi," she said, wiping the sleep dust from her eyes. I could see the thin outline of her boobs pressing underneath her shirt, and it further reinforced my new mission. This was definitely the right path for me. "What time is it?"

"About one-fifteen," I said. She glanced back inside the house for some reason and then turned back to me.

"This isn't such a good time." There was no enthusiasm in her voice. "Why don't you come back some other day?"

"Oh, yeah, sure."

"Well, bye."

She shut the door in my face. Kaboom. Just call me Hiroshima. I stood there in a helpless fog and tried to figure out what went wrong. I became angry and without consideration for the consequences, my finger shot out, and I rang the doorbell again. She opened the door more hastily this time, perhaps a little perturbed.

"Did I do something wrong?" I said with a touch of resentment.

"No, not at all," she said.

"Then what's going on? You said to come by and see you during the day."

"I know, but my dad's home, and he's trying to rest. He's not feeling well." I felt like a complete idiot even though she kindly offered me a soft smile. "Listen, wait outside for a few minutes. I'll get dressed."

She closed the door, and I felt elated. She came to my rescue. I walked over to the curb and sat down, waiting for her. I had plenty of time to think and ponder my lousy timing. Had I just been patient and waited one more day, Shelly might've been more enthused to see me. At the very least, I would've seemed less impatient and clingy. When she reappeared moments later I was treated to the delightful vision of her movement; everything jiggled just right.

"Let's go have some breakfast," she said.

"But it's lunchtime," I replied.

"Not to me."

&#x6b6;

We sat across from each other at a greasy spoon coffee shop called the Pie King, just a few blocks south of Shelly's house. It was a drab and no frills restaurant decorated in salmon-colored walls and oversized, off-white vinyl booth seating. They served huge helpings of food for about three bucks. I ordered a burger and fries, and Shelly had the French toast and scrambled eggs. She drenched her French toast in maple syrup and let the syrup run over into her eggs, which made me cringe. I protected my eggs from anything sweet at all costs; eggs should be salty.

"You know what I heard?" she said. "Remember that guy from the bathroom, Craig?"

"Yeah."

"After he left the party, he got into a car accident. It was pretty bad, too. They took him to the hospital. I guess he broke his ribs and stuff. They said he almost died from the internal bleeding."

I must've blanked out for a few seconds because she waved her hand across my face. Even though I was blasted that night, I recalled his offer to drive me to another party.

"Hello, anyone there?" she said.

"Wow," I said, still in a daze.

"I bet they'll take away his license for at least a year... what a drag."

We both paused to continue eating.

"Do you have any brothers and sisters?" she asked.

"Uh, yeah. Three. An older brother and two older sisters."

"So you're the baby."

Everyone made that comment when they heard I was the youngest. I detested it.

"What about you?" I asked.

"An older brother. He goes to college at Santa Barbara. That's all right for him, but I wanna go to school out of the state, somewhere interesting, like New York or Florida. Where are you planning to go to college?"

"I just wanna get through high school first."

She poured more syrup on her French toast and swirled a piece of it around the plate until it was soaking. Then before she plunged the fork and bread into her mouth she said, "I keep waiting for you to ask me, but you never do."

"Ask you what?"

"Aren't you the least bit curious about my mother and whether we've talked or not...about your dad?"

I was deeply curious but wanted to keep the conversation light. I swiped a French fry through some ketchup as a diversion, hoping to buy some time.

"I figured you'd tell me when you wanted to," I said, shoving the fry into my mouth.

"You're never gonna get anywhere in this world with that kind of attitude. You have to reach out and take what you want." Her eyes implied something other than the topic of conversation.

"So, what did she say?" I said.

"We haven't talked yet. I'm waiting for the right time."

"Then why'd you ask me about it?"

"You don't seem at all interested in keeping your dad and my mom apart," she said, exasperated. "First, you come looking for my mother to do... I can't imagine what, and now you could care less. What's the deal?"

"I care," I said defensively, not knowing exactly how to communicate my caring. "I want it to end just like you do."

"Well you don't seem very concerned about it," she said. "I'm always the one who brings them up."

I was at a loss for words, trying to find the sentence that would bring this troubling subject to a close. She pushed out a short guffaw that felt totally misplaced, considering the conversation. She always kept me off balance.

"What if they saw us together, you know, making out or

something. Wouldn't that be a trip? I wonder what they'd do," she said. Her eyes detached from mine, as if trying to figure out a way to make it happen. I had my own thoughts, of the two of us embraced like long lost lovers, exchanging saliva and touching body parts until the wee hours of morning. "Would serve them right if we flaunted it in their face," she added, almost gleefully.

We finished our meals and I paid the check with my allowance. Riding our bikes through town, we decided to stop inside the Valley Vista Bowling alley for some pinball and video games, and seeing the lanes were clear, opted to roll a few frames instead. I was having so much fun with Shelly that I almost forgot about our conversation in the coffee shop and the fact that my sister ran away from home.

"If I get a strike, that means I win," she said, cradling the electric blue ball in her hands and preparing to roll.

"Yeah, but you'll blow it. I feel a gutter ball coming on."

"That's only because you roll them so often."

She stuck out her butt and although I should've been offended, it made my skin tingle. She made her approach to the lane and swung the ball into the air, slipping and almost falling over herself. It bounced off the polished wood and cut a slight diagonal path toward the left side of the front pin. It connected in the sweet spot of what they call the New Jersey side, terminology I've never quite understood, and ricocheted through the pins and knocked every one down. She jumped and screeched in delight, and even though she'd beaten me, as highly competitive as I was, I'd rather lose if it meant seeing her eject her body into the air. I guess that was the moment I knew that without a doubt, I'd fallen madly in love with the daughter of my father's mistress.

"You owe me an ice cream," she demanded.

"You stepped over the line, that's a foul," I said.

"I did not."

"I saw you. I was sitting right here watching you."

"Right, Kevin, like you were actually looking at my feet," she said knowingly.

I relished it so when she said my name, and she was right, my eyesight was nowhere near her feet. Just then we heard the explosion of pins crashing together, and we turned our heads to the lane next to us. An older guy, in the neighborhood of eighteen, had just bowled a strike and was strutting back to the scorer's table, making sure we'd witnessed his brilliant roll. I didn't know him although I was all too familiar with his type. He was a rugged jock with perfectly combed brown hair, probably had more brawn than brains, and he moved around as though a red carpet should be rolled out underneath his feet. He looked over at Shelly as if to imply that she could do a lot better than me.

"What are you looking at, punk?" he said to me.

"I was just admiring your excellent bowling technique," I said, which made Shelly giggle.

"Are you jerkin' me around, man, 'cause if you are, I'll come over there and kick your pasty white ass."

His bruiser buddy at the scorer's table grinned like Opie, hoping, I was sure, that a fight would break out. Maybe he could make himself useful that way. Unlike his better-looking friend, he was a roly-poly kind of guy with heavy arms and a permanent, shit-eating grin. He'd frizzed his hair into a puffy, light brown Afro ball, which was the new style, although it wasn't a look I found flattering on white guys. Sure, it looked great on Dr. J as he glided like a superhero through the lane, or on those funky dancers shaking their groove thing on *Soul Train*, but not on white guys.

"No thanks, she's doing a fine job of that already," I said. Two for two, I thought, although I was pushing my luck.

"You let a girl beat you?" said the bruiser, "what a chump." I turned to Shelly, and although I'd only known her for a few days, I knew his comment wouldn't fly, not even for one second, off the ground.

"I bet I could beat you, Porky," she said. Enraged, the Afro bruiser ejected from his seat and the plastic chair tipped over.

"You calling me a pig?" he said.

"Here, I'll speak in a language you can understand…oink, oink," she said. Either it was my imagination or steam had begun to filter out the Afro bruiser's nostrils, which were flaring, appropriately enough, as wide as well…a pig's.

"Pick up a ball, and let's roll," the bruiser said. He plucked a heavy black ball from the circular rack like it was a volleyball and shoved his fingers hard into the holes, his eyes aflame.

"Wait a minute," said the taller one. "There has to be something on the line, otherwise, who gives a shit?"

"Name it," asserted Shelly.

The two dopes conferred for a moment, putting their big heads together and whispering. I could only imagine what their pea-sized brains were concocting. Being a guy I was fairly confident the payoff would fall somewhere in the general vicinity of three possible areas: money, food, or sex. These were certainly the areas on which I would concentrate.

"Okay, we got it," began the taller one. "It's us against you two twerps. Losers have to streak through the bowling alley."

Streaking, what a concept. Now, I'd seen some of those idiots on television streaking naked through the Academy Awards and on the streets of New York City, but I'd never actually seen one live and in full streak mode. I had to admit the idea of throwing the match so I could see Shelly's naked body crossed my mind, until I connected the dots and realized that she'd be seeing my naked body, too. I wasn't prepared to make that trade, especially in a bowling alley.

"You are on," said Shelly, before I could disagree.

"What?" I gasped, turning my back to them. "You'd really streak through this bowling alley?"

"Don't worry, we won't have to," she said, hushed. "We can take these jerks."

"But I'm no good and you're a…" I stopped myself short.

"A girl?" she said with a slicing glare. "If you don't wanna play, fine, I'll bowl without you. But I'm not letting these buttheads get away with thinking they're better than us."

She didn't hesitate a moment in retrieving her ball from the rack and stepped right up to the lane.

"By all means, ladies first," said the taller one, who was doing his best imitation of a gentleman. He flared a smug grin while something dawned on me that should've long before I agreed to this match: this asshole couldn't lose. His sculpted body would undoubtedly look fabulous in the buff, especially next to his slob of a friend. And, if he won the game, he'd have the pleasure of seeing Shelly in her birthday suit and reducing me to the likes of a child compared to him. A guy like him probably had a bushy mound of pubic hair sprouting from his loins, while my guy was more similar to a young tree after a windy day; some branches but not a whole

150

heck of a lot of leaves. This was a disaster waiting to happen. I decided that winning and avoiding the humiliation was the far better option of the two. I urgently turned to Shelly just before she rolled and shouted, "Come on, Shelly, blast those fucking pins!" The force of my encouragement took everyone by surprise. "I mean, come on, roll a good one," I said more calmly.

Shelly's first roll was a dead-center strike, and we cheered and hugged each other, which was always a plus. The taller guy with the bushy pubes (no doubt), rolled after Shelly and countered with a strike of his own. The game was a seesaw battle down to the last frame. Shelly actually bowled a strong game, much better than her game against me, and it agitated Bushy Pubes. Within Shelly festered a fighting spirit that I hadn't seen in many girls, with the exception of Rachel, and I wondered how this would play out in our relationship. Was she a man-eater? She was certainly eating *these* guys for lunch.

Bushy Pubes applied the pressure by knocking in a spare on his final frame, and I had the last roll for our team.

"If you get a strike, we win. The pig won't even get a chance," said Shelly.

"If I don't?"

"We'll still have a chance with a spare, but it means the pig can beat us if he gets lucky."

"I guess the pressure's on, huh?"

"I know you can do it, Kevin." With that one sentence from her sumptuous lips, I prepared to roll. I could feel all the eyes glued to my back while beads of sweat formed on my forehead. I began my approach to the foul line. As I felt my body lunge and hunker down low to release the ball, the extra adrenaline in my system kicked in, and I rolled the ball with some high octane juice. Unfortunately, the extra juice spun the ball across the lane, right to left, and it slammed the side wall and barely grazed the corner pin, rocking it gently before it regained its steadiness. Not one lousy pin fell. I didn't want to turn around and face them, nor face her, since I could hear the guys busting out in a riotous laughter.

"Hey dude, the idea is to *hit* the pins," said Bushy Pubes, making the Pig laugh harder.

"Yeah, maybe next time you should roll two balls…get it, two balls?" said the Pig, gushing at his lame joke. I was humiliated.

"The game's not over, meathead," shouted Shelly.

"Ooohh, somebody's getting hot under the collar over there. Well, don't worry, blondie, in a few minutes you'll be able to take off all your clothes," said the Pig. They laughed and snorted again, and I couldn't take it any longer.

"I have another roll, Charlie Brown," I said. The Pig lunged forward, but Bushy Pubes held him back, thankfully.

"Just cool your heels, dude," said Bushy Pubes to the Pig. "You still have to roll, and you'd better not fuck up."

"That's right, this isn't over by a long shot," said Shelly. "Go ahead, Kevin."

"Go ahead, Kevin," the Pig said in a girlish, mocking voice.

I picked up the ball from the rack and approached the lane. I made the same exact approach to the foul line in terms of speed, but this time I had a nice, smooth backswing and didn't rush the follow-through. The ball left my fingers in excellent position on the boards and turned over and over with a slight sideways spin, picking up speed and curving ever so slightly toward the center, and then smash, wiped out all the pins in one, fatal blow. I heard a screeching cheer from Shelly and nothing from the two stooges. When I pivoted Shelly was cheering and clapping, so naturally I took a bow. She loved it.

Since it was my last frame, I got an extra ball, and I converted it into nine more pins for our team. The Pig would have to strike on his first ball and then spare out to beat us.

"Come on, man," said Bushy Pubes urgently while the Pig prepared to roll. He lumbered down toward the foul line and whipped the ball hard like a slingshot. It moved with a blistering pace and busted up the pins with such finality that two of them spun in tight circles, looking dizzy from the impact, and then fell down; a monstrous strike.

"Yeah!" the Pig shouted, making a fist.

"Fuckin'-a," said Bushy Pubes. They slapped high fives, and the Pig sneered at us.

"Get ready to let it all hang loose, girls," said the Pig.

He made his second approach to the foul line and let the ball fly with equal power. This time the ball slid to the left and wiped out the entire left side, kicking out one pin on the right. Four pins remained in a line, not bunched together, which gave me hope. Just as he approached the lane for his last roll, Shelly coughed out loud. They looked at her with disdain.

"Excuse me, I was choking on something," she said.

"Choke on this," said the Pig, yanking up on his crotch.

"Just bowl, all right?" I said, trying to defend my woman's honor and having absolutely no way of doing so.

"Shut up, gutter boy," said the Pig.

He nailed me there. I had no comeback for the gutter ball I rolled. He took aim and made his approach, firing another speeding bullet down the lane. Jesus, I thought, didn't this guy believe in touch? He gave it some air as it bounced once off the boards and made its way toward the pins. As the ball struck the first pin, it kicked out the pin right next to it, bounced high off the wall, and sideswiped the remaining two pins for a spare. The game was over, and I was cooked.

Bushy Pubes and the Pig were so elated I thought they were going to smooch, but they stopped short of that and simply gloated. Bushy Pubes strutted right up to Shelly, and she stood defiantly with her arms crossed.

"Can I watch you undress too?" he said.

"Back off, slime ball," she said, pushing him in the chest.

"Yeah, just back off," I blurted for some ridiculous reason. He rifled his eyes my direction, then stepped nose to nose with me, or should I say, chin to nose.

"You just make sure you're not blocking our view, you catch my drift?" he said.

"Jeez, and all this time I thought you guys really just wanted to see me," I said, dripping with sarcasm. Bushy Pubes lunged for my throat and choked me hard, his eyes strained with the fire of hatred.

"I could take you out right now, you faggot," he spewed.

"Stop it," shouted Shelly, trying to break his stronghold. "Let him go!" He finally released his chokehold, and it took several seconds for my throat to recover.

"Come on, Kevin, let's get this over with." Shelly grabbed my arm and started to lead me away.

"Where you going?" said Bushy Pubes.

"You don't expect us to undress right here, do you?" said Shelly.

"Hell yes, right here and now, lover girl," said the Pig.

"Yeah, come on, let's see the goods," said Bushy Pubes.

"No way, we're going in the bathrooms," said Shelly. "Take it or leave it."

Shelly and I walked away and the guys, really having no choice, followed right behind us like a couple of baby chicks following their mother.

"We're gonna be right outside the doors, and we want full nudity. None of this underwear shit," said Bushy Pubes. Shelly paused and faced him with a steely expression of cool resolve.

"Tell you what, champ. I'll hand you my underwear on the way out, would you like that?" said Shelly in a sexy, Marilyn Monroe-style voice. I thought the morons were going to cream right there in their pants.

"I'll keep it under my pillow," said Bushy Pubes.

"I'm sure you will," mocked Shelly.

We calmly continued toward the bathrooms with the guys trailing us. I was starting to panic and saw flashes of myself streaking side by side next to Shelly, who appeared horrified and repulsed in my flashes. There was nothing wrong with my body, although just the idea of letting her see me naked and running through this building with my peter bouncing around scared the living daylights out of me. Shelly fidgeted with her earlobe and then froze in place.

"Damn," she said.

"What?" I said.

"I dropped my earring. Help me look." She clutched my arm and yanked me down to the floor. We were on our knees when she whispered, "Climb out." Then she said more for them, "Oh, I found it," pretending to pick up her earring. She tossed me a reassuring glance just before we both disappeared into our respective bathrooms.

⚲

Once inside I surveyed the scene and noticed a window just large enough for me to squeeze through. I'd have to climb on the cracked and rusty sink, hoping it didn't cave in, and wiggle myself through the opening. The drop would be about ten feet to the ground. I had to assume that Shelly had a similar situation in the girls' bathroom.

I climbed carefully onto the sink and then stood erect. The woeful sink was unsteady, but I was mildly confident it would support me. I could barely see over the window opening and to my dismay, I looked down upon a huge trash dumpster bulging to the green metal rims. The trash would break my fall, although the idea of landing in a dumpster made me queasy. I popped out the metal screen and pushed open the adjustable glass frame as far up as possible. I hoisted myself on the ledge with a grunt and tried to slither my upper body through the opening. I squeezed most of my upper body through and peered across to the other bathroom, but there was no sign of Shelly. I inhaled deeply and let my body fall out the window. I plunged headfirst into the dumpster, hitting a large trash bag and sinking inside the bin, wedging in between something that smelled like a dead rat and yesterday's chili cheeseburger. I pushed myself up and climbed out, then hustled over to the girls' side.

"Shelly," I whispered urgently.

"Kevin, is that you?" I heard her say.

"Yeah, I'm out. What are you waiting for?"

"I can't get myself up on the window ledge."

Shelly's head was just barely poking over the edge of the window and her hands were clutched to the frame, but she couldn't get adequate leverage.

"Come on, you can do it," I encouraged. I could her her grunting and trying, but to no avail.

"What are you doing?" I heard someone say behind me. Two young girls about twelve years old were curiously watching.

"My friend is trying to get out. Some guys inside are stalking her," I said.

"Really?" she responded, totally enthralled.

"Yeah, one of the guys is crazy, you know? He could do something really horrible, like bite her, or worse, pull out all her hair!"

In tandem they both reacted in horror, hands covering their mouths as they gasped, "Uhh!," flabbergasted by the idea that a girl could lose her precious hair.

"They're right outside the bathroom. She could use your help, you know?"

"Okay," she said, checking with her friend for agreement.

"Yeah, we'll help," said her friend.

"Don't tell those guys why you're going in the bathroom, all right? Don't even say a word, they might get suspicious," I added.

They nodded and hurried into the bowling alley. A few moments later I could hear some more voices in the bathroom.

"Come on, come on," I urged them. Soon Shelly's upper body was shoved through the opening and she was leaning halfway over.

"Come on, I'll break your fall," I said.

She positioned her hands on the frame, balanced herself, and prepared for the drop.

"Get ready," she said.

"Just hurry up," I responded.

"Are you sure you can catch me?"

"Yeah, come on, just do it!"

She lunged out the window, and this golden body came hurtling down at a speed and size I wasn't physically equipped to stop. She plunged into my arms and we went crashing together to the cement. The full thrust of her weight slammed me as my right hip pounded the pavement and my right elbow hit a split-second later. I grunted and instantly felt the sting of pain shoot up the right side of my body and all the way up to my shoulder.

"Are you all right?" she said.

"Yeah, are you?" I said.

"Yeah, I think so."

She looked at her hands, and they were scraped with cement and showed traces of blood, but nothing too serious. Suddenly, we heard some commotion in the boys' bathroom. I saw Bushy Pubes extend his head over the window ledge.

"Son of a bitch!" he yelled.

"Let's get outta here," I said urgently.

We hustled to our feet and sprinted around to the front of the building. We unlocked our bikes and just as we hopped on the seats, the two Neanderthals pushed out the front glass doors of the bowling alley, thirsting for blood.

"There they are!" the Pig shouted. They took off after us and gained ground swiftly, drawing to within several feet of us. Shelly and I motored to high speed and eventually, thankfully, started to pull away.

"We'll nail you motherfuckers!" yelled one as we rode away.

"You're dead meat!" shouted the other.

Now free from any danger, Shelly and I—for some odd reason—broke into a giggle and then started to laugh uncontrollably. As we cruised at top speed and headed into the quieter residential streets, we just kept laughing. When we finally stopped laughing and just rode, both drawn inward and reflecting on our masterful escape, the pain started again, a dull, aching pain. What a contrast in feelings, I thought. Ever since I'd met this girl, my body had been bruised and pained, but my heart had never felt more energized and alive. Unlike the threat of streaking in the bowling alley, I decided that it was a fair trade-off to make.

# Chapter Fifteen

*There were three things about the summer I enjoyed more than* anything else. First and most importantly, there was no homework. Secondly, we usually took a family vacation, maybe to the beach or a lake, where we would ski on the glassy water and my father would spend half his time either repairing the engine on the boat or station wagon. And third, my birthday was in August.

When I was a kid my parents would take Rachel and me, since our birthdays were only five days apart, to Magic Mountain, the new theme park in Los Angeles. We were allowed to bring one friend and gorge ourselves all day and night on junk food and try out every ride in the sprawling park. A few years ago I reluctantly went on the new Spin Out ride and promptly barfed up my hamburger and fries just moments after I stepped off. I never went on that tortuous ride again. All it did was spin around in a circle so fast that your body would cling to the walls, and you'd become horribly nauseous. It was a cruel and senseless contraption, and there was even something mind-altering about the way it worked. Perhaps it was a government experiment for mind control and little bespectacled men in white jumpsuits were sitting behind a huge console and recording their findings. In my estimation it was pointless, just spinning around in circles, and I knew I never wanted to set foot inside that ride again.

My parents tried hard to make our birthdays extra special since they came together, and we always celebrated with one family party for both of us. When I was younger it didn't bother me. However, now that I was older I wanted my own party. I think Rachel felt the same way. We'd outgrown the tandem party, even though it made the day more convenient for our family.

"We've already decided this. We're going to Lacy Park for a barbecue," said my father.

"But there's nothing to do there," I said.

"Listen, we'll bring the football, the baseball stuff, all the Frisbees…we'll have a great time, you'll see."

"Is Rachel coming?" I asked.

"That's the only way she would show up, if it was on neutral turf," said Sarah, who was helping my mother pack some food in the kitchen. I could tell by my father's defiant expression that he didn't appreciate her comment and putting a stopgap on his enthusiasm. "Well, it's true, isn't it? She doesn't wanna be here. She's made that pretty clear."

"Rachel is lost right now, and we have to make things easy for her so she can find her way back," said my mother.

"That's another way of saying we have to accommodate her every wish," said Sarah. "She takes off, and we spend all our time trying to make everything perfect for her."

"We?" said my mother, raising her eyebrows at Sarah.

"Okay, you and Dad," said Sarah. "But I still don't think it's fair to us."

My father was stuffing an old army duffel bag with sports equipment, keeping busy so he could sidestep the conversation. My father served in the Army during the Korean War, though he never saw action. When they asked the men in the division before they were shipped off to fight if anyone could type, he shot up his hand in a flash, despite no formal training in typing. He probably thought he could fake his way through the job. After all, he had to either fake typing or dodge bullets. He was stationed in a remote copy room miles from the combat zone, mostly typing up death notices on soldiers, some of whom he knew from training. My mother once told us it was a time he'd rather forget and to best leave the subject alone. I couldn't blame him. He must've felt guilty about typing in a cozy office while his buddies were fighting for their lives at the front.

"We'd do the same thing for all of you," said my mother.

"The rest of us wouldn't run away from home," said Sarah. "I actually liked it here. All the apartments my friends and I can afford are dumps. You should see some of these places, shoeboxes with a toilet."

"Yeah, why would I leave a place with free food, clean clothes, and a color television?" I tossed in. My father grinned and punched me lightly on the arm, enjoying my comment.

"I seem to recall a few difficult moments when you were her age," said my mother.

"Yeah, maybe, but I never got this hands-off treatment. You

two were harder on me and Jay."

"Well, I'm not so sure about that. If we *were* harder, it's only because we were new parents. Everything tends to get amplified when you're a new parent. But we always strive for equality around here, right John?"

"Uh-huh," my father said absently, not bothering to raise his head while still packing. He had this magical way of flowing alongside the molten lava of a heated family conversation without actually getting in the way and being burned by it. Undoubtedly he passed that gene to my brother, who also excelled in that area.

"Doesn't matter anyway. I was a saint compared to Rachel," said Sarah.

"A saint? You had your vices and still do," said my mother.

"Vices... like what?"

My mother hesitated, clearly uncomfortable with the answer that came to her mind.

"Come on, mom, you made that statement, so tell me, like what?" Sarah pressed, growing more agitated.

"Well, if you must know, the male gender, for one," my mother said. "You always had your eye on a boy."

Sarah huffed. "So, that's not a vice. It's natural for me to like boys. Rachel's the same way."

In that instant I caught my mother slicing an apprehensive glance at my father, who just kept packing. My mother returned to making the sandwiches.

"Well... 'like' is probably the wrong word. More like an obsession, and it's carried right over into adulthood."

"That's crazy, I don't have an obsession for boys."

"Hand me the mayo," said my mother.

Displeased, Sarah extended the jar of mayonnaise to my mother. "I have a healthy attraction to men, just like all my other friends," she said.

"Fine, whatever you say. I don't know why we're arguing about this anyway," conceded my mother.

Sarah paused from making the food and resentfully rolled her eyes. Getting no response from my mother, she resumed preparation of the food. I thought the conversation was over, but it's never really over with the females in my family. These conversations often started with a gentle debate and then festered on boil until someone exploded.

"I can't believe you'd say something like that," shouted Sarah. Prepare for liftoff, I thought.

"All I'm saying is that we all have our issues and vices, and no one in this house is any different. The important thing is to find ways to deal with them. If you're not learning, then you're not growing, and we could all do a little more growing around here."

Again my mother snuck a cutting glance at my father, who was swimming right along unscathed. "I'm not a kid anymore, mother," said Sarah, slapping down the knife and exiting the kitchen. My mother's tired sigh was a telling sign of parental exhaustion.

"Okay, it's all here. It's gonna be a great day," said my father cheerfully, heaving the bag over his shoulder and looking at my mother.

My mother just scowled at him with disgusted disbelief.

"You don't catch a darn thing, do you?" she said. She slammed a jar against the kitchen counter and stormed out of the kitchen, firing another cold look at my father.

"What?" said my father, perplexed. "What'd I do?"

※

We packed the station wagon with enough food and junk to last through winter hibernation and drove off to Lacy Park. My parents had recently discovered the park a few years ago and now it was their favorite place to take the family. It was a huge, open space with a wide grass field about the size of two football fields, enclosed by tall palm trees and dotted with picnic tables in the shaded outskirts. It was a beautiful and peaceful place, although I was hoping for something more exciting for my fifteenth birthday. Actually, I would've rather been spending the day with Shelly. Under normal circumstances I could've invited her to the celebration, but these circumstances were anything but normal.

My mother and sister began setting up the table and spreading out all the food, paper plates, and plastic utensils.

"How are they gonna know where to find us?" I asked.

"I told them we'd be on the northeast side. They'll figure it out," said my father. "Come on, Kevin, let's go!"

My father pulled out a football and motioned for me to run for a pass, and instinctively I started to move. It was almost a reflex action to run whenever my father held a football in his hands. The language of sports was something we both understood and respected. As individuals, we communicated and connected mostly through the clear-cut lens of a sporting event or moment. It was easier for us, so he indulged all my athletic interests and exposed his youngest son to opportunities whenever he could. After the UCLA Bruins, my father's alma mater, won the NCAA basketball

166

championship in 1972, we drove to the Los Angeles International airport to welcome home the winning team. I stood in awe of Bill Walton, his towering stature and size, as he and the Wizard himself, coach John Wooden, emerged together from the terminal tunnel. I was dumbstruck, but as they approached, my father nudged my arm, and I meekly held out a piece of paper and pen, praying they would notice the shy, little boy well beneath their line of vision. Thankfully coach Wooden paused, snatched the paper and pen from my hand, smiled grandfatherly, and scribbled his name. Then he shoved the paper in Walton's gut, his star pupil, who was busy lapping up all the loving attention from his adoring fans. After Walton signed he glanced down and said, "Here you go, kid," in a garbled, deep voice, pushing the paper and pen back into my face. I don't remember uttering a single word, my mouth agape, but just staring upward at a red-headed skyscraper of a man.

About a year before, my father somehow found out that Jerry West from the Los Angeles Lakers would be making a charitable appearance at a Christmas tree lot organized by the Boy's Club. When we left the house, I thought the plan was to pick out a tree and help some kids at the same time. To my wondrous surprise, Mr. Clutch stood near the entrance of the lot, wearing tight-fitting bell bottom slacks, a black leather belt with a silver buckle, and a checkered blue and beige blazer, shaking hands with other young boys and their fathers. He emitted the shining glow of a Hollywood movie star. I couldn't believe that I'd soon be meeting my pro basketball hero. I was so excited that I could barely stand still. I kept my eyes glued to his every move and gesture, much like I studied his moves and jump shots on the basketball court. Inching ever closer, and finally hearing his humble voice, I was struck by the peculiar notion that the successful athlete I idolized was, in fact, a discontented soul. He never displayed a smile or playful grin, despite the numerous boys and fathers who beamed in his presence. As I finally stepped up before him, the impression hit me even harder. I was a young lad, and I didn't know why, and he didn't seem angry or upset about anything in particular, but the quiet despair in his demeanor was obvious. I recall leaving that day and wondering how a star athlete with so much abundance in his life, a confident and skilled player who wanted the ball in his hands with the game on the line, could appear so completely lost and alone among a crowd of devoted fans. Back then, of course, I didn't have the advantage of hindsight. A basketball player only competes in two or three games a week, along with some practices, during a season that lasts a little more than half a year. The remainder of his time is spent dealing with the same mundane or annoying or possibly tragic life issues as everyone else. Maybe Mr. West needed a basketball in his hands to feel immune to all that and to feel good about himself. I could certainly relate, considering I always felt better with a football in my hands.

My father and I tossed the football until Rachel emerged from the shade under the palm trees on the far side of the park, walking side by side with Jamie. I was irritated that Rachel was allowed to bring a friend since this was supposed to be a family event. Then it dawned on me that she probably didn't ask my parents for permission. Part of the advantage of running away, I guess, was being able to play by your own rules.

🚲

It was quieter around the picnic table than usual while we munched on thick hamburgers and potato salad and juicy watermelon. Jay joined us about ten minutes after Rachel arrived. He was always the last to arrive and the first to leave any family gathering. I spent a fair amount of my time stealing quick, studying glances at Jamie, who was more withdrawn and uptight than usual. Her eyes had a detached, glassy glaze to them, and it made me wonder if she'd taken drugs. I couldn't imagine, however, that Rachel would show up to a family gathering with a friend who was stoned. Then it dawned on me that perhaps Rachel was stoned, too.

"I might get a gig producing a band called Crackers," said Jay. "They're pretty good. They've already lined up a deal with a small label."

"Who do they sound like?" said Sarah.

"Kind of a mixture between Rod Stewart and David Bowie, hard-driving rock with a little bit of jazz mixed in," said Jay.

"How's the engineering job working out with that other group?" my father asked.

"Steely Dan?" said Jay.

"That would be so amazing if you worked with them," said Sarah, excited. "Could we come to the studio one night and watch?"

"It's dead. They went with a different producer," said Jay.

Jay promptly withdrew from the conversation and shoveled a big bite of potato salad into his mouth, looking into the distance. We all knew how much he wanted that job.

"Something will come up, maybe this other group," said my father.

"The industry runs hot and cold," said Jay. "I just have to keep my name circulating out there."

"When did you decide to become a vegetarian, Jamie?" asked my mother, deftly changing the subject.

"A few months ago," she said. "I sliced into this undercooked piece of steak, and it started bleeding. I imagined some cow in the field getting its head chopped off, and that was the end for me."

We all paused from eating, staring down at the food, the disgusting visual hitting us simultaneously.

"You look a little pale, Jamie, maybe you're not getting enough iron," said my mother.

"I'd rather look pale than eat meat," said Jamie. "It's disgusting what they do to those animals."

"They're just cows, probably the dumbest animals on the planet," said Sarah.

"That doesn't give people the right to slaughter them for food," said Jamie.

"But that's just the tip of the iceberg," added Jay. "Scientists conduct all these bizarre experiments on animals, tortuous stuff that's very painful and sometimes fatal. That's the real cruelty. Killing for food seems more natural and humane than torturing creatures for our own personal knowledge."

"Suddenly I'm not so hungry anymore," said Rachel, dropping her hamburger to the paper plate with a soft whack.

"I'll take another hamburger, Dad," I said cheerfully.

"Coming right up, birthday boy," said my father, smiling. My father rose from the table and flipped a burger on the grill. Standing there, fussing with the meat on the grill, he appeared more at ease and in his element. Maybe all men felt more comfortable when they were cooking meat over a fire.

"How does it feel to be seventeen?" my mother said, again changing the subject.

"Not so great since I don't have a car, like all my other friends," said Rachel, swiping a sideways glance at my father.

"Do all your other friends work?" said my father, returning to the table with a burger on a plate and setting it down for me.

"I'm seventeen now. You said when I was seventeen you'd buy me a car. You never said anything about having to get a job first."

Sarah leaned in as if eagerly awaiting the response with every cell in her body.

"When you come back home we'll talk about a car," he said.

"That's so lame. Why do I have to be home to get a car?" Rachel asked.

"Because I'm still responsible for you and what you do with that car, and if you want one, you'll have to live at home."

"I can get you a car," said Jamie, prompting my father to pause in mid-bite and toss a scornful expression at her.

"See, even Jamie can get me a car," said Rachel.

"It won't be a hotrod or anything, but it'll get you around town. Some of the guys I know fix up old cars all the time."

"No offense, Jamie, but I don't want my daughter driving around in some broken-down jalopy," said my father.

"Car's a car, Dad," chimed in Jay.

"What about the insurance? I'll have to pay for insurance," said my father, glad that he'd found a loophole.

"It'll be cheaper on an old car," said Jay, always ready with a retort.

"I don't know why Rachel should get a car when Jay and I

didn't," said Sarah, annoyed.

"But wait a minute, didn't Jay have a motorcycle when he was sixteen?" I chimed in.

"Yeah, that's right, Jay had a motorcycle. You and Mom let him ride around on that thing without a helmet, too," said Rachel.

"Yeah, well..." said my father, trying to formulate a comeback, "that was different."

"Different because it's worse, you mean," said Sarah.

"No, different because..."

"Don't say it, Dad," said Rachel. "Don't use the G-word."

"It's not because you're a girl. Your mother and I were broke then. We couldn't afford a car for Jay so we let him find an old motorcycle he could fix up," said my father. "Maybe it wasn't the best decision, but he took good care of it and never crashed it once," he added, pointing his fork at Rachel for emphasis.

"So we have money now?" I asked. "Because I'd like a car, too, when I get my license. And I'll take something nice. A Porsche would work."

"Get real, pal," said Jay.

"I'm just laying the groundwork, that's all."

"You're building on the wrong property."

Jamie busted into laughter until she realized nobody else was amused, then stopped and hastily plowed a bite of potato salad into her mouth.

"Then it's settled. Jamie will help me get a car," said Rachel.

"No it's not settled. We'll talk when you come home," said my father.

"I knew you'd start using that against me."

"Using what?"

"The fact that I'm living somewhere else," said Rachel. "Every important decision that concerns me will have to take place at home. You won't let me make any major decisions on my own."

"This decision doesn't concern just you," said my father.

"That's just another way of saying that you don't think I can handle the responsibility of a car." My father didn't respond and buried his eyes in his plate of food. Rachel repositioned in her seat and I could see the tide of anger beginning to rise up in her face. "You don't think I can handle a car, do you?" said Rachel.

"I didn't say that," said my father.

"You think I'll get loaded one night and wrap it around a telephone pole."

"Rachel…" said my mother, trying to derail the exchange.

"You do, Dad, just admit it."

"No, I will *not* admit it!" my father shouted in a rare outburst, pounding his fist on the table. It caught everyone off guard, and nobody moved a muscle while he tried to compose himself. "I just don't think we should be having this conversation right now. This is a birthday party. We're here to have a good time, not talk about buying cars. So let's just drop it and—"

"—And what, talk about it when I get home?" interrupted Rachel. Nobody chewed a morsel; the air was thicker than peanut butter. "Just forget it. I'm not coming home…ever!" Rachel ejected from the table. "Come on, Jamie, let's ditch this bogus party."

She grabbed Jamie's arm and yanked her from the table, almost causing her to trip and fall. Jamie was terribly embarrassed and tried to communicate that she was sorry with her skittish eyes.

"Peace," said Jamie timidly, holding up the sign.

"Come on, Rachel, don't leave," implored Sarah. "We haven't

even cut the cake!"

They never turned around and simply kept walking across the grassy field, exchanging some hushed and heated words. I think Jamie was trying to convince Rachel to change her mind. But we've all been down that road before with Rachel, one that swirls around until it finally becomes a dead end. Welcome to my fifteenth year of life.

# Chapter Sixteen

*There were two words in the English language that when spoken together conjured images of slave-like torture and humiliation: hell week.* I was told that it was something similar to getting a root canal for five days in a row. It would be the ultimate test of my courage, strength, desire, and manhood, and I wasn't certain I had enough of any of these to make the grade. I got a taste of hell week in junior high except that it was juvenile compared to the big school, from what I'd heard. In high school, it was all about endurance, and finding out who had the guts and intestinal fortitude to withstand five straight days of physical and mental abuse. It was about taking a bunch of cocky, rebellious, and summer-dazed teenagers and pounding them into submission. It was about permanently removing that chip on each guy's shoulder and preparing them to receive instructions. The coaches knew exactly how to accomplish this feat, too. For two hours a day, twice a day, they'd snap their commanding voices like whips and make us run, jump, and push until we either gave up or stood up. Either way, they didn't really give a damn. They simply wanted to see who was left standing, knowing that those athletes still around would be the battle-tested young men who would fight their wars for them on the gridiron.

"Come on, come on, let's go, move it gentlemen, move it!" yelled Coach Bower from his station, in my opinion the worst station of all. Coach Bower made us run in place and drop to the turf in a push-up position, only to immediately spring to our feet again, called thrust-squats. They were torture, not to mention horribly mundane. I was certain by the wry grin he wore under his thick, sandy-colored moustache, that he derived some sick, sadistic pleasure from them. I bet all the coaches took pleasure in hell week. Their coaches must've tortured them, and now they were exacting their revenge, a sweet, wet, early morning dew revenge.

My group filtered right into line, still sucking gasps of air from ten minutes of non-stop hurdles during the last station.

"Get those feet moving, gentlemen, come on, let's go, let's go," fired Bower.

I felt sorry for some of the heavier guys. They didn't heed the warning from graduates gone before and entered hell week in terrible shape. Some had already dropped out, unable to handle the pounding. I was lean and sturdy, having spent the last month or so playing hour upon hour of basketball. But it was only the first day, and I was ready to puke.

"Down...up!" barked Bower. He nonchalantly walked the line with his hands clasped behind his back and pivoted occasionally to view the other stations, as though he could care less about his own group of men. Bower carried himself proudly, with a slight forward lean and purposeful walk, and kept himself in excellent physical condition. He had the physique of a fullback, bulging thighs and beefy calves, although his upper body was less muscular. He exaggerated his short strides with the flip of his feet so that his thigh muscles would ripple into place. His sandy blond hair was beach-boy straight and rather long for a coach, a couple of inches below his ears. He parted his hair so far down on the left side of his skull that he was constantly swiping his fingers across his forehead to push his bangs to the side. Place one of those horned helmets on his head and a sword in his hand, and he'd make the prototypical Viking.

"Down...up!" He delivered these words without passion or compassion. Somehow I viewed his disinterest in our agony as a telling sign of his ruthless brutality as a person. Even though he was head coach, he'd be spending most of his time with the defense, since he played outside linebacker in college. I was trying out for quarterback, so Bower wouldn't be my practice coach once the season began. Although he rarely waited more than a few seconds before he barked a command, every so often his mind would drift away and he'd leave us lying flat on the turf, teasing us into believing the torture was over. I cherished each restful moment on the ground, and like a soldier keeping low in the foxhole, I checked on my comrades in arms. I looked to my left and noticed that big Tony was pale and beaten, his eyelids shut and his head resting on the grass as if he were sleeping, or dead.

"Come on, dude, suck it up," I said to him.

Tony barely cracked opened his eyes and appeared to have no recollection of where he was or what he was doing. He was on death row.

"Up!" yelled Bower. I sprang to my feet as if someone pressed a button on my ass. Bower wasn't going to beat me, not today, not the very first day. Tony didn't move.

"Get up, son, get up!" shouted Bower. Tony pressed his hands to the turf and strained to push, but his shoulders were the only parts that moved. The rest of his large body stayed firmly sucked to the ground. *Another one bites the dust.*

After football practice, I rode home and cruised into the driveway. I was weary and my muscles ached, and I knew that tomorrow morning my body would feel even worse. I noticed a familiar bike in the driveway, although I couldn't place it with an owner. I couldn't concentrate on anything else except the thought of gobbling up a thick grilled cheese sandwich and some potato chips with a tall glass of chocolate milk, and planting my butt on the sofa. I parked my bike and lumbered toward the front door when I heard some voices. I peered inside the living room through our large, rectangular front window. Now it was possible that the long day of grueling workouts had caused my listless mind to play tricks with my vision. I could've sworn that the young woman talking to my mother was none other than Shelly. I blinked, hoping it was a mirage, but the image remained clear. Then the young woman waved pleasantly. *Oh shit, oh major shit, it was Shelly.* My mother turned her head and smiled so wide and proud I thought she was going to leap through the window and tackle me with joy.

I still had the chance to escape on my bike, I thought. I could say that I forgot something at school or dropped something in the street. Then I remembered Shelly's words after our near hazardous encounter with her mom; that I chickened out and failed her test. Was this another one? Was she just playing games with me? After our conquest at the bowling alley I thought I'd proven myself worthy. Jesus, what was it going to take with this girl, broken bones?

"Are you gonna stand there all day? You have a visitor," said my mother, holding the front door open and leaning outside.

As I tentatively approached my mother at the door, I was trying to formulate some type of plan, but the only words that came to my mind's viewer screen were, "Oh shit, oh shit, oh shit."

"Why didn't you tell us you had a new friend... a new *girl* friend?" my mother said, beaming.

"Um, guess I forgot."

My mother rolled her eyes, snickered and shut the front door, which sounded like a steel-casted dungeon door. I turned and stood at the edge of the living room. Shelly glistened with pride and rose to her feet. I was so uncomfortable I'd rather listen to an hour of someone scraping their long fingernails across a chalkboard. And yet Shelly stood there, calm and collected, strangely gratified by this whole situation.

"How was football practice?" said Shelly in her bubbly voice.

"Uh, tiring, very tiring." I faked a yawn and stretched my arms into the air. "I really need a long nap."

I started to turn for the hallway and my room when my mother pushed me from behind and forced me into the living room.

"Oh, he's just kidding, Shelly," said my mother.

"I know, he teases me all the time," said Shelly.

"All the time?" asked my mother. "How much time have you two spent together?" And at the exact same time I uttered the words "not much," Shelly said "a lot."

"There seems to be some confusion here," said my mother. "Which is it?"

"It's probably somewhere in between," I said, firing a disapproving glance at Shelly, which bounced off her happy defector shield like a Superball.

"I was just telling your mom how we met," said Shelly.

"You were?" I said in a tone of warning.

"In Thrifty's at the ice cream counter. He ordered Rocky Road, and I ordered Rainbow sherbet. Like they say, Viva la difference."

"Are you two the same age?" asked my mother.

"I'm the older woman," said Shelly, tipping her head and batting an eyelash. "But only by a year. Besides, Kevin is much more mature than most of the boys my age. He's very sweet to me, and always the gentleman. You should be very proud."

If my mother had been a male peacock—creatures we have in abundance in the foothills of Rossmoor—her colorful feathers would have fanned out in dazzling style. I wanted to conk Shelly on the head with my club like Fred Flintstone and drag her out of my house by her thick mane, except that I had no club and I wasn't a barbarian (not to imply that Fred was, only that in general, cavemen were).

"Oh shoot!" my mother said, slapping her hands together the way she often did when she remembered something. It rattled my already jumpy nerves. "You've been here ten minutes, and I haven't offered you a cold drink. Do you like 7-Up?"

"Sure, that would be great," said Shelly.

"Okay, one 7-Up it is." My mother started to leave us. "You too, Kevin?"

"If it comes with a grilled cheese, yeah."

"It doesn't. We'll be having dinner in a little while, after your dad comes home. Will you be staying for dinner, Shelly?"

I nearly blacked out. I saw my life flash before my eyes, my very short life with too few memories and none of them involving sex.

"Uh… I can't, but thanks anyway," said Shelly.

"Maybe some other time," said my mother, then she left us. When we were alone, I leveled my eyes at Shelly, who wasn't about to back down to me.

"Before you say anything," she started in a hushed voice, holding up her hands, "I just wanna say that she has no idea who I am."

"But my dad could be home any minute," I countered.

"I'll be gone by the time he comes home, and even if I'm not, what's the big deal?"

"What's the big deal—are you kidding me?"

"Look at you, you're like a frightened squirrel. Don't be such a spaz, Kevin. Just relax and let the moment take you away for a change."

She paused and noticed a framed photograph on the coffee table. "Are these your sisters and brother?" she asked, holding up the photo. I firmly grabbed the frame and set it back down.

"Is this some kind of test?" I said, "Because if it is, I think it really sucks."

"Why would I be testing you?"

"Then what are you doing here?"

"I wanted to see your house, where you live, is that so wrong?"

She burned me with those stunning green eyes and made the kind of innocent baby face that a person of my limited emotional strength couldn't possibly disappoint. "Besides, I think it's about time we tell them about us, don't you?"

"Here we are," said my mother, entering the room with bubbling glasses of soda. She handed us our sodas and I immediately took a long, thirst-quenching gulp. I was panic-stricken that Shelly was about to divulge our relationship and her identity in front of my mother, and yet I was helpless to control the moment. I was just a spectator now.

"So, Shelly, do I know your parents?" asked my mother.

I coughed up some soda and sprinkled liquid all over the carpet, the soda dripping down my shirt.

"Kevin," my mother said, "slow down, for heaven's sake."

"Sorry, wrong pipe," I said, banging my chest and coughing. Shelly paused, glanced my direction, and then opened her mouth to speak.

"Uh…," she began.

"No!" I shouted. "No, you don't," I repeated, more calmly, trying to redeem myself. Shelly furrowed her eyebrows, either disappointed or confused, or maybe both.

"We're fairly new to the area," said Shelly.

"Oh, well, maybe we'll meet them soon, and invite them over for a barbecue, okay?"

"Sure, they'd love that," said Shelly, playing the girlfriend role so well it unnerved me. Several seconds elapsed without conversation. My outburst turned the moment into something odd and uncomfortable, but I didn't care. I wanted this gathering to end. "Well, I guess I should get back home," said Shelly, just the words I wanted to hear. "My mother doesn't know where I am."

"Well, okay, I enjoyed meeting you, Shelly."

"You too, Mrs. Copeland." Shelly took a huge gulp from the drink and said, "Thanks for the soda," then set it down on the coffee table.

"Don't be a stranger, okay?" said my mother. "You're welcome here any time."

Shelly smiled and moved toward the front door. I filed in right behind her, close enough that she couldn't pivot and say anything else without meeting my steadfast eyes. I was enormously relieved when we set foot outside and approached her bike. We had escaped another treacherous moment.

"Your mom is nice," said Shelly.

"Yeah, super, so it's time to go," I said, anxious.

"I feel kind of sorry for her, don't you?"

"Yeah, yeah, okay, bye now."

"I mean, she probably still loves your dad. It's so... tragic."

"Right, tragic, see ya later."

"Think about what I said, about telling them the truth. We can't go on forever like this," she said.

"I can. My father and your mother are."

"That's different. They're married, they have to hide it." She paused and searched my eyes. "Don't you want people to know about us? Are you ashamed of me?"

"Ashamed of…hell no, you're the prettiest…" and I paused, aware of the flood of exuberance about to exit my mouth. She broke into a coy smile at my half admission.

I froze, hearing a big car engine, low and chugging, in the distance. I kept my eyes fixed to the airspace just left of the house on the corner, and then it appeared, the unmistakable nose of our lime green station wagon.

"Oh shit, it's my dad, go, go!" I shouted at Shelly.

She kissed me on the mouth and hopped on her bike. "Come by my house tomorrow after practice," she said, starting to peddle away.

"Yeah, yeah, just go!"

My father slowed to pull in. The two of them spent a good, long moment, the longest of my life, exchanging gapes. I feared the worst, that he recognized her. My father parked the car, and Shelly disappeared around the corner.

"Who was that?" my father asked.

"Just a friend," I said.

"Uh-huh," he said with a knowing grin. "She's a pretty girl, what's she doing with you?"

"Real funny, Dad."

"Well, did you make it?" I had no idea what he was referring to, still shaken by a near collision of fate. "Through your first day of hell week?"

"Oh yeah, no sweat."

"What's the competition look like?"

"Hard to tell. It's all just endurance training right now."

"That's the toughest part. They're testing your strength of will. You make it through this and you'll be okay."

"Right."

"Well, don't forget about your chores. You don't get a free ride through football season."

"Like Rachel does," I said under my breath.

"What was that?" asked my father.

"Maybe I should run away like Rachel did, then I wouldn't have to do chores."

My father paused and dropped his eyes to the pavement. I wasn't sure which bothered him more, the content of my sentence or the fact that I was the one who said it. I knew it was a rotten thing to say, and yet I felt a certain vindication by having said it.

"I certainly hope you don't mean that, Kevin," he said in a meaningful, fatherly tone. I despondently lowered my head, feeling ashamed. He reached out and squeezed my shoulder, a gesture he often added to a particularly tender moment between us, and then brushed by me.

"Put your bike away. You don't want it to get stolen," he said, walking up the steps.

Even though nothing ever got stolen in this isolated neighborhood, my father always felt compelled to warn me anyway. I suppose it was part of his job, to warn his children of the dangers lurking around the bend. But who warned him? Who told a father how to cope with life's unpredictable twists and turns? I thought about Shelly and what she said about telling the truth. Despite seeing her kiss me and getting a good, close look, my father had no clue about her identity, or what was lurking just around the bend.

&#x1F6B2;

That night after dinner I sank into the sofa, put on my headphones, and listened to Crosby, Stills, and Nash. The group's multi-layered vocals and harmonies always soothed my mind. I finally reached a relaxed, dreamy state when the last song ended on the first side, and the needle automatically lifted and returned to the arm holder. I heard some shouting, and I removed my headphones to listen.

"It's not the right time, John," my mother shouted from down the hallway.

"Then when is the right time?" my father said, his voice strained and hard.

"I don't know, but this family is falling apart as it is. I don't think it's right to dump all your shit on them, too."

"My shit? Are you blaming everything on me?"

"No, I just want you to take some responsibility for your actions, that's all," said my mother.

"I've always taken responsibility for my actions. But this is not just about me, it's about us," replied my father.

"There is no 'us' anymore!" shouted my mother. I heard a door slam shut.

"Audrey!" my father yelled, and then the door opened and shut again. Now their voices were more muffled, although I could still make out most of the words.

"Don't push a guilt trip on me, Audrey. We got in this thing together."

"But you never got out. You were supposed to get out!"

"I can't suddenly just change how I feel," said my father.

"Neither can I! But the last thing I want to do is involve the kids. They deserve better than to be dragged through the dirt of our screwed-up relationship."

"I just think we should practice what we preach," said my father. "You're always harping on the fact that we don't share enough with the kids. Well here's our chance."

"Well maybe I'm not preaching it anymore. Maybe all that crap about new age parenting is just bullshit, John. Did that ever occur to you? Have you even noticed what's happening around here?"

"Oh here we go again. You're always gonna find fault with how we handle the kids. Nothing we do is ever good enough."

"It's not good enough, John. Just because our kids are old enough to take care of themselves doesn't mean we get to start acting like children again."

"That's not fair, Audrey, and you know it. We've always acted responsibly with the kids. Besides, you were just as enthusiastic as I was, if not more."

"Well guess what? I'm not anymore! I hate it, and I want it to stop!" my mother screamed.

The argument ended abruptly, and I wondered what they were doing. Did they simply realize they'd been shouting and were now speaking in hushed tones? Was he holding her in his arms while she cried? Were they just standing apart in silent agony, trying to make sense of a dreadful phase in their relationship?

I turned the record over to side two and set the needle on the first song. I felt a heavy sadness in my chest as I sank lower into the sofa. The irony of the moment wasn't lost on me, that while my parents were struggling to keep their marriage and love alive, I was falling in love for the first time. I shut my eyes and tried to settle in to the music, but I no longer had a settled mind.

# Chapter Seventeen

*I dreamt about the movie* Papillon *in the early morning.* My father took me to see the film several months ago and the gruesome images stayed with me for weeks. In my dream I saw Steve McQueen's steady poker face while he took the burning cigar from the leper inside the dark, smoky tent and inhaled an anxious puff. As the main character, Papillon, he was trying to make his escape down the river by securing a boat from the leper's village. He didn't have a dime to his name, relying only on his wits and courage. After Papillon smoked the cigar, the leper asked him in a gruff, weakened voice, "How did you know that leprosy wasn't contagious?" Papillon swallowed nervously and replied, "I didn't." The leper laughed in the film, and in my dream it was a loud and maniacal laugh. Even in his enormous relief, Papillon displayed no real emotion, just barely a relieved grin, not wanting to reveal his fear. Papillon was so desperate to gain his freedom that he was willing to risk contracting one of the ugliest and most brutal diseases known to man. He was given the boat, only to be captured later and sent to Devil's Island, where he made a final, reckless escape by jumping off a towering cliff and into the roaring sea, floating away on his makeshift raft.

I had no idea how this dream related to my situation. Maybe I needed to break free like Papillon, to forge my own direction and discover what was waiting at the other end of the river. I knew there was something important at stake here—relationships hung in balance, and families were susceptible to ruins. Every move I made would have serious repercussions. If I wanted Shelly in my life I might have to sacrifice the manageable relationships I had with my parents. I might have to expose us, which would likely unleash a chaos never seen before in my family.

Football practice ended and I was relishing a few relaxing hours at home before the next workout. I concluded the key to surviving hell week was to conserve as much energy as possible before the next beating. While I bent down to unlock my bike I heard a woman's voice, which was rare around the football field, especially during the summer.

"Kevin Copeland?" I barely glanced upward while bending over and unwrapping the chain-link lock from my bike. The voice was hauntingly familiar. "Are you Kevin?"

"Yeah," I said, the glare from the harsh late morning sun obstructing my vision.

"I'm Mrs. Vaughn, Shelly's mother." I paused, stunned by the mention of her name. Jesus, how should I respond? Ignoring her, hoping she'd go away, I finished wrapping my lock around the center bar on my bike. "I need to talk to you," she said.

Damn, I thought, these Vaughn women were always sneaking up on me.

"I can't, I have to get home," I said.

"This won't take long. It's very important."

I felt trapped and as usual, totally unprepared. My heart thumped against my ribcage, and my mind raced with competing thoughts. I could've just bolted away, except I had to assume that Shelly caved in and revealed us, or her mom had finally recognized me, which left me little choice except to stand my ground and face her. At some point, I'd have to walk through this dark tunnel anyway. It might as well be today, and on my turf.

A few moments later I found myself sitting in the far top corner of the football bleachers and talking privately to Mrs. Vaughn, gazing below at the field on which I hoped to score touchdowns and impress the girls. This was the first time I'd ever sat alone with a female in these stands. Somehow, I never pictured the moment quite like this.

"Shelly told me everything about your relationship," she said. The statement was shocking, initially, before I remembered that Shelly had wanted to spill the beans. But where was my warning? Why couldn't Shelly have alerted me that our secret had been released into the great, wide open? "You realize that it has to stop, don't you?"

I paused a long time before responding, "No."

Her eyes flickered oddly after my response, as though she was suddenly aware of something new.

"Well it does. I want this relationship to end and right now… today." I felt the skin on my face and around my eyes squeeze tighter. I studied her while she lifted her purse and dug through the contents like a dog digging for a bone. She had a determined and focused demeanor about her, as if every thought was driven by a purpose. Maybe my perception was distorted, but every word and movement seemed cold and calculating. "Where is that…oh, here it is."

She whipped out a package of spearmint gum and offered me a stick. I shook my head. I wanted nothing from this woman, except her daughter. "Suit yourself… Roger," she said, glancing shrewdly at me, knowing I lied about my name and trying to stir a reaction. I didn't bite on her comment. She unwrapped the stick of gum and stuffed it hastily into her mouth. "So, do we understand each other?"

"But you don't even know me."

"Oh yes I"—and then she paused, averting her eyes. "It doesn't matter. Believe me, she'll only end up hurting you, and I know you don't want that."

I huffed indignantly. "You're wrong, she won't."

"I've already told her she's forbidden from seeing you anymore. I suggest you forget about her and move on."

"That's crazy. This isn't the Soviet Union. You can't stop her from seeing me."

"Yes I can, and I did," she said with a tone of desperation. "I'm her mother and she still takes direction from me. And I want you to stay away from her, too. Is that clear?"

I gazed out at the green, empty field and considered all the battles I would wage there, and about the strength and courage it would take to win them. For some reason, and even though I was sitting motionless in the bleachers, I adopted this contest as my first one and Mrs. Vaughn as my opponent.

"I don't think so," I said with a stern resolve. "You're not *my* mother."

"Okay, if that's how you feel. Then, I guess I'll have to talk to your dad," she countered. Pow—sacked for a ten yard loss. "He doesn't know about you and Shelly but he will, and he won't like it, not one bit."

"How do you know?"

"Because I know him."

"Yeah, so I've heard," I said, injecting a childish tone.

"You and Shelly would only make things worse," she said, sweeping her fingers through her hair. "I just can't deal with that right now."

"For who? It won't make things any worse for me."

"Believe me, it can't work. Not now, not ever."

Truth be told, she was probably right. How could we possibly have a normal relationship, given we were still so dependent upon our parents? On the other hand, I couldn't let this woman bully me into something that I didn't want.

"I'll stop seeing Shelly if you stop seeing my dad."

She was stunned by my comeback shot and then promptly recovered.

"That's not an option," she said.

"That's my option, take it or leave it."

As I stood up, preparing to descend the stands, she released a gentle grin that seemed both painful and pleasing. She took a deep breath and then laid her next words on very thick.

"Your father never told me how strong you were. He said you were a good son, thoughtful and considerate, helpful around the house. But he never said anything about your strength. That's a wonderful trait to have as a young man."

"Does that mean we have a deal?"

Waiting for her response, I realized that I wasn't certain which answer I wanted to hear. In the beginning, my intentions were iron clad: I wanted to drive a wedge between them so my parents would gain a fighting chance. Now, as if there was such a concept as cosmic justice or karma, Mrs. Vaughn was attempting to end *my* relationship. I reasoned, though, that either way I couldn't lose. Shelly and I could always lay low for a few months and then pick up where the relationship left off. Who would care after the storm had blown over?

"I'm sorry you had to find out about me and your dad, but I can't leave him. We have a deep connection, you know? A spiritual bond. You just don't find that every day. I know that's very hard for you to understand at your age."

"Doesn't make it right," I said.

"He loves your mother, too, you know."

"Shut up!" I shouted uncontrollably. "Just…shut up about my mom."

Mrs. Vaughn sighed with defeat, then rose from the bench and stepped down toward me. I couldn't look at her. She leaned close to me, too close, so that I could smell her flowery perfume.

"I don't expect you to understand right now. It's complicated. As for you and Shelly, it's going to stop. So if you choose to go against my wishes, then it's out of my hands. I'll have to tell your father about you two. This situation could get very…

uncomfortable." She glanced out at the football field, and a thought seemed to bubble in her mind. "Who knows, if he really wants to punish you, he might pull you from the football team. All that hard work you put in, all your athletic hopes and dreams. Well, it would be devastating, wouldn't it?"

She let loose a wicked grin, then continued down the steps and toward the field.

"He wouldn't do that... and Shelly wouldn't dump me because of you!" I shouted.

Mrs. Vaughn turned and delivered an expression of sympathy that parents often gave to misinformed young children, and it boiled my blood with rage. She reached the cement pathway between the bleachers and the field fence, and I watched her stride away with those long, well-toned legs. I tried to imagine her body vanishing into thin air, as if Scotty had beamed her up to the Enterprise and whisked her away at warp speed. No such luck. More power, Scotty, I need more power.

⚲

During the ride home I tried to convince myself that Shelly would remain strong. I had to believe she'd disobey her mother and stay with me. I knew it was wishful thinking, but it got me through the long ride home.

As I made the sweeping turn onto my street, I noticed a vehicle parked in front of my house. It was a dirty and dented old Mustang, with severely scratched white paint and rusty tire rims; a real pile.

I quietly entered my house since I knew my father was working and my mother said she wouldn't be home until the late afternoon. I made my way down the hallway and overheard some voices in the back part of the house. One was Rachel's, and the other voice sounded like Jamie's.

Rachel's door was cracked open several inches. As I approached within the dimly lit hallway, I saw their bodies moving back and forth inside the room. They were giggling and talking. I moved closer, stealthily, and like a lion sneaking up on its prey, I bent down low. I leaned against the wall and peered inside. It was rare that I could catch a glimpse of Jamie in her natural, unguarded state. She was usually quite careful of the way she acted in my house, for fear of being forbidden to return. I was intrigued.

"Take this, I like this top," said Jamie, holding up a blue piece of clothing.

"I don't wanna ruin that, it's one of my favorites," said Rachel.

"They gave you some space in the closet, didn't they?" said Jamie.

"Yeah, but I'd rather just keep that here, so I know it's safe. I can get it whenever I want to."

"You're not doing this right."

"Doing what right?"

"Running away. You have to pretend like you're never coming back. Otherwise they won't take you seriously."

"What does that have to do with taking all my favorite clothes?" asked Rachel.

"If you take all your favorite stuff, they'll know you're serious."

"Not my parents. When I got my ears pierced they didn't notice for a week."

Rachel began stuffing clothes into a pillowcase while Jamie

surveyed the room.

"Do your parents keep any money around the house?" Jamie asked.

"Sometimes in their dresser drawer," said Rachel, stuffing more clothing into a pillowcase.

"We should look before we leave," said Jamie. "We're getting low on cash."

"It's not cool to steal from my parents," said Rachel.

"We're runaways now. We do what we have to."

"I guess," Rachel shrugged.

"What about Kevin, does he have any?"

"I'm not taking money from my little brother. Besides, he hides it like a miser. If I took it he'd know it was me."

"We can always return it when we make more."

"How are we gonna make money?"

"It's easy. I can make a hundred bucks just like that. The only problem is that it can be kind of dangerous."

"I don't wanna do anything crazy. Running away was crazy enough for me."

"That's why we should check your house, we need every penny we can get."

"I think you should steal from your stepdad," said Rachel. "He deserves it, the pervert." With downtrodden eyes Jamie looked at her hands and readjusted a silver ring on her finger, evidently stung by Rachel's comment. "I'm sorry," backtracked Rachel. "It's just that I wish you'd talk to me about it, or get some help. Jesus, at least tell your mom. What he did was sickening."

"I don't need any help. I'm fine. I can handle that prick on my own, all right?" said Jamie forcefully, trying hard to end the discussion.

"Jamie, he should be put away for what he's—"

"That fucker doesn't exist to me!" blasted Jamie, her face flushed red. "Just forget about him, okay, can you do that, for me?"

"Yeah, sure," said Rachel tenderly, realizing she'd gone too far.

They were silent for a few moments before Rachel turned and started to pack more clothes into the pillowcase. Jamie appeared remorseful about the moment and then moved right up behind Rachel, as if needing to distract herself. I saw Jamie lift both hands and cradle Rachel's long, golden brown hair, and let the hair sift and fall through her pale white hands.

Without exchanging words Rachel corralled her own hair and pulled it aside and over her shoulder. Jamie began to gently knead Rachel's shoulders, and I heard my sister moan softly, tilting her head. Jamie was methodical about the way she rubbed Rachel's shoulders, and then she moved her hands up the base of the neck and under the ears, pushing her fingertips into Rachel's flesh.

"Does that feel good?" asked Jamie softly.

"Heavenly," said Rachel.

I watched with an acute fascination. I was frozen in my hunkered down position and realized that I hadn't moved a muscle in a long while. My thighs burned. Jamie dragged her hands back down the shoulders, around the shoulder blades, and down along the spine with one, long continuous movement. Rachel groaned in a pleasing way that for some reason made me shudder from discomfort. Jamie started to move up the back again, and then she split her hands apart and massaged Rachel's sides. She made smooth, round motions with her fingertips, then moments later, her left hand disappeared from my view and slid in front and around Rachel, so all I could see was Jamie's elbow and bicep muscle flexing and moving. Jamie slowly leaned closer to Rachel and kissed her gently on the nape of the neck. The vision was so incredible to my eyes, so inconceivable, that the meaning of the kiss never completely registered in my mind, as if the entire scene was an abstract painting. Rachel moaned again and then turned around towards Jamie. They shared a deep, probing stare, then leaned towards each other and tenderly met their lips. I was stunned. I tried to reposition myself to get a better view when I felt a shooting sting of pain in my thigh and my left leg gave out. I fell on my butt and made a loud thump.

"What was that?" said Jamie.

I sprang to my feet and dashed into my room, just moments before I heard some steps toward Rachel's door and into the hallway. I opened my closet with a loud thrust and removed my sweaty football t-shirt. Rachel appeared at my door.

"Oh, it's only you," said Rachel.

"Yeah," I said nervously, trying to contain my emotions. Could it have been just a sweet, caring moment between two close girlfriends? Perhaps girls shared these kinds of moments, for all I knew. I mean, how much did I really know about the female species?

"What are you doing here? I thought you ran away."

"I'm getting some more clothes," she said.

"Whose car is out front?"

"Mine and Jamie's. It's ours. We bought it. Well, some guys we know helped us."

"Looks like a real piece of junk."

"At least I'm not riding around on a bike."

We said nothing for a few moments, both deciding that it was better to end this childish line of conversation.

"How's Mom and Dad?" she said. I shrugged. "They don't call me anymore."

"Why should they?" I said. "You keep telling them to back off."

"Do they ever talk about me?"

"They can't believe how easy it was to get you outta the house." I kept a straight face until Rachel's drooped with disappointment. "I'm kidding…duh."

"Right," she said, smiling weakly and skirting her gaze aside. She was strangely vulnerable at this moment, far from the cantankerous and stubborn girl who occupied this house a couple of weeks ago. Perhaps being away from the comfort and familiarity of home had weakened her resolve.

"I don't know why you had to run away. Mom and Dad let us do almost anything we want anyway," I said. "It's not like they keep you chained up or anything."

"I need my space," she said. "Every time I set foot in this house I feel like they're watching me, waiting for me to screw up. I don't like that feeling."

"So don't screw up," I said.

"That's so typical of you to say something like that. You couldn't screw up if you tried."

"Bullshit," I blurted, thinking about everything that had happened lately. I wanted to tell her everything and prove her wrong. I wanted her to know she wasn't the only one with problems around here. "I've messed up before."

"When?" she said.

My mind suddenly went blank. I couldn't think of a single event that would compete with some of Rachel's monstrous mishaps. She blew out regular high school and attended continuation school. She came home blitzed on more than one occasion. And her most glaring mistake came several months ago, when my parents had to shorten our best vacation ever in Hawaii to take Rachel home for an abortion.

"Okay, fine, so you beat me. It's not something I'd be real proud of," I countered in a mean tone, which wiped the knowing grin right off her face. Whenever she cornered me I had this uncontrollable urge to retaliate, and I usually said something regrettable. Dejected, Rachel turned around and left my view in the hallway. A few moments later I heard her call out, "Jamie?"

"I'm out here," Jamie shouted from the backyard.

I moved into the hallway and saw Rachel walk through Jay's door and outside onto the patio. I leaned over just enough to see through Jay's door and watched them from behind the wall. Rachel grabbed Jamie's cigarette and took a long and needful drag.

"Let's get some and get outta here," said Jamie.

"Yeah," said Rachel. "I hate it here."

I saw them walk behind the corner of Rachel's room, the far rear end of the backyard, which I found unusual. What were they retrieving back there? I stepped onto the porch, and then crept along the side wall, keeping out of sight. Suddenly Rachel cursed out loud.

"Fuck, they're gone, they took 'em," said Rachel.

"Your parents?" asked Jamie.

"Yeah, they pulled 'em out."

"But you said they agreed to it."

"They did…damn them. This is all because I ran away," Rachel said bitterly. "They make me so fuckin' pissed off. Let's get outta here."

I hopped up on the porch, and then dashed through Jay's door and into the house. Through the doorway I watched them step up onto the porch and enter the house through the sliding glass door. Rachel was fighting mad. I snuck back outside onto the porch, made sure they'd vacated the house, then treaded lightly behind Rachel's room. For as long as I could remember there'd been a strip of dirt underneath Rachel's window where my mother occasionally tried to grow tomatoes or flowers, without much success. This part of the yard only caught a few hours of sunlight a day, if that. For most of the year it was just a ragged strip of dry, lifeless dirt. But a few weeks ago I noticed some small green plants that sprang up from the far end of the strip, though I figured they were just weeds. When I checked this area again I noticed the plants had been excavated and only a few scattered leaves remained. Curious, I kneeled down and dug my fingers through the unusually moist dirt, scooped up a handful of small broken leaves and dirt, and brought them to my nose. I let the soil sift through my fluttering fingers while I breathed in a huge whiff of something strangely sweet and musty, almost like burnt sugar. There was something very familiar about the smell; too familiar. Then, as if the soil was crawling with cockroaches, I dropped what remained in my hands to the ground. It couldn't be. There had to be a mistake here, some kind of misunderstanding. I probably confused Rachel's words somehow. She must've been lying, although the reasons for doing so were unclear. It wasn't possible to conceive of the alternative, that my parents had permitted this junk to grow in our backyard. If they allowed this to grow at their home, then no doubt they were smoking it, too. I was mystified. I couldn't conceive the image of my parents smoking a joint with friends and giggling like stoned teenagers. I stood there for the longest time and stared blankly into the soil. I must've been wrong. I had to be.

# Chapter Eighteen

*My head felt like a water balloon ready to explode. I was being* bombarded with distressing facts I couldn't interpret or transmit through the logical processes of my mind. I was a big snowball rolling down the slippery slope, picking up patches of icy truth and cold facts, praying that I wouldn't crash head first into a pine tree. I tried to concentrate on Shelly—her lovely face, her sexy, puffy lips, and her delicious, chest-heaving walk—and I tried to imagine us together, eliminating all negative thoughts from my mind. I knew that images were not enough, though. I needed to see Shelly, to hear her voice, and talk to her about our situation. I decided to call her and find out if she could meet me before the late afternoon practice. We only spoke briefly, and she agreed.

When I arrived at the A&W Root Beer hamburger stand not far from the high school, I noticed four people at one of the patio picnic tables. Moving closer, I saw that one was Shelly, sitting with two guys and one girl. I recognized the handsome, dark-haired guy from the party, the one who made such a commotion when he and his girlfriend arrived. Only this time the girlfriend was nowhere in sight. The other two were familiar except I was intoxicated that night, so I couldn't recall their names. I pretended not to see them and went directly to the order window for a root beer.

"Kevin," I heard Shelly shout. I pivoted without showing any enthusiasm. "Come over," she said, waving. I nodded real James Dean-like and paid the clerk for my drink. I realized the best way to handle this situation was to appear completely unaffected.

"Look who I ran into," said Shelly. "You know Pete and David, from the party. And this is Robin."

"You play football?" asked Pete, the one I'd remembered. I was dressed in my workout gear.

"Yeah," I responded.

"What position?"

"Quarterback."

"How far can you throw?"

"Probably around fifty yards."

"Not bad. I can throw sixty, but football's not my sport," Pete gloated.

"Pete plays baseball," said Shelly with enthusiasm. "Shortstop, right?"

"Yeah. You trying out for the sophomore baseball team this year?"

"I don't know, maybe. Baseball's not really my best sport," I said.

"Hey, not everyone can hit a ninety-mile an hour fastball," said Pete smugly.

"Yeah, or throw one," added David.

"One more year, Shelly, and we'll be able to try out for song girl," pitched in Robin.

"I like the pep squad better," said Shelly. "They get to do jumps and stunts with the guys."

"You wanna jump around with those guys, in front of people?" said David.

"Yeah, why not?" said Shelly.

"They're guys… doing cheers, in frilly costumes," said David. "Don't you think that's a little gay?"

"Forget that, I'd be worried they might drop you on your head," said Pete.

"You're such jocks. It's not gay at all, and they have to keep in great shape. Besides, think about this… they get to spend hours practicing with us, lifting us, and touching our bodies. They get to know who we are and what we like. Not such a bad deal while you jocks are out there sweating your butts off, knocking each other around, and for what, a ball game?" said Shelly smartly.

Ouch, what a killer comeback. Pete and David were stumped, their brains working overtime trying to conceive of the possibilities. I had to admire Shelly for the way she countered utter stupidity with her own brand of teenage wisdom.

"Hey, let's blow this joint and head for your house," said David, coming out of his stupor.

"You guys coming?" said Pete, looking at Shelly. She hesitated, and then turned to me.

"Where?" I said.

"Pete has a big pool, and his parents are gone for the day. He's having some friends over. You wanna go?" said Shelly.

"I have football practice later," I said.

"Just split when you have to, no big deal," offered Pete.

'Yeah, come on, man," said David. "What are you afraid of?"

"But I don't have a bathing suit."

"No sweat, dude, just take one of mine," said Pete. "One-seventy-two Highland Oaks drive. Be there, my man."

Before I could move a muscle or respond they ejected from the table and trampled right by. Apparently Shelly walked to A&W, because she followed them to Pete's car, a bright, clean BMW. It was the kind of car my father would never buy, fancy and foreign.

"See you there, right?" said Shelly just before getting in.

I gave Shelly a half-hearted grin before she leaned inside. Pete started the car and they drove away, the stereo blaring from within. I looked at my bike, and somehow it seemed pathetically inadequate to me.

Pete's house was several blocks from the high school, going northeast and straight up into the foothills, where the highlanders lived. There were two distinct geographic divisions to Rossmoor: the highlands and the lowlands. My family lived in the lowlands, where the earth was flat, the paved roads ran in perpendicular lines, and the houses were smaller and more modest. Above Foothill Boulevard, the dividing line between the haves and the have-nots, was an entire community of highland dwellers with their impressive ranch-style homes, neatly designed front yards, swimming pools, spacious backyards, and circular driveways. Here, local gardeners and pool cleaners and tree trimmers and maids could be found on any given day. In my neighborhood, everyone did their own yard maintenance. Although the highlands comprised about one-fifth of the city's landmass, it was my guess that it held about half of the aggregate wealth.

During the latter part of December, the highlanders would bind together in a glowing display of spirit and pride to decorate their homes in elaborate fashion. Every holiday season the lowlanders would migrate into the foothills to view this extravagant demonstration of good tidings. The endless string of lights and jolly bright Santa's and expensive nativity scenes were small consolation, in my opinion, for the bumper-to-bumper traffic, hand-waving policemen and their street blocks, and mothers pushing strollers across the street, seemingly oblivious to traffic. While their children admired the brilliant festival of lights, blurry-eyed fathers honked their horns and tried to navigate through a confusing maze of twisting streets without crashing into one another, and mothers mumbled anxiously about the shopping and wrapping they still had to do. All this took place while the highlanders sat snugly inside their cozy homes, sipping eggnog and rum, peeking out from behind curtains at the steady stream of headlights and taillights, exchanging small talk about the spirit of Christmas.

As I peddled the grueling grade uphill, I considered turning back for home. This decision was costing me valuable nuggets of energy, and I was annoyed with Shelly for sidestepping our meeting. I thought it demonstrated a lack of respect for our new relationship. On the other hand, who was I to deny her a cool dip on a hot summer's day?

Pete's house was spectacular. The backyard was about half the size of a football field in width and length; the biggest I'd ever seen. The lawn stretched about twenty yards beyond the pool, while a tall wooden fence enclosed the entire yard. The perimeter was lined with neatly groomed azalea bushes. There was a stable barn along the left side, although I couldn't find a horse or animal. In front of the stable was a tangerine tree, and just steps in front of the tree was a regulation basketball backboard. There was plenty of space between the hoop and the garage for a half-court game. A large oak tree with thick roots sprang up from the center of the yard and mushroomed over almost the entire lawn with its long branches. There was a tool shed along the right side of the fence, and just beyond the shed and to the right of the oak tree was a colorful rose garden about seven yards in diameter, encircled by a cement path. A big patio area extended from the house to about the midway point of the pool, which had a flattened out u-shape and a diving board, along with a circular Jacuzzi in the shallow end. As I finished soaking in the ultimate backyard, I noticed Shelly stepping onto the diving board and launching herself into mid-air, her hot pink two-piece bathing suit clinging to every curvaceous part of her body.

In the next half hour, more people arrived and the backyard started to fill up with bodies. Some were playing Whiffle ball on the back lawn, some playing basketball, some stuffing their faces with chips and dip, and some swam in the pool. Every few minutes another group would show up with grocery bags of beer and hard liquor and food under their arms, and at one point, I thought I caught a whiff of pot. Pete let me borrow a pair of trunks, and even though they hung loosely on me, I didn't mind. I was in paradise, amongst the privileged few, frolicking with young girls in dripping wet bathing suits, and feeling the cold water on my warm skin. This had all the makings of a full-fledged, hard-core party.

"Hey, Kevin, catch," I heard, turning to find a beer can that was hurtling at my head. I caught it just before it smacked me as David grinned and turned away. There I was, standing in the shallow end of the pool, with an ice-cold can of Coors in my hand. I stared absently at it.

"Come on, dude, crack it open," shouted David, which caught Pete's attention from nearby.

"Come on, one beer won't hurt you," said Pete. "It'll kill the pain."

"Yeah, you'll be more relaxed for practice," said David.

"Drink, drink, drink," Pete chanted, and a few moments later several people joined him in a peer pressure display that really left me no choice. "Drink, drink, drink," they all chanted simultaneously. It was powerful stuff.

I pulled back the tab and took a hefty gulp that proved my boldness, or at least that I was willing. They roared with approval and then went about their business. I've had beer before, but this was the first one that actually tasted good. Perhaps it was the moment—the cheers, the quenching coolness—or it could've been Shelly cascading out of the clear, shimmering water, beaming that million-dollar smile.

"Wow, drinking a beer before practice. It's so daring of you, Kevin. What will you do next?" she said with a mischievous twinkle. I leaned into her and planted a gentle kiss on her lips. Perhaps I was marking my territory for all the other guys or letting her know that I forgave her for telling her mother about us. In any case, I was pleased when she didn't pull back or seem embarrassed. She snatched my beer, chugging a big gulp. She winced as it went down.

"Ooh, I'd rather have a cocktail," she said.

"It's more of a man's drink," I said.

"So, are you man enough to drink that entire beer in one go?"

Keeping my eyes on her, I put the beer to my lips and tilted the can, letting the suds fill up my throat and slide into my stomach.

"Come on, Kevin, do it," said Shelly with a lusty tone.

I let my head fall back and was nearing the end when a backlog started to push up my throat and into my nostrils, and I coughed up some suds. Shelly chortled while I wiped my mouth, and then grabbed the can from me, tilted her head way back and let the remaining drops fall onto her extended tongue, flicking to catch every golden drop. As I observed this with the deepest admiration and pleasure, I was thankful that the lower half of my body was submerged in water. Shelly tossed the empty can onto the patio and shouted, "Another beer for my friend, please," swimming away from me.

"All right, dude," said David excitedly, "now you're in the groove." He tossed me another can, and not more than a couple of minutes after the first one, I had beer number two in my hand.

The party rapidly went ballistic. The beers and kamikazes and Jack Daniel's shooters made the rounds more than a couple of times, and the backyard was beginning to resemble a mini-version of Woodstock, bathing suit style. Apparently Pete didn't mind, because beer cans and pool toys and sporting balls of all shapes and sizes were flying haphazardly like misguided missiles through the air. He brought stereo speakers the size of filing cabinets just outside the sliding glass door of the living room, pumping the likes of Aerosmith and Jethro Tull into the yard. It was the garden of good and evil, mostly evil, and before I knew it I was halfway through my third beer, with two kamikazes already tumbling around in my stomach.

"Come here," said Shelly, pulling me away from the chips and dips, where I'd just begun to graze. She led me along the front side of the house. We found ourselves tucked away in a private area, mostly out of sight, underneath a healthy lemon tree. Shelly plucked a lemon from a low branch and bit into it, ripping away pieces of the skin as the juice sprayed around her face. The primal way she ripped into the lemon really got my own juices stirred up.

"Open your mouth," she said. She raised the lemon above my head and squeezed the juice inside my mouth, the light droplets smacking my tongue with a sour burn. "Don't swallow," she said. She squeezed the lemon juice into her own mouth, dropped the lemon to the grass, and moved into me. She placed her lips on mine and swirled her tongue around until the lemon juices mixed together and tickled my mouth. She pressed her body against mine, and as we kissed the juice dribbled out the sides of our mouths. She started to moan, so naturally, I started to moan, too. As her hips pushed stronger into mine, my shorts began to pitch, but I realized this was a moment to be bold, not shy. When Shelly felt me pushing against her hips, she dropped her hand over my crotch and gently and repeatedly squeezed my growing hard-on, as if milking a cow, on the outside of my bathing suit. I thought I should reciprocate, so I raised my hand along her side and eased over to her breast. She kept squeezing and touching and moaning, so I slid my hand underneath her bathing suit and gently rubbed and pinched her hard nipple. I wasn't sure how far to take this since we were outdoors and well within the boundaries of discovery. Just then something thudded on the wood shingle roof, and a football tumbled over the edge and bounced near our feet, rolling against the fence. We froze, and then released our hands, and some dude appeared in the opening along the side of the house. I picked up the ball and flipped it his direction. "Thanks," he said. He smirked and added before leaving, "Carry on."

"Oh shit," I said, "what time is it?"

"Why?" said Shelly, totally confused.

"Football practice!" I took three running strides before I froze. I wanted to get something off my chest all day, but never really had the chance. "I just want you to know that I'm cool with it," I said.

"Cool with what?" she said.

"You telling your mom about us."

"What?"

"She told me, that you told her."

"You spoke to my mother about us?" she said, flabbergasted.

"Yeah."

"And she knows who you are?"

"Didn't you know?" I asked.

"I never said a word about us."

I was floored. "But she said you told her everything."

"She tricked you, Kevin. She must've been suspicious of you. She got you to admit the truth."

"You really didn't tell her anything?"

"Just that I was seeing a football player, the guy who fell off his bike. That's all."

"She threatened me. She wants me to stay away from you."

"She said that?" said Shelly, intrigued.

"Yeah, but I said no way, stay out of our business."

"Oh, yeah, of course you did. Hey, you'd better go."

I hustled into the house, slashing through people and around furniture like O.J. Simpson did in the Hertz car commercial. I glanced at the clock and realized practice started about a half hour ago. I hurriedly changed into my workout clothes and bolted out of the driveway on my bike with a burst of speed. I figured I could be there in five minutes, if I really flew. I cranked my wheels full tilt, ran through a yellow light turning red in a main intersection and drew the honking horn of an angry motorist swerving by me.

My head felt dizzy, and my stomach grumbled. I didn't have much to eat and now all that alcohol, not to mention a sour shot of lemon juice, was gurgling in my gut and making me light-headed. My mind was racing with thoughts that competed between the hot kissing with Shelly and my impending doom on the football field. Our coaches warned us that tardiness would not be tolerated.

🚲

I arrived at the field and saw the players had already begun their circuits. I locked my bike to the rack and sprinted to the practice field. I tried to slide into the nearest circuit group without drawing too much attention, except the ever-present Coach Bower spotted me.

"Looks like someone is late, gentlemen!" he shouted. "Coaches, take a time out." Each group was told to stop by their coach and the attention focused on Coach Bower and me. "Is that you, Mr. Copeland?" I was shielding myself behind Todd Miller, a large lineman with a wide body.

"Step out, step out," whispered Miller.

"I said, is that you, Mr. Copeland?" said Bower louder.

I slid out reluctantly from behind Miller. "Yes sir," I shouted.

"We're a team here, Mr. Copeland. Would you like to share with the team why you're late?"

"I have no excuse, sir."

"Is that so?"

"Yes, sir…I mean, no sir."

"But everybody has an excuse. See Taylor over there," said Coach Bower, pointing and moving in my direction with a slow death march, "he doesn't have the proper uniform today because his mother forgot to wash his clothes. And Halstrom over there, he says he can't do any sit-ups today because of a muscle pull in his stomach. And Dixon over there, he can't practice tomorrow morning because he has a dentist appointment. See, everyone has an excuse, Mr. Copeland, everyone but you. Problem is, I don't like excuses. There isn't a coach on God's green earth who likes excuses. Excuses," he emphasized, "do not make champions. They make losers."

Now he was near me, still speaking loud enough for the entire team to hear.

"We're hearing too many excuses, gentlemen," he shouted. "Excuses will not earn you a position on this team. Excuses will not win you any football games. At least Mr. Copeland here had the guts to admit that he *had* no excuse. How refreshing. But that doesn't mean he gets off easy. It only means that I respect him just a little bit more for not making up some idiotic story." Then he turned to me with his cold, steely eyes and shouted, "Now get your legs moving son!"

His deep voice nearly blasted the hair right off my skull and I immediately started to run in place.

"Faster! Faster! Down…up! Down…up! Down…up!"

The pace was relentless, and all I could feel was the alcohol sloshing around like a blender on high speed. "Down…up! Move those feet!" It was brutal, and after a minute or so of squat-thrusts I was exhausted, my throat dry and tight, unable to catch my breath. The morning practice, the bike riding, the pool party, the alcohol, had all come together and left me weak and queasy. "Down…up!" Bower took another step closer to me. I was sucking in and expelling enough air to inflate a blimp.

"Plan on being late again, Mr. Copeland?"

"No sir," I shouted like a soldier.

I thought I'd survived when something made him furrow his eyebrows. He eyeballed me with an odd awareness. I just kept running in place.

"Stop!" he barked. I bent over in fatigue, my hands on my knees, inhaling all the air I could trap. I was moments away from puking right on his black Puma football shoes. "Stand up straight, son." I straightened and clenched my hands behind my head. Coach Bower leaned his face right into mine and then he sniffed. Oh shit, he sniffed. I closed my mouth and tried to breathe through my nose.

With a slow urgency, he said, "Open your mouth."

I complied with his orders, still trying to take in air through my nose, but I was severely winded. Suspicious, he leaned in even closer, his bushy moustache nearly scraping against my skin, and deliberately sniffed my mouth. I tried not to let out even a whisper of air, but it was too late. He glared with a knowing disapproval and turned away from me.

"My group split up and filter into the other circuits," commanded Coach Bower. His group of players just stood around, utterly confused. "Now!" he shouted, and somehow this made his directive clearer. They split apart like a bowling ball had cracked between them and dashed to the other groups on the field. With a grave expression, he turned back to me.

"Follow me," he said, disappointedly.

I saw my football career spiraling down the toilet. I envisioned my father's disillusioned face upon hearing the news that his son was kicked off the football team for being drunk at practice. I saw myself sitting in the stands on Friday nights, watching the team compete on the field for a championship, while I munched on gobs of candy, chips, and chili dogs, becoming a big, fat, disgusting slob. Worst of all, I saw myself becoming the laughing stock and disgrace of Rossmoor High, and with that moniker, totally unappealing to the female population.

I tracked Coach Bower into the quiet locker rooms, empty and eerie, through the lockers and by the showers, and into the back offices. He didn't utter a word nor did he even glance in my direction. He was all business.

"Take a seat," he said. He sat down behind his desk and picked up the phone while I sat in the chair opposite him. "What's your phone number?" I gave him the number and he dialed, sighing heavily and pinching the bridge of his nose, exasperated by this moment.

"Mrs. Copeland? Hello, this is Coach Bower at Rossmoor High. I think it'd be a good idea to come out to the football field as soon as possible and pick up your son. Well, I'd rather talk to you about it here. No, no, he's not hurt or anything. Okay, we'll see you soon."

He hung up the phone and stared at me, concentrating on the

words he was forming in his mind.

"You know what, Copeland? I should make an example of you. I should kick your butt right off the team and tell everyone why." He paused and made some distracting popping sounds with his tongue. "But I'm not going to make that decision…yet." I felt my body exhale. "I'm gonna let your parents decide. And if they let you play, I want you to know this: I'll be watching you like a hawk, a mean and hungry hawk. You so much as put your chin strap on wrong, and I'll swoop down on you and snatch you right off the field." He swiped his hand across the air as if catching something, then paused. "Sound fair?"

"Yes, Coach."

Coach Bower leaned back in his chair and gazed out the window. He placed the palms of his hands together as though starting a prayer and flipped them back and forth against his lips. Still staring out the window, he said, "Alcohol is the devil's brew, son. It'll steal every ounce of dignity and pride you have. And it'll turn your body into a piece of dog shit. I know, I've been in the belly of the beast." Then he swiveled around to me. "Do you hear what I'm sayin' to you?"

"Yes, sir."

Coach Bower rose from his chair and moved near the wall where several plaques and awards hung. He removed one from the nail and extended it to me. I presumed he wanted me to grab it so I did. It was the varsity football team picture from 1964. Coach Bower had no moustache then and was probably fifteen pounds lighter, and he was actually smiling. What had turned his smile into a scowl, I wondered.

"Number fifty-eight, he's dead and buried now. Got drunk and ran his car right off the road up near Landry Flats. He and his girlfriend went up in a ball of flames." Number fifty-eight glowed strength and vitality, so alive and ready for his football season. Coach Bower grabbed the plaque from me, replaced it on the wall, and handed me another; varsity team, 1970.

"Number twenty-three, he's in a drug rehab program. One minute he's pumpin' a few harmless beers at parties, smokin' a little grass, then the next he's doin' crack cocaine. Nearly exploded his heart one night." I looked at number twenty-three and pondered how he could fall such a long distance from the time and place captured in this hopeful picture. Coach Bower returned the plaque to the wall and then faced me with his hands on his waist.

"I don't wanna be telling some kid a sad story about you, son. Got that?"

"You won't have to, Coach."

He stared so intently into my eyes that I was compelled to fidget. "If I see you back here at practice tomorrow, be prepared to get your butt kicked all over the field. We're gonna be extra tough on you. Now you just sit there for a few minutes and think real hard about what I've said." Coach Bower leaned down so his face was right across from my left ear. I kept deathly still. "And one more thing," he said, slowing and hushing his words, "if just one word of this conversation ever leaves this room, then I'll make sure you get real acquainted with mister sideline bench and his sharp pine needles all season long, understand?" He lingered for a moment while I nodded with a petrified urgency. I could feel his warm breath on my skin. Then he straightened, turned and exited the office, his plastic cleats clicking against the cement.

When he was gone, I exhaled in relief and looked again at the other team pictures on the wall. I tried to imagine what other tragedies and maladies had befallen the hopeful young men pictured in them. Surely there had to be more, unknown perhaps to the community; secret, unspeakable horrors that families tried to keep private. My mistake may have been fatal to my football career, but certainly not to my life. For that, I was very thankful.

# Chapter Nineteen

*My father came home from work earlier than usual that evening.*
Evidently, my mother called him at the office and shared the news.
It wasn't my parents' style to scold me for errors in judgment,
especially since this was a problem normally associated with
Rachel, and they'd scolded her enough without any tangible
results. My mother tried to speak calmly and reasonably during the
drive home from school. Our conversation was strange, much too
civil and misdirected for the act I committed. And then it
transitioned into the usual topic.

"Your Aunt Mary has trouble with liquor, did you know that?"
said my mother. I nodded in a disinterested way. "So did my
father, although Mary is a jolly drunk and my father, well, let's just
say it didn't bring out the best in him. What worries me, and I'm
telling you this because I know you'll understand, is that Rachel is
heading down the same path as Mary. I see so many similarities

between the two."

"Mom, I'm the one who messed up today, not Rachel."

"I know, and I'm grateful you're okay. And I know you won't do something like this again, right?" she said, eyeing me for the response.

"Right," I muttered.

"But Rachel is the one having real problems, not you."

"What?" I gushed reactively. "What exactly are her problems, because I'd like to know? She's seventeen years old, she's pretty, she has lots of friends, and she doesn't even have to go to a real school. I don't understand where the big problems enter the picture."

My mother arched her eyebrows and was genuinely caught off guard by my forceful reaction. "It's very difficult to understand, I know, even harder to explain. It has to do with family dynamics and the way kids grow up in big families," she said.

"That's psycho-bullshit, Mom, and you know it."

"Kevin," she said, ashamed of me, "watch your mouth."

"But this is crazy. I'm the one who got drunk, and you start talking about Rachel and how worried you are about her. She's probably off shopping somewhere with Jamie, having a grand old time."

"The alcohol is making you say these things," she started. "We'll talk more when you're sober. You're not yourself right now."

"Fine, whatever."

We both focused straight ahead. My mother's stiffness indicated that she was reflecting on our exchange and how she might add some insight to our conversation. She re-gripped the steering wheel, as if preparing to make a statement of importance.

"If your dad and I spend a lot of time talking about Rachel, it's only because we're worried about her," said my mother. "You don't know what it's like for a parent to worry every day and night, to not know where your child is or what she's doing."

"You must not be *that* worried," I said under my breath.

"Why would you say that?" she asked.

"Forget it," I mumbled.

"Don't play games with me, Kevin, I'm in no mood. Just tell me what you're talking about."

"Fine, I'm talking about the pot plants in the backyard," I said, raising my voice. My mother inadvertently stepped on the brakes, and we lunged forward, quickly releasing them. The driver behind us punched his horn, unleashing a long and loud honk and then accelerated around us. The young male driver flipped the finger at my mother, but she was too afraid to look in his direction. She was flustered and trying to compose herself before reacting. "So it's true? You let her grow those?" I said, exasperated.

"We ripped out those plants several days ago," she tried to say calmly, although it came out stuttered and nervous.

"So you could smoke the stuff yourselves, right?" I said sarcastically.

"Okay, listen, Kevin, you're old enough to know that your parents have…experimented with marijuana, but it's not something we do often. Actually, we really don't care for it all that much."

"Then why'd you grow it?"

"That's not an easy answer. When Rachel brought us the idea, naturally, we were opposed. Then we thought about it. She kept pressuring us. We knew that if we denied her, she'd find someplace else to grow it. You know how she gets when her mind is made up, bound and determined. This way, we thought we could at least keep her out of trouble."

"Didn't help much," I said.

"It was a horrible decision, totally misguided, and we'll never do something like that again. I promise. And I know you'll make better decisions about drugs, right?" I didn't respond, and it unnerved my mother. "Right, Kevin?"

"Yeah... sure," I replied without any conviction.

🚲

My father didn't mumble a word for the first half hour he was home. He just tossed me a disappointed glance or two as he brushed by me, going the opposite direction. Then he shouted my name from outside the garage. He was tinkering on the boat, which he often did in the early evening before nightfall. He was cleaning some junk from inside the hull and paused when I appeared, standing tall and staring down at me. Here it comes, I thought, the demeaning sermon; it had to come from somebody.

"Grab a trashcan for me, will ya?" he said.

I ducked inside to the garage and clutched a trashcan by the handle, hauling it out near the boat. My father began to dump various items into the metal trashcan—a ripped life vest, a broken paddle, some rusty tools, and a worn ski rope.

"That ski rope's still good," I said.

"It's shot. We'll get a new one," he said.

I picked up the ski rope from the trashcan and he was right. Certain parts of the rope had begun to unravel.

"I guess it wouldn't be cool if it suddenly snapped on someone in the middle of a run. Could you imagine the scream from Sarah?" I said, attempting to inject a little levity into the situation. My father barely flashed a grin. "It held up for a pretty long time, though." I said.

"Yeah, sure did," he said. This was going surprisingly well.

"Is that all?" I said. He paused and sighed, standing with his hands on his hips, just like Coach Bower; the captain of the ship.

"When I'm through I want you to wash the boat. I'll be done soon."

"Ah come on, Dad," I complained.

"And wax it. It hasn't had a wax in a year."

"Do I have to…tonight?"

"If you hurry you can get it all done before dark."

"But I—"

"Kevin, don't argue with me," he interrupted.

"I never see Rachel doing any work as punishment," I charged.

"Leave her outta this. Besides, this is not punishment."

"Then what is it?"

"It's you doing something for me. Could you do something for your father, huh?"

He turned and locked hard on my eyes, like a gunner pilot who swivels in his chair and takes aim on his victim. I didn't give him any reasons to fire.

"Yeah," I finally moped.

My father released his gaze and dumped the remaining items into the trashcan. He swung his leg over the side of the boat and onto the trailer tire rim and then hopped to the ground. He wiped his hands on a cloth towel.

"Your mother and I were planning to talk to you kids about…our situation. But I guess you beat us to the punch."

"Huh?" I said. He switched topics on me and my slow brain, still fighting the alcohol, didn't recognize it.

"It's not so easy to talk about. But the last thing we need is for you to make it harder."

"I won't mess up like that again," I said, figuring that he was referring to the alcohol.

He didn't seem satisfied with my answer and entered the garage. I watched him search through piles of junk, and after several seconds he grew agitated. More time elapsed and he started to mumble words such as "Where is that…?" and "Damn this…" and "I know it was here somewhere." Then he started tossing random items aside and pushing cans of paint against the wall. Finally, he reached into a corner pile of dirty rags, rusted cans, and discarded garden tools and withdrew a small, round tin can.

"Here, use this wax," he said, tossing the can to me. He moved away from the wall of junk and stood near the center of the garage. Surveying the messy surroundings I could sense he was troubled by something.

"I should organize this garage," he said, more to himself. "Makes your life so much easier when everything is in order."

The tired way he stood, the helpless lilt in his voice, the aimless way he scanned the garage, somehow made my father seem vulnerable to life, to plain, old, everyday life. I'd never thought of him that way before. He always had the right answers and knew exactly what he was doing, or so it seemed. He had direction, a sure-fire plan, and he knew where the first step should be. But at this moment he was lost, turned around, in unfamiliar territory.

He aimed his gaze at the station wagon parked in the driveway and said, "Do you really like her, or is this about me and your mom?"

I should've seen this coming, except my mind was a useless pile of slush. He found out about Shelly and me. I knew this moment had to happen, but why today of all days? I was trying to sober up, my coach had sent me home early from practice for disciplinary reasons, and I was so exhausted I could barely think straight. He faced me and waited, his eyes drenched in worried anticipation.

"Yeah, I like her," I finally said, simply going with the first response that entered my mind. He pursed his lips in disappointment and barely nodded.

"It's bad timing, Kevin, bad as it can get."

The only bad timing in this scenario, I thought, was my father's and the choices he made about women. How could he dump the label of bad timing on me? I was simply a victim of circumstance, a kid who ventured into the unknown, into something dark and murky, and came out the other side to find a girl, a bright, shining, blonde beacon of light and hope. A strong surge of pride welled up in my throat, but I suppressed it, letting it settle back into my chest. The topic of conversation compelled me to sharpen my thoughts and focus on standing my ground, no matter how shaky I felt. This was a critical moment between us that I couldn't take lightly.

"What am I supposed to do?" I asked.

"You can end it. Give us one less thing to worry about. Your mom and I...well, we have enough to worry about right now."

"But I don't want to."

I saw no reason to sugarcoat my words, not now. He grunted in a bemused way and shook his head in disbelief. It must've all seemed pretty bizarre to him. Heck, it was to me, too. He sighed heavily and looked outside again, the bright light of day such a contrast to the dank and shadowy darkness of our garage.

"It won't be a normal relationship, Kevin," he said. "You can't bring her around the house or the family. You'll have to keep her away from here."

"It's not so hard, right?" I said, resolutely. The alcohol had given me a false confidence, but so be it. He nodded solemnly, his eyes lowered, as if stung by my implication.

"Are you trying to prove something to me, Kevin? Trying to teach your old man a lesson?"

"Call it whatever you want, Dad, but I haven't done anything wrong... except for, you know, today."

I left my eyesight aimed at him and didn't waiver or display weakness. I was the gunner now. Between the two of us, I was the innocent one here, and he knew it. That was my anchor.

"Wash the boat," he said flatly.

He started to exit the garage when my voice stopped him.

"I need to know," I hesitated, unable to keep the confidence I had just moments ago. I was about to ask permission for something and this put him right back in the driver's seat; father and son. "Can I go back to practice tomorrow?"

I'd given him ample reason to deny me, except I knew how badly he wanted to see his son compete at the high school level. He played tight end in high school and loved the game of football as much as I did.

"Yeah... but I'm expecting a stronger commitment from you than what you showed today. You can't play a sport in high school and just do whatever you feel like doing. You'll never make it. You have to be dedicated and make personal sacrifices for the team."

"I know," I said.

He hardly acknowledged my response and left the garage, heading into the laundry room that led into the kitchen. I picked up a bucket and sponge, grabbed the bottle of boat wash from the shelf, and headed out to the boat. I should've felt fortunate for my light sentence. I kept everything I wanted and only had to wash and wax the boat as penance. Instead, I just felt dismal.

🚲

It was still relatively early when I turned off the lights and rolled into bed. I was totally spent. My head was swimming with thoughts, doing the backstroke, butterfly, and breaststroke all at once. So much information to process and none of it made much sense. I was starting to believe that adults lacked the answers, too, that part of being human was feeling constantly confused. This thought scared the bejesus out of me, especially with so much on the line. Someone rapped lightly on my door.

"Are you awake?" said my mother.

"Yeah."

"Can I come in?"

"Sure."

My mother pushed through the door, and the light from the hallway caught her face just enough to show her angst. She likely knew everything my father did, and of everyone involved, this situation probably pained her the most. It was possible that she considered my relationship with Shelly as a betrayal, as if dealing with one betrayal were not enough. She didn't turn on the bedroom light and instead left my door open. We could see each other, except the subtle nuances of her expressions, which I'd begun to interpret with better clarity, were not discernible.

"Here's some clean clothes for tomorrow's practice," she said, laying them on my dresser. She sat down gently at the edge of my bed and didn't speak for quite some time. "Want me to scratch your back?"

"You don't have to."

"I know, I want to."

I flipped over on my stomach, which was how I slept anyway, and my mother peeled back the sheet. The first touch of her nails on my back always brought goose bumps to my skin. She applied just the right amount of pressure.

"It's been a long time since I did this," she said.

"I'm not a little boy anymore."

"I know, but even big boys deserve a good scratch now and then."

I could feel my weight sink into the mattress and my scalp tingle while her long nails glided over my skin. I waited for her to continue the conversation and mention something about Shelly, or my behavior before practice and during the drive home, but she was silent. So I closed my eyes, deeply inhaling and exhaling. With each stroke of my mother's hand another troubling thought floated from my head. For a moment I wondered why my parents had chosen to keep the peace instead of trying to discipline me, but it no longer made any difference. I must've drifted off to sleep, because the next moment I remembered was waking up to a rattling window from a windstorm outside. I closed my eyes again and tried not to let the wind bother me.

# Chapter Twenty

*"Down...up! Down...up!" Coach Bower was merciless. I* should've expected nothing less, though. He warned me. I sensed some of the guys resented me for ticking off Coach Bower and making him even tougher. I had to assume that the word had spread about my party escapade, since so many kids had seen me drinking that day, although none of my teammates made any comments. The other coaches didn't tread lightly, either. I bet Coach Bower told them to crank up the heat. They singled me out whenever they had the chance. They wanted to break me, push me to quit, but I was more determined than ever. The alcohol was flushed from my system, and I was well rested after a long slumber.

"Down...up!" Bower boomed.

I kept telling myself to suck it up, like the coaches always yelled at us. I made it through morning practice and actually felt strong and revived, even accomplished. I handled everything they dished out and more. I was unlocking my bike when Coach Bower exited the locker rooms.

"See you this afternoon, Mr. Copeland," he said, passing me.

"Sure thing, Coach," I said.

He never paused nor even glanced in my direction, although the tone of his voice implied that he was pleased with my effort.

🚲

When I turned onto our street, I noticed Kyle shooting hoops in the driveway and his father working in the garage. I found it unusual that Mr. Bollinger was home during the late morning. He laid bathroom and kitchen flooring for a living and always had a steady stream of clients. He was one of those fathers who wore denim jeans, a cotton, short sleeve shirt, and leather boots to work. I imagined he was the secret envy of every white collar, briefcase-carrying dad on the street, including my own.

Kyle spotted me and waved me in. Even though he pulled a cheap stunt the other day, and had pulled many over my short lifetime, I always found myself returning to the scene of the crime. I was drawn to him and connected in ways I couldn't comprehend. Maybe I was fascinated by his chameleon personality, or by the unpredictability of his words and deeds. My blood raced a little faster around him, and this, perhaps more than anything else, drew me to him. I considered how I felt around Shelly, a pulse that quickened and skin that tingled, and while I knew I was attracted to each individual for entirely different reasons, the bottom line was the same: they electrified me, brought a little mystery into my life, and I suppose I needed that. I was beginning to believe all humans needed that.

I parked my bike in Kyle's driveway and hopped off, and he immediately fired a chest pass my way. We shot baskets while Mr. Bollinger tinkered with some sort of radio on his raised workbench inside the garage.

"Did you know Bill Sharman once made a hundred free throws in a row?" said Kyle. "It's the record."

"Best I've ever done is about ten," I replied.

"Wilt Chamberlain scored a hundred points in one game. He scored just about every time he touched the ball."

"It's not so hard when you're seven-foot-two," I said.

"Kareem Abdul-Jabbar will break a hundred one day. He's got the sky-hook. Nobody can stop it."

Kyle demonstrated the hook from the far right side of the driveway, looping the ball in an arc above his head. It clanked off the rim and bounced over onto the lawn. As Kyle retrieved the ball I observed Mr. Bollinger, so laser focused on his task and equally as oblivious to us. I felt compelled to speak to him.

"Hey Mr. Bollinger," I blurted.

Devoid of any energy, Mr. Bollinger just grunted. He and Kyle were similar in many ways. Mr. Bollinger moved methodically and walked with a plodding, heavy stride. He had wide, square shoulders, and his arms hung from his body without swinging, like an ape's. His voice was barely audible at times, and he spoke with a drowsy slur. He always seemed in need of a refreshing nap. He rarely smiled or laughed, and when he did it was in response to the strangest things. When he wasn't working in his yard or garage, I often caught him in front of the television, sitting in his cloth recliner sofa chair, drinking a beer and watching with a hypnotic, disinterested gaze. He was drinking today, too. As Kyle took another shot I watched Mr. Bollinger chug down a Coors. He wiped his mouth with the top side of his forearm and returned to his workbench.

Just as Kyle was about to launch a shot, Mr. Bollinger yelled, "Goddamn it!" and smacked a tool against his work table. It clanked, reminding me of the sound I'd heard from Mr. Resnik almost every night next door. In the midst of his shot, Kyle launched an air ball that pounded the backboard and bounced high on the asphalt. Mr. Bollinger bent over and picked up the BB gun, his face puffing red, his jaw clenched, and chills ran up my spine. "I told you to put this Goddamn gun away in its case when you were through with it."

"I was going to," pleaded Kyle.

"That's a lie, and you know it," said Mr. Bollinger. "It's been sitting here for days."

"I'll put it away right now," said Kyle. He dashed inside the garage and tried to take the gun from his father, but Mr. Bollinger yanked it away. "You don't know how to take care of a Goddamn thing, do ya? Everything I give you gets ruined," said Mr. Bollinger.

Kyle was embarrassed and glanced awkwardly at me. He probably wanted me to leave, and quickly, but I was glued to the pavement. "I said I'd put it away," said Kyle carefully.

"Do you know what could happen if some little kid came in here and played around with his thing? Do you, son?" said Mr. Bollinger, rapping the barrel of the gun against Kyle's chest, making him wince with pain. "It should be locked away in its case and put somewhere high."

"It's just a BB gun, Dad," responded Kyle, a little too smartly.

To my alarming surprise, Mr. Bollinger stepped backwards and jerked the BB gun to the right side of his head, aiming directly at his son's noggin. Kyle flinched and instinctively raised his arms in front of his face, then no doubt feeling foolish, cautiously lowered them. The end of the gun's barrel was about a foot from Kyle's nose.

"Jesus, Dad, that thing's loaded," said Kyle, glancing back at me, this time with a silent plea for help.

"If this gun is so harmless, then why'd you flinch?" said Mr. Bollinger, still aiming the gun.

"I don't know, I just did," said Kyle.

"Fear. You were protecting yourself. You know this gun can hurt you real bad," said Mr. Bollinger.

After making his point I expected Mr. Bollinger to lower the gun, but he didn't. For a flickering moment I caught a twitch in his cheek, a nervous tick, and I thought he might just be crazy enough to pull the trigger. I considered leaving but I was a witness now. I had to stay and watch how this bizarre scene would play out.

Mr. Bollinger's chest expanded from a deep breath and he finally lowered the gun from Kyle's head. He pushed it with a firm thrust into Kyle's chest, leaving an impression on his son that he wouldn't soon forget. I couldn't imagine my own father ever pulling this kind of a stunt.

"Now put the Goddamn gun away and don't ever let me see it lying around here again." Mr. Bollinger snatched his beer can from the work table, fired one last disapproving glance at his son, and left the garage, chugging his beer just before going inside the house.

I'd seen enough, preferring not to face Kyle. I straddled my bike seat and started for home. I glanced behind and saw that Kyle was packing the gun in its case, being extra careful. For the most part, Mr. Bollinger seemed like a mild-mannered man, though somewhat withdrawn. But during the last few years I noticed there was something menacing lurking inside him, maybe something that would cause him to point a loaded weapon at his youngest son. Considering recent events, I knew that every man had his deep, dark secrets, and his share of unresolved mistakes. I also knew that to a certain degree, children had to live with those mistakes.

For the better part of my life Kyle had bullied and humiliated me, and yet he always managed to magically balance these hurts with random acts of kindness and friendship, just enough to bandage the wounds. Part of me wanted Kyle's father to pull that trigger and blast a hole in his face. I wasn't proud of admitting that, and yet I felt he deserved it. Despite all that Kyle had inflicted upon me, I'd dutifully carried on with a stiff upper lip and tried to keep the friendship alive. Yet we both knew it was dying fast. We both knew the dynamics we developed early in our lives were transforming into something unrecognizable. He was older and more aggressive, and I was younger and more compliant; he was the leader, and I was the follower. That was the pattern we'd followed since the moment we could walk, talk, and throw a football. But as I grew bigger and more self-confident, and became interested in other people and activities, Kyle would have no place in my life, and he knew it. I think he resented me, too, for venturing outside his safe and familiar kingdom. More often than not, when I left Kyle's house, I was consumed by anger and confusion. Today, for the first time, I rode away from his house and actually felt sorry for Kyle Bollinger.

⚏

Later that day, I gazed around my room with a burning discontent. I ripped down my pictures of Barbara and Raquel, admired them for a last, few precious seconds, then crumpled them into paper balls and tossed them into my Rams trashcan. The wall was bare, and I had nothing to replace them, although it was more important that they be removed from my sight. In fact, I would've preferred to redesign my entire room. Almost everything irritated me now, from the row of first place blue ribbons hanging from my bookshelf, to the dry and dusty abalone shell I kept on my desk, filled to the rim with stupid trinkets. I tried to scrape the old motorcycle and sports stickers from my headboard, but it was useless. They'd been stuck there for years, and without the proper tools, they weren't coming off. Something else annoyed me, too. It had annoyed me for a long time, and today was the day I'd finally do something about it. I marched into the kitchen, where my mother was fixing some lunch, and stood resolutely before her.

"I want some curtains on my windows," I demanded. My mother wrinkled her brow and paused from her food preparation. "Why don't I have any curtains?"

"I never thought it bothered you," she replied.

"Well it does. I need some privacy. And I don't like trying to sleep knowing my windows aren't covered."

"Alright, we'll get you some curtains."

"When?"

"Well, soon."

"Today?"

"Kevin, they're not like a carton of milk you can pick up at the grocery store. You have to measure the window frames, decide what kind you want, find a store that carries them. It takes some time."

She sliced some cheddar cheese and spread a thick layer of mayonnaise on Wonder white bread. Then she slapped two pieces of bologna on top of the cheese. My stomach growled.

"Could you work on that?" I asked.

"Is something wrong? You sound upset," said my mother.

"I hate my room. It's just so... lame."

It was strange timing, but my mother smirked in a way she had many times before. She thought I was cute, but it only served to make me feel childish.

"Okay, we can change your room if you want," she said.

I nodded crisply as though I'd given my orders and knew they'd be carried out. Then I started to leave the kitchen.

"Don't you want your sandwich?" my mother said, holding it up.

"Oh, yeah," I said. She placed it back on the plate.

"Some chips and chocolate milk?" she added. I nodded. My mother smiled and poured a big pile of potato chips on my plate. As she retrieved the milk and Nestle chocolate mix, I took my seat at the kitchen table. I watched her stir the powder into the milk, the spoon clinking against the glass, and then she stopped.

"All the lumps gone?" I asked. My mother nodded and briskly stirred a few more times. She knew I hated lumps in my food, especially in my chocolate milk and tomato soup. She carried my lunch to the table.

"I'll work on getting you those curtains, okay?"

Then she put a gentle hand on my shoulder, bent down, and kissed me on the cheek. I felt guilty for demanding the curtains, and worse, for dating the daughter of the woman who was stealing her husband away.

She left the kitchen and paused in front of the television set. I heard a broadcaster report something about the White House, although I didn't pay much attention. I could see my mother's head through the rectangular opening in the kitchen wall, which opened into the living room. I kept an eye on her while I ate my lunch. I didn't listen carefully to the report since I'd seen and heard too much already about Nixon and the Watergate scandal. I was sick of it, and I got the impression that my parents were, too. At this moment, however, my mother was drawn in completely to the report. I thought I heard the sound switch from a reporter to President Ford's monotone voice. I glanced every so often to my mother, who moved a step closer to the TV. Then suddenly I heard my mother shout, "Asshole!"

"Mom!" I shouted back.

"Oh, Kevin, I'm sorry about that. It's just this idiot Ford, he makes me so angry."

I set down my glass and entered the living room. President Ford stood behind the official podium inside the White House pressroom, the familiar blue curtain with the presidential seal behind him, addressing the media. This was the first time I'd noticed how bright and clean those blue curtains were. I thought that same color would look real nice in my room.

"What'd he do?" I asked.

"He just pardoned Nixon, that jerk."

"What does that mean?"

"It means, basically, that he's letting Nixon off the hook for the Watergate break-in."

"But I thought all those hearings proved him guilty," I said.

"They did."

"And what about all those tapes?"

"It's totally despicable. Those damn politicians, they'll do anything to save face. They all know he orchestrated the whole thing, they just won't admit it."

"But how can Ford pardon him?"

"Because he's the president now. He has that power. I'm sure he got bullied into it. No one in his right mind believes Nixon deserves a pardon. Well, he just lost the last ounce of respect I had for him. I thought he was a pretty decent man, until now. Now he's just another spineless politician."

My mother huffed and left the room. It caught me by surprise, the way she reacted so vocally. Politics was more a topic for moderate philosophical debate around my house, and rarely inspired the kind of passion displayed by my mother. As I returned my focus to the television, it occurred to me while watching President Ford, that maybe her outburst had nothing whatsoever to do with politics. Maybe it was far more personal than that. Somewhere between the lies and rhetoric, the double talk and polished speeches, was the bitter, ugly truth, and the suffering it caused. I was certain that the people and families nearest the truth suffered the most from it; in private, behind closed doors and pulled curtains, face to face, where there was no place to hide and no chance to rehearse any lines.

# Chapter Twenty-One

*Sitting outside on the porch steps, I considered my next move* with Shelly after our passionate encounter under the lemon tree. I heard the familiar high-pitched whistle from Matt in the Resnik's yard, the cattle call from my eager neighbor.

"Hey Kevin, check these out," shouted Matt. Through our chain link fence, mostly covered by bushes, I could see portions of Matt and his brother Ronnie moving around and exchanging gentle body punches.

I entered the Resnik's yard to find Matt and Ronnie wearing puffy brown boxing gloves that were wrinkled and dusty. I'd only seen boxing gloves in sporting goods stores before, but never had I slipped them on my hands with the intention of actually punching someone.

"Where'd you get those?" I asked.

"My dad brought 'em down from the attic," said Matt.

"Let me try 'em," I said to Ronnie. He held out his arms, and I pulled the gloves off his hands.

The laces were missing, and the material that wrapped around the wrists was ragged and worn.

"These aren't regulation, but they can still sting pretty good if you connect just right," said Matt. "They're sixteeen ounces. The pros use twelve ounces."

I shoved my hands all the way into the soft inners of the gloves. They felt snug on my hands and were much lighter than they appeared. Without the laces they'd probably shift around somewhat, though if I clenched my fingers real tight, I could grab enough material to keep the gloves securely on my hand. A well-placed punch with everything I had could do some damage. I squared off with Matt, who probably weighed several pounds less and was a couple of inches shorter. I was ready to land a punch and find out what the old gloves could do.

"My money's on Kevin," said Ronnie.

"We're not fighting for real," said Matt.

"We're not?" I said in all seriousness. Matt went pale, and then I grinned, easing his worry.

I put up my hands in front of my face like a real boxer, and we playfully bobbed around. I made the first punch, a strong jab at his head that I telegraphed on purpose. He had plenty of time to move his glove and intercept the punch, and the impact made a brief and sharp "whoosh." The sound reminded me of the boxing matches on TV, only with more air in it. Matt let loose a jab that hit my guarding glove, which pushed into my face, and the force surprised me.

"Come on, you wimps, hit each other harder," urged Matt,

always trying to instigate fights between his brother and me. I was certain he'd been waiting for this moment his entire ten years of life, which now that I thought of it, was the reason he promptly turned the gloves over to me. I lunged forward, making a big roundhouse right and to my surprise, connected almost full thrust on Matt's ear. His head jerked to the side, and he wobbled for just a moment, then he steadied again.

"Whoa, good one," he said, a little dazed.

He backed away from me. With that telling blow he probably realized I could knock him down. It felt good to land a punch, although I had no intentions of knocking Matt to the ground. I liked him. I had no beefs with him. Kyle, on the other hand, could've unleashed my killer animal instincts. Although it was more likely I'd be the first one lying flat on the ground for the eight count, not Kyle.

"What do you two think you're doing?" we heard a woman say. We paused and turned our heads toward the front door. Mrs. Resnik held a basket of laundry and seemed bewildered by what she saw. Her dishwater blonde hair was hidden underneath a creamy yellow silk scarf. "Your father told you not to fight with those unless he was here to supervise."

"They're not fighting for real, Mom," said Ronnie.

"Yeah, we're just goofing around," added Matt.

"I don't care. I want those gloves put away until your father comes home. Someone could get hurt." We all stood there as if the words never connected, like an errant punch. "Did you hear me?" she said louder.

Matt shrugged and held his gloves out to Ronnie, who pulled them off.

245

"You're lucky. He would've kicked your butt," said Ronnie to his brother.

"Naw, just landed a lucky punch, that's all," I said.

"It was a pretty good one," said Matt. "With professional gloves, that might have knocked me over."

"Think so?" I said.

"I've tried on a pair of the real ones. There's not much padding there."

"Not much in your head, either," said Ronnie, swinging the glove and smacking his older brother's head. Ronnie ran away, and Matt bolted right after him, a sight I'd witnessed on many occasions.

"You little shit," said Matt chasing him.

"Mom, Matt said a cuss word!" shouted Ronnie, racing into the house. Matt rumbled right in after him while Mrs. Resnik reappeared from the laundry room.

"No running in the house, boys," she shouted with a hopeless undertone.

With a heavy sigh, Mrs. Resnik paused on the cement walkway between the laundry room and the work shed, hesitant to reenter the house. She wiped her forehead with the back of her hand and pulled in a deep breath, trying to catch her wind. There was an overworked droopiness about the way she stood, as if one more pair of pants in her laundry basket might just be enough to make her drop the entire load. A gust of wind rolled through the yard and the scarf began to unfurl and break loose from her head. She hooted sharply, trying to grab it in mid-air with her small, left hand. The basket slipped from her right hand and the clothes tumbled over the edge to the ground. She grunted in discontent and scooped the laundry back into her basket, while the scarf drifted into the leafy air and finally landed halfway between us on the lawn. I started to move toward the scarf, and she paused, smiled graciously, and nodded her head ever so slightly, like royalty acknowledging a servant. I retrieved the scarf and approached her while she fixed her hair, a thick scalp of matted blonde curls that had been trapped for so many hours that no springy rebound remained. I held out the scarf, and to my surprise, she blushed, her gaze shifting away from mine, and her cheeks puffing from a sheepish grin.

"Thank you, Kevin, that was very kind of you," she said in a demure voice, lowering the basket to the ground and taking the scarf.

"You're welcome," I said.

"You boys can play with the gloves when their father gets home."

"Sure."

Neither one of us knew how to fill the silent air, but the conversation felt incomplete.

"So... how's your mom and dad?"

"Um, they're okay," I said, glossing over the truth.

"Good... I'm real happy to hear that. Say hello to them for me."

I nodded gently. I couldn't recall a longer conversation between us, and it crashed into a brick wall nearly as fast as it had begun.

"Well, have a nice evening," she said.

"You too."

She tied the scarf around her head, picked up the laundry basket, tossed one final grateful smile my way, and entered the house with a reluctant, tired walk. Mrs. Resnik always gave off the air of a burdened woman, much like Matt was a burdened son. Perhaps the weight of moral responsibility and the unbendable boundaries of religion, devout as they tried to be, pressed heavily against their frames. The entire family walked around with the same tired gloom about them; heavy. That was the right word to describe them; heavy without being fat.

I turned and noticed the boxing gloves strewn on the lawn, so aged and soiled. I wondered how many different hands had filled them, hands of courage and hands of brute strength, and how many of those fighters had succumbed to their opponent's punches. Although I'd once been involved in a feisty wrestling match with a seventh grade adversary, I pinned him to the grass and never had to throw a punch. As a new student to our school, I think he considered the fight a challenge for playground supremacy.

"Come on, you little twerp, throw a punch," I remembered him spewing, trying to break free from my grip.

"I don't need to, man, I got you down," I had said. He squirmed and grunted and pushed with every muscle in his body, but he wasn't budging from my grip. My knees were straddled over his shoulders, and I had his wrists planted to the grass.

"This is no fight, it's a Girl Scout meeting," he'd shouted.

"Call it what you want, but I'm not throwing punches with you."

"Let me up you fuck face, I'll kick your ass," he spat at me.

I still don't recall why we wrestled or understood why he so vehemently wanted to exchange blows, especially when I had proven the more capable fighter. I reasoned with him, waited for him to cool off, and finally walked away from the fight without a single punch being thrown and only a few bloody scratches on my limbs. Until today, I've never thrown a punch at someone's face. I secretly envied the boys at school who brawled and hobbled away bloody and beaten, for even though they lacked a certain awareness and perception about their actions, and always attracted punishment, they were fearless and without hesitation. They didn't seem to fear the pain of a punch, and I found that intriguing.

"Kevin, you have a phone call," I heard my mother shout from our yard. I left the gloves on the grass and headed for my house. I was excited to learn that Shelly was on the other line. After some awkward pleasantries, she revealed the reason for her call.

"I just had a huge fight with my mom. She came home for lunch and we had it out. It got pretty nasty."

"About me?"

"Yeah, well, about everything."

"What'd she say?" I heard her sniffle, as if she'd been crying.

"Listen, can I see you tonight, after practice?"

"Sure, where?"

"Meet me at Rossmoor Park at eight, by the playground."

"Okay, but what are we gonna do?"

"Just meet me, all right?" she said, exasperated by my question.

I hung up the phone with a feeling of dread. It wasn't the kind of phone call that inspired confidence.

# Chapter Twenty-Two

*All through football practice, our last one for hell week, I couldn't* concentrate on anything except Shelly. Coincidentally, it might have been this preoccupation with Shelly and our impending rendezvous that kept me distracted from the exhaustion. I was going through the motions of the workouts without any mental connection to them whatsoever. It worked amazingly well, and as I rode away from the field I thought of ways to integrate this strategy at future practices, especially during wind sprints. I had enough time to grab a burrito at my favorite fast food restaurant, Taco Lita, just a couple of blocks east of campus. While I devoured my food I tried to envision how the night with Shelly would unfold. Before I knew it the burrito was gone, and I never once thought about the taste. So, I stepped up to the bright, orange tiled counter and ordered another one, this time slowing down to savor each bite.

�🚲

The top edge of the sun had almost disappeared from the horizon while I guided my bike into the park. This particular park was nothing like Lacy Park. It had several lighted tennis courts, an enclosed baseball field with grandstands, an adjacent full-length golf course, an Olympic size swimming pool, and a large sand playground for youngsters. It was fully functional, and unlike Lacy Park, was landscaped sporadically with huge oak and pine trees in no particular order or fashion. It made the park more open overall and unblocked from the streets, but on the flip side, rendered it almost useless for organized sporting activities of any significant size.

From the cement walkway I plowed my bike through a wide strip of grass before I reached the playground. It was deserted except for a girl, who I presumed to be Shelly, lying on her back on the silver carousel wheel and pushing it around with the balls of her bare feet. I approached her quietly while she kept circling around, and then I stepped up to the rim, the thick handlebars rolling by in parallel lines like a spinning wheel, and we caught glances as she twirled by. She didn't respond, clearly contained and thoughtful. When she rounded toward me again, I hopped up right above and straddled her between my legs. I push-kicked the carousel and we spun around faster while I gazed down at her. It seemed no greeting was necessary, just the greeting of our eyes, and I was content to stay there until she was ready to speak.

"How's everything going with the team?" she said in a flat voice.

"Not so bad. Hell week is finally over. Now we start real practices."

"That's good." I sensed by the tone in her response that hell week had just begun for us. "Will you make the team?"

"I think so. They pretty much take everyone, unless you're a real klutz." The carousel kept spinning, then Shelly leaned up, and for an awkward moment her mouth was inches away from my crotch. She stared at my crotch, expressionless, then up at me, with no embarrassment or concern at all. I jumped down off the carousel and grabbed a hold of a handlebar, bringing the big silver wheel to a stop.

"My mom said she won't let me drive if I keep seeing you," said Shelly. "She said she'll take away my license when it comes in the mail." I didn't know how to respond. She was obviously distraught about this. "I told her I'm old enough to date who I want, but she said not you, not right now. She thinks we're doing this to get back at them."

"What'd your dad say?" I asked.

"Saves him the trouble of buying me a new car."

"He was gonna buy you a new car?"

"Not anymore."

Shelly stood from the carousel and walked dejectedly over to the swing set and plopped into a swing. The first, deep blue shade of darkness had fallen over the city and only a thin layer of slate gray smog laid on the horizon, as it did almost every night in the summer. I joined Shelly and sat down in the swing next to her. She gently swayed back and forth while I kept still and glanced inconspicuously at her. I couldn't think of anything to say that would improve her mood.

"Wasn't gonna be anything fancy, just a little Ford or Chevy. Maybe even one of those cute foreign cars. But I was gonna fix it up and give it character, you know?" she said, gazing off into the distance. "I'd get some of those shiny custom rims for the tires, a killer stereo, maybe even string some beads from the rear-view mirror. I'd keep a little make-up box with perfume in the glove box, you know, for emergencies, and for my girlfriends. And my car would always smell nice, like spring flowers. Not all smoky like some cars."

I kept waiting for the inevitable change of subject, the dramatic pause in her voice, and then the slice of the blade. While she spoke I envisioned my head in a guillotine and my wrists locked in the circular wooden holes, the shiny and razor sharp blade positioned several feet above my outstretched neck. My head would drop into a wicker basket and put an end to a rather unremarkable life. Maybe if I demonstrated enough enthusiasm or kept her talking about other subjects, I might just escape my death, for tonight. I was quite certain of one thing: I couldn't measure up to a brand new car, and if she really stopped to think about it, she'd reach the exact same conclusion.

She pushed real hard and sprang backwards, and her body lofted behind, then swung upwards. She pushed again on her way back up for the second time and sent herself even higher.

I planted my feet and pushed from the ground as hard as I could. In a few seconds I'd reached her same height of arc. Admittedly I felt a little childish, until I reached full tilt and the chill of the air whipped through my hair, and it felt refreshing. As a child this movement held a hypnotic magic for me, and I always headed directly for the swing set before anything else. I heard

Shelly screech at the top of the arc and then she tried to push me, but only brushed my shoulder. She kept trying with each crossing, but I blocked her attacks without retaliating. I was afraid of pushing her off entirely. We laughed and fired playful verbal jibes going opposite directions. For a few moments we'd completely forgotten about the storm whipping around us. I was content to swing with Shelly for as long as she wanted and pretend we were kids again. And truthfully, in so many ways that defined a person, we *were* kids. We'd somehow submerged ourselves into an adult world with grown up problems, and skipped over the best part of being young and falling in love: the drug-like euphoria, the excitement, the discovery, and the freedom to act wildly upon our heart's desires. We were always stealing these brief moments of freedom away from our families, and for me, they were never long enough.

Just when I relaxed and my body felt free and light, Shelly ejected from the swing and plunged into the sand like a long jumper. On my next swing upward I launched myself into the air, felt the tingling sensation of weightless suspension at the top of my leap, and landed right beside her, rolling against her side in a cloud of swirling sand.

"I'll give you points for the routine, but your landing sucked. Seven point nine overall score," said Shelly.

"Who made you judge and jury?" I asked.

"I took three years of gymnastics, and then I got sort of…too big in certain areas," she said, glancing down at her chest.

"What was your best event?"

"The uneven bars."

Pleasingly, the guillotine vision was replaced by a new one:

Shelly wrapping her finely tuned body around those uneven bars and swinging in perfect symmetry, every curve of her form highlighted by a skin-tight leotard. She rose to her feet and brushed herself off. I enjoyed watching her swipe at her legs, encumbered only by a pair of white cotton shorts, and brush away the sand from her arms and chest.

"Race you to the rocket," she said, darting away.

I dashed behind her and pinched her bottom just steps before she reached the rocket. She squealed playfully and started to climb up inside. The city had purchased a huge steel space ship rocket that had a spiral staircase that ran up through the center and a slide that extended from the middle level. The entry holes were tight, but I was pleased to learn that I could still squeeze through them. The rocket stood about twenty feet tall and was approximately seven feet in diameter at its widest. It had small portholes about the size of a cantaloupe at each of its three levels so kids could gaze out over the park. The top level was somewhat cramped and we couldn't stand up, so we sat down on the cool steel floor and leaned against the frame of the rocket. It was quiet inside, and except for the ever-present drone of the rushing cars in the distance, I felt completely shut off from the outside world.

"Don't you wish this was a real rocket and we could just press a button and blast off?" she said.

"Yeah, but where would you go?" I asked.

"All the way to the end of the universe," she said with a gleam.

"But they say there is no end to the universe."

"There has to be, don't you think? Everything has to end."

Her eyes trailed away sadly, and I feared that I'd taken her to the one place I wanted to avoid most.

"Then what's on the outside of the universe?" I said, quickly adding another piece of track to the current topic.

"Well, maybe it's God. Maybe she's just standing on the outside holding everything in her arms, like a big beach ball."

"She?" I replied with a grin.

"Yeah, I'm pretty sure if there *is* one, God is female. We're the more compassionate and loving gender. It makes sense."

"Okay, I'll buy that logic. But then what's on the outside of her?" I asked.

"Nothing, I suppose. Just total emptiness."

"There has to be something, don't you think?"

"Maybe it's just white space, forever white and shining."

"Well, is that heaven?" I said, trying to keep this going.

"I guess so, if you wanna call it that."

"So what's on the outside of heaven? There has to be something. Does it just go on forever and ever?" I pressed again.

"You know, I just realized something about you," she said. "You like to argue, don't you?"

"I don't know, not really."

"Yes you do. You like to push things a little, see where they go." I didn't know how to respond. If I agreed, she might've thought I was lying, and if I disagreed, I was arguing again. Then she bailed me out. "It's okay, I like people who speak their mind and question things."

"You do?"

"Yeah, sure, they're more interesting, don't you think?"

"I guess so."

"That's probably one of the reasons you like me, right? I'm pretty outspoken."

"It's not the only reason," I said, realizing I'd left myself wide open for scrutiny.

"Really? What are some other reasons?" she asked. I was tongue-tied. "Come on, at least one or two."

"There's way too many to name," I stalled.

"You're not getting off *that* easy, mister quarterback. Come on, now, you're gonna have to think quickly on your feet. The defense is comin' after you, here they come."

She threw her hands up in my face and made hectic, growling noises, like I was being chased by an angry linebacker. It was effective.

"Okay..." I said, caving in. She paused and dropped her hands, awaiting my response. "Your lips, I really like your lips."

"Okay, why do you like my lips?"

"Now I have to tell you why?"

"Yeah, come on," she pleaded. "What good is that information if I don't know the reason why?"

She was right. I was cornered, and by my own doing. I cleared my throat and tried to concoct an answer. Nothing suitable came to mind, at least nothing that wouldn't sound ridiculous or trite. Soft streams of moonlight funneled through the portholes and offered just enough light to make out the details of her lovely face, and I was transfixed. I let my gaze linger on her eyes while she waited with a longing that seemed more substantial than mere words could satisfy. She was hanging on my every breath, every movement, awaiting a response that would somehow transform her and whisk her away from here. It was then I realized that no words I knew or could piece together in a line would fulfill the expectations we shared. In just a few seconds we somehow crossed a line, and words would only drift aimlessly without attachment or meaning, like debris and random particles in space. I had nowhere else to go, nothing left to contribute, so I reached up slowly with my right hand and gently ran my fingertips over her lips. Her cherry gloss made it easy to slide my fingers all the way across. She kept very still, and I knew that I responded correctly. She placed her hand over mine and lightly kissed my fingers, closing her eyes. I leaned over and gently replaced my fingers with my mouth, and just as I made contact with her sweet cherry lips, I closed my eyes. She parted her lips and slipped her tongue into my mouth. We kissed delicately for several minutes, swirling our tongues together in rhythms of delight without too much force or speed. Our hands began to explore each other's arms and chests and thighs, matching the deliberate pace of our kiss. She paused and opened her eyes to mine, then pulled away from my mouth, kept her eyes fixed on me, and for a brief, excruciating moment, I thought the end was near. Her expression was so intent that I suspected the worst. Then she crossed her hands in front of her waist and slowly removed her t-shirt over her head, and I felt myself exhale. I was surprised to find her wearing a fancy red lace bra that appeared far too extravagant for a night such as this. The visual, however, was enticing, and I was thankful she chose to wear it. The bra brought clarity and purpose to our evening together. I knew that red, in this instance, did not mean stop. We carefully removed each other's clothes, careful in a way that ensures momentum and conclusion, and I became acutely aware of every point of physical contact on my body, whether from the cool hard steel of the rocket or the warm smoothness of her skin. I became totally disconnected from my thoughts, separated from this dark and dusty place, until all the blackness and dull silver metal and pale blue light beams and specks of floating dust spun away in a hazy blur that left nothing in my view except the golden frame around her form. It was just her and me; her moving on me, her touching me, her kissing me; and me, making motions and touching her wonderful body in ways that pleased her most. The universe, as I knew it then, expanded no wider than beyond this steel cylinder cave.

# Chapter Twenty-Three

*"Kevin, come on, wake up,"* I thought I heard someone say. Maybe I'd been dreaming. Maybe the last couple of weeks had just been an extraordinary dream. Then someone shook my shoulder. "Kevin, wake up, it's eight o'clock." I gradually opened my eyes to a blurry vision of my father lifting a pair of shorts from my dresser drawer and tossing them on my bed. I closed my eyes again without moving or responding, hoping he'd go away.

"We have a tennis match," he said. "Rachel agreed to play doubles with us. It's a start."

"Huh?" I slogged.

"I told you about this yesterday. We're meeting Rachel to play tennis at Rossmoor Park. Get a move-on."

He tossed a t-shirt at me that draped over my face.

Since I was raised by two tennis fanatics who constantly dragged me to the courts, I was a solid tennis player. But there were a few elements not in my favor on this particular morning. For one, I could see the nose of the rocket over the fence from the court. Knowing I lost my virginity in that rocket the night before was a thought I couldn't eradicate from my mind, nor did I want to. Also, I was dead tired, not only from last night but from a week of grueling, two-a-day football practices. Thirdly, my sister Rachel, who was teamed with my father, looked ridiculously out of place in a pair of flip flop sandals and ragged cut-off shorts, embroidered with rainbows and sunflowers. Even though she had a tennis outfit at home, I think her selection this morning was meant more as a personal statement than a fashion statement; she wouldn't comply with standards of any kind. In any case, it was a distraction every time she flapped her way to the ball.

I shuffled back for an overhead smash that should've been easy, but the ball fell right in line with the rocket and I pulled it down and hard into the bottom of the net.

"Kevin," my mother complained, "what's wrong with you this morning?"

I just shrugged, knowing full well that the explanation would not be well received.

"I think I'll keep sending up those big lobs," my father gloated.

"Go ahead, Pops. I'll pound the next one down your throat," I said, making him chuckle.

"Ooh, we're so scared," said Rachel tauntingly, shaking her hips for emphasis.

"You should be, dressed like that," I said.

"You're just pissed off because we're beating you," she said.

"It ain't over yet," I countered.

"All right, pipe down, let's just play tennis," my mother tossed in.

My father served to me, and I blasted a gorgeous return right down the doubles line and passed Rachel, and my father snapped, "Out!" I darted to the net.

"You're insane, that was right on the line," I protested.

"Kevin, it was out by half a foot," he answered.

"You're starting to lose your eyesight, Dad."

"It was out, Kevy, just accept it," said Rachel.

"Don't you start on me with that name," I threatened.

"That's game, five to three. Your serve," said my father.

He hit the balls over to our side and turned his back to us while I sneered at Rachel. She just flipped the upper corner of her lip at me. What really ticked me off was that winning this match meant practically nothing to Rachel, and yet she'd use it in every conceivable way as a means to infuriate me. I retrieved the balls, still fuming from his call. I only had a banana in my stomach that I grabbed before leaving, and the lack of fuel was beginning to make me irritable.

I was serving to Rachel's side, and even though I'd eased up on my first serves to her, I was angry and in no mood for tiptoeing around. I blasted a big serve right at her body that caromed off her errant racquet and into the other court.

"Kevin," my father said, "ease up on the serve to your sister."

"Why should I?" I asked.

"You know she can't return those serves."

"Well then she'd better learn fast."

My father sneered and walked back to the end line to return my serve. I tried to power a big ace down the centerline.

"Fault!" my father shouted. I had no problem with that call.

I put some extra spin on the second serve, and my father sliced it back at my mother. The rally lasted for several shots until my mother tried to short drop shot on Rachel, but it went too far beyond the net and bounced high. Rachel hustled to the ball, her sandals flapping against the pavement, and slammed it deep into the corner of the court, right by me.

"Out!" I yelled.

"What?" Rachel shouted.

"Having trouble with your hearing?" I said.

"No, I'm having trouble with your calls. That was good, and you know it."

"I saw it out, so it's out."

"Kevin, what are you doing?" accused my father.

"I'm making a call. The ball was out."

"It's his call, John, and he saw it out," said my mother.

"Mom, are you gonna let him get away with this?" said Rachel.

"We all make our own calls, that's the rule we play by," said my mother.

"That's right, but let's keep things fair and square," said my father.

"Fair and square?" said my mother, exasperated. "You've been serving hard to me all match, and yet you tell Kevin to ease up on Rachel."

"That's because you're a good player," countered my fatherly gingerly.

"I'm not a good player?" said Rachel, offended.

"No, I–I just meant that your mom is used to my hard serves."

"Typical," my mother said under her breath.

"What was that?" said my father.

"You know, John, you used to serve a little easier to me so we could have a real game with rallies." I saw that my father was taken aback by her comment. My mother had ventured into new, uncharted waters in front of Rachel and me. It felt too personal, especially in a public place. "Now everything is about winning."

"That's ridiculous, Audrey, we have great matches."

"No, John, *you* have great matches, I just play in them," she said. I realized the people on the courts on either side had stopped playing and were pretending to take a break and gather some balls. I was greatly relieved to see they were all strangers.

"I don't know what you're talking about," said my father.

"You know perfectly well what I'm talking about. You're just as competitive as your two sons. In fact, the apples didn't fall far from the tree."

"All right, if that's the way you feel, I'll ease up on my serve."

"Just forget it."

"No, I will."

"Forget it, John, just serve the way you always do."

"No, no, if it's bothering you then I'll ease up."

"Then you'll complain it's not fun anymore. I wouldn't want that on my conscience, that you weren't having fun anymore. God forbid you shouldn't have any fun in your life!" my mother suddenly shouted. The long and silent seconds after my mother's outburst were excruciating.

"Oh this is so stupid, we can't even play tennis right," said

Rachel. She threw her racquet against the net and flapped away. My mother and father exchanged frustrated glances, and my mother dropped her racquet on the court and trotted after Rachel.

"Rachel," shouted my mother.

"Get away from me!" screamed Rachel.

Only as two males can, my father and I stood and stared with a blank confusion at the scene. Rachel disappeared first through the fence gate, followed shortly thereafter by my mother. Then my father turned toward me. I thought this would be the part where we'd commiserate over the hyper-sensitivity of the women in our family and our plight as the men who tried to appease them.

"Why'd you have to serve so hard to Rachel, huh?" he said.

"What?" I said in disbelief.

"You heard me. Now she's run off again."

"Are you blaming *me* for this?"

"You can't take it out on other people just because you're losing."

"Hey, I can handle losing, I just can't handle cheaters."

"You think I would cheat you?" he asked, genuinely troubled by my implication. My father had this sincere way of looking offended when he wanted to.

"Maybe not on purpose, but subconsciously."

My father huffed and grinned. "What do you know about the subconscious mind?" he asked.

"I know it makes you do weird things, things you can't explain. I know it controls you in ways you can't understand." His grin ran away from his face, shocked that I had a legitimate answer.

"Just the same, you should take it easy on your sister. She's going through a difficult time right now."

"Where have I heard that before? Oh yeah, just about every day of my stupid life."

"Keep your voice down."

I walked closer to my father. "I didn't even wanna play this morning. You dragged me here."

"I thought it would be good for us and for Rachel."

"See, that's just it. Everything's about her. She's fine, she's having the time of her life. She gets to do whatever the hell she wants."

"Kevin, you really have a lot to learn about the female species," he said in a condescending tone.

"You think so, huh? I've been finding out a lot lately."

He eyed me curiously, swallowing hard. He knew exactly what I meant. "Listen, things at your age, well, they tend to get outta control," he said.

"What are you so worried about?" I asked.

"You, her, both families. I don't think you realize what kind of strain you've put on everyone."

"I'm just following in the footsteps of my father. Aren't you proud of me?" I said sarcastically.

He narrowed his eyes, sighing disappointedly. Then he glanced away and returned my gaze with a serious expression, and I knew this was the part he wanted me to listen to most carefully.

"Just because we've agreed to let you explore this relationship doesn't mean it's not affecting us, or her family. Especially her family. Whether you like it or not, you and—"

"Shelly."

"Right. You two are right in the middle of this. The last thing we need is for something to go wrong."

"I think it's a little too late for that, Dad."

"What do you mean?" he said.

"I think something went wrong a long time ago," I said. My father was affected by my comment, impressed by his son's understanding of matters close to the heart.

"Yeah, okay. You're pissed off at your father, huh? Feeling hurt and angry?" I didn't look at him. "Go ahead, you can say it. Get it off your chest."

"Let's just play some tennis." I started to turn away.

"Kevin, I really hope you're seeing this girl for the right reasons."

"It's Shelly, her name is Shelly," I said. "And who cares about the reasons anyway? You're just afraid we'll last longer than you and that…that…witch," I said vehemently.

"Kevin!" My father glanced around nervously and said in a more controlled voice, "Don't talk about her that way. It's not fair to her or me."

"How could you pick her over Mom? Bad move, Dad, really bad move."

He stepped closer to me, not wanting our words to be overheard. "This is not about choice or choosing sides. Your mom and I, we're trying to deal with this in our own way. We still care about each other very much, that will never change."

"And I care about Shelly. So I guess we'll both just keep going until something blows up. Maybe it has to happen that way."

"I know how you ran into her at the store. I know you were trying to track down her mom."

"So? I was curious, big deal."

"I can't blame you for being curious," he said. "But now you're involved in all this, and that means you have a responsibility. Your relationship is bigger than just the two of you. It's about two families now. You have to handle it with discretion and dignity and most importantly, with respect. You have to consider other people's feelings and not just your own."

I stared into my father's eyes and listened to him speak, words which rang true and made real sense to me, perhaps more than anything he'd ever said. Deep down, I knew he tried to keep his other relationship from infecting the family. He tried to keep the peace and never relinquished his role as father and caretaker. Even so, I couldn't escape the restless anguish I harbored inside, the agony of knowing that he pushed aside his wife of twenty-five years; the woman who raised me. I could rationalize his behavior and choices in a logical manner, even extend him some credit for trying to maintain the family dynamics. Yet I could never forgive or forget that he made it all happen, and that he seemed unwilling to end it.

# Chapter Twenty-Four

*Not a word was spoken during the ride home in the car. Rachel* never returned to the courts, and it dashed all the high hopes my parents had for the day. When we pulled into our driveway, I noticed Helen working in her garden. I slid across the seat so I could exit on the far side. I didn't feel like making conversation with anyone, let alone the chatterbox queen. Matt was raking the leaves in his front yard, and Mr. Bollinger was tinkering at his workbench in the garage. Even the father of the mysterious family at the enclosed end of the street, who rarely came outside for anything and spoke to no one, was outside waxing his expensive Buick four-door. When we plowed out of the station wagon, Helen wasted no time in corralling my mother.

"Audrey, would you listen to that?" said a frantic Helen, tilting her head toward the neighbor's house across the street. My mother cranked her head to the Morgan's house. "It started just a few minutes ago. I thought this would finally be a nice, quiet Saturday morning."

The yelling was louder than usual. I couldn't hear a male voice, only two women and a screaming child.

"I heard a door slam and then a big crash," said Helen. "It's like the devil himself lives in there."

"That poor child," said my mother. "What's going to become of him?"

"I wouldn't be surprised if they carted that kid away in an ambulance someday," said Helen. "It's only a matter of time before disaster strikes. They're just counting the days, that's all."

My father was appalled and shook his head in disapproval, then started for the front door. He has a resigned, live and let live quality about him that in some ways I admire, and in other ways, truly despise.

"Kevin, are you coming inside?" my father asked.

I couldn't accurately describe the mixture of feelings that overheated my system at that moment. Maybe it was the lack of nourishment or the faintness I felt when I stood too fast from the car. I was feeling disoriented and edgy, that much was true. Maybe it was the look of resignation on my father's face, and the words he spoke that sounded so indifferent in light of the troubling shrills and screams emanating from across the street. Whatever the case, I glanced around and noticed my neighbors carrying on with business as usual, without a care in the world, and finally to Helen, the only soul showing any real concern, and something stirred inside me. It felt like a groundswell of all the most despicable and heinous feelings a person could have for something, wound tightly together in a compact ball in the pit of an empty stomach, then snapping at the core and rapidly unwinding. I felt my skin tingle and my grip tighten around the racquet handle.

"Come on, Kevin, I'll make you some breakfast," said my mother, crossing the driveway and moving toward our front steps. My father paused at the base of the steps and pivoted.

"Kevin, you heard your mother, let's eat," he said.

I was transfixed on the Morgan's house, in particular, on the front door. I felt a spasm in my right tricep. The baby kept crying, and the adults kept shouting. The noise reverberated in my head and consumed my every thought. The neighborhood had a fuzzy, surrealistic glow in the warm mid-morning sun, and my head spun briefly from vertigo.

"Kevin, are you listening to us?" I thought I heard my mother ask. I could decipher the words, but they sounded jumbled and unimportant.

I took the first step toward the house, and then a second. By the third step I was committed to an action for which I had no comprehension or plans of any sort.

"Where are you going?" asked my father.

I stepped down from our lawn onto the concrete with a heavy and determined stride. From the corner of my eye I could see Matt pause from raking the leaves and the mysterious neighbor lift his head from waxing his car to check things out. My pace quickened, and my stride lengthened. I tried to clear my mind, for I knew that rational thoughts—in these situations—were eventually the death of action.

I heard my father's voice and I thought he shouted, "Kevin, come back here. That's none of your business."

Nothing anyone could say or do could deter me. My body was

leaning forward with an unstoppable thrust. I stepped up firmly on the front porch of the Morgan's house and right to the front door. I rapped real hard on the door three times with my racquet, leaving a scratch mark. The adult voices silenced inside, but the baby kept wailing bloody murder. My mind was an absolute blank, yet there I stood at the doorstep of the Morgan's house, a family everybody avoided like the plague, a Jimmy Conners T-3 aluminum tennis racquet in my right hand, and an uncoiled ball of rage in my gut. A few seconds later the door propped open, and Mrs. Morgan stood there. She was shorter and heavier than she appeared from afar, and her brick red lipstick was smudged and her royal blue mascara was applied too heavily. Her short, dyed black hair was messy and oily, and her teeth were stained from smoking. Her cheap five-and-dime clothes were wrinkled and showing signs of wear, and she squeezed a cigarette between her fingers that had almost burnt down to the filter. Her sun-baked skin was shriveled, and her mouth had frozen to a scowl; the right clown costume and she was ready for the circus. I'd never seen her up close and the sheer ugliness of her face startled me. But it was more than just her appearance; everything about her was wretched.

"What do you want?" she demanded, her voice gruff from years of smoking.

Truthfully, I didn't really know. Lately I'd been reacting to events without thinking, making mistakes, and then scrambling to recover and regain my balance. My first instinct was to swat her across the head, like I was killing a fly. I decided to stop and think, and I went with my second instinct, which was to say the first thought that came to my mind.

"I want you and your daughter to shut the hell up!" It came out in a slow, threatening tone that gradually picked up steam and force, ending with an emphatic bang.

She blinked and flinched in astonishment, as if someone had zapped her with a stun gun. I had her back on her heels and reeling. I raised the racquet for emphasis and intimidation.

"Can't you hear the baby crying? I can! The whole damn neighborhood can!" I shouted. "Now you and your daughter stop yelling at each other and start looking after that boy or I'll report you to the police, *got that*?"

I popped her on top of the head with my racquet on the word "got." Instinct, I suppose. I hit her with the sweet spot of the strings, which was fortunate for her. She was so flabbergasted by my aggression that she just stood still with her black-and-blue painted eyes bugged wide open, as if she'd seen a ghost.

"Good!" I shouted right in her face, brushing her backwards.

I pivoted sharply and started to leave when I noticed that the baby had quit wailing and all the neighbors had now ventured curiously to the end of their driveways.

"Get the hell off my property, or I'll report *you* to the police!" she yelled, slamming the door.

I flipped the racquet and rested it on my shoulder and made my way across the Morgan's dried-out lawn. The mysterious neighbor at the end of our street started to applaud, and I heard Helen shout "Bravo! Bravo!" and clap her hands repeatedly. Then Matt unleashed one of his famous finger whistles that practically scorched the trees with its power and sound. Even Mr. Bollinger, subdued to the core, flashed a big thumbs-up from his driveway and yelled in his husky voice, "Way to go, kid, way to go!"

My father grinned broadly and chuckled, shaking his head in

disbelief. He wasn't easily or genuinely surprised by anything his children did, yet I knew that I'd totally blown his mind with this stunt. As for my mother, I wouldn't have traded the pride in her eyes and the brilliance of her smile for all the Super Bowl rings in the world. For the first time in a long while, as my mother glowed and exchanged a proud, loving glance with my father, I felt as though we were a family again—a unit, a team. I didn't turn back toward the Morgan's house, although after I heard the door slam shut, I knew that victory was mine.

"Winner and still champion by a knockout, Kid Copeland!" my dad shouted like a boxing ring announcer, thrusting my arm into the air.

"That was unbelievable," praised my mother, "absolutely unbelievable."

"What in the heck got into you?" asked my father.

I considered the question and the only logical conclusion I could reach was, "I'm just really hungry."

My parents broke into a raucous laughter, and my father proudly rubbed my head.

"God bless you, Kevin Copeland," shouted Helen, throwing me a big kiss. Then Helen darted into her house, no doubt excited to tell her husband that the mean, old grandma of Lyncrest Road had finally met her match.

The three of us receded into our house and about a half hour later I was treated to a meal composed of four strips of bacon, two thick pancakes smothered in maple syrup and butter, and three scrambled eggs with cheddar cheese sprinkled on top. Oh yeah, and a huge, frosty cold glass of Carnation instant chocolate drink.

# Chapter Twenty-Five

*Unfortunately, the shining afterglow of my triumph didn't last* nearly long enough. Later in the day, walking down the hallway, I heard my mother in her bedroom on the phone and using her serious tone. I presumed the other caller on the line was Rachel. I could see through the crack in the doorway that my mother was trying to contain her emotions. I'd begun to believe that Rachel had left home indefinitely and wouldn't return; my parents probably feared the same. I continued into the living room to watch some television, and just as I leaned over for the knob, my mother stormed by and hurried into the kitchen, hell bent on something. When *The Newlywed Game* appeared on the screen I lowered the volume just enough to hear my parents and listen to the show at the same time. Those clueless newlywed couples had no idea what they were in for, I thought.

"John, would you get in here and talk to your daughter, please!"

she shouted into the garage from the laundry room.

"Is she coming home?" I heard my father shout.

"I don't know, but you need to talk to her."

"Why, so I can become frustrated all over again, like you are now?"

"I'm not frustrated, I'm just tired of going around in circles with her."

"That's frustration, and now you're asking me to feel the same way."

"Listen to you, John. You've given up. You've left this all up to me, and I resent that."

"Oh that's nonsense, Audrey," my father said, moving closer to my mother and the door. "I haven't given up. But talking to her over the phone while she's in that house hasn't done a bit of good. As soon as she hangs up she runs right to that family for support, and they give it to her. Then we sit here and feel like failures."

"So what do we do, just stop talking to her?" I heard a long pause. "John, you're not suggesting we cut her off, are you?"

"Why should she come home if we just treat her the same way over the phone, and she can do whatever the hell she wants over there? She doesn't see anything wrong with this."

"So that's it, we just turn a deaf ear and stop talking to our daughter? I can't do that, John. Maybe you can, but I can't."

"Tell her if she wants to talk to me she can come home first. That's where I'll do all my talking."

"Why don't you tell her yourself?"

I heard my father step up to the laundry room and into the kitchen with a hard and determined stride. He picked up the phone while my mother stood nearby. I watched and listened from the living room, although from where I sat on the sofa I could only see parts of them, their upper bodies shifting and moving in and out of my eyesight.

"Hi, Rachel," he said calmly. "Yeah, I know, I know. Listen, I was just telling Mom that I'd prefer to have these talks face to face. Yes, that means you come here. Mom feels the same way."

My father glanced uneasily at my mother, who nodded her head briefly to reinforce his new plan.

"Yes, I know. Well, we think it would work best this way. Uh-huh…yeah…well, Rachel, you've had it pretty much your way so far, and you know that. I know, right." My father didn't speak for a long while, and I thought this was a definite sign that indicated trouble ahead. I couldn't see my father's expression, nor did I need to. I knew exactly how this would turn out.

"Well then, I don't think I'm prepared to keep this going over the phone. We never get anywhere. No…I don't think so. Rachel, wait, just listen. We're not shutting you out…no, it's not like that. We're not—"

The walls of fortitude had begun to crack. My father was nothing if not sympathetic, even when buoyed by his beliefs.

"I never said that," he said louder and with more urgency. "No, that's not what I meant …no. Rachel, listen… okay, fine, we don't have to, just don't start crying, okay? It's all right. No… not if it upsets you this much."

I leaned sideways enough to see my father rub his forehead. The new plan was officially dead in the water before it had even set sail.

"Okay, we'll talk later."

My father hung up the phone and sighed.

"We're just pushing her further and further away," said my

mother.

"I just wanted to see how she would handle it. We can go back to the phone conversations," said my father.

"Just don't complain about having to talk to her," needled my mother.

"Oh, would you stop with that!" he shouted angrily. "I talked to her, all right? Why is everything such an ordeal with you? We'll get through this just like we get through everything else."

"In case it hasn't sunk into your thick skull, John, we're *not* getting through everything else," my mother said insistently. "Maybe you can shut everything out around here, but I can't. Our daughter has run away from home and we're... just..."

My mother paused and choked up. She squealed briefly in a way that releases a build-up of anguish and then began to sob. They weren't aware of my presence in the living room, or if they were, they no longer cared to hide anything from me. I knew just about everything there was to know, anyway. My mother wiped her eyes and sniffled. My father stepped closer and wrapped his arms around her. This was the first real affection I'd seen between them in months, and it was much too personal and intense, so I quietly left the living room.

⚲

When I walked outside I anticipated the sun would feel much warmer. The weather had cooled off during the last couple of days, and I took this as a sign that summer was fading fast. A stiff breeze brushed back our huge ash tree and made for the rise and fall of the leaves' whistling rush. As a child, the sound of the wind through the trees unnerved me, especially when dark, foreboding clouds drifted in over the purple mountains.

When I was nine, my mother asked Rachel to watch me for about an hour while she went down to visit with Mrs. Bollinger, her best friend in the neighborhood. It was a dark and cloudy day in the winter, and after a while Rachel became bored with babysitting. She mentioned that she needed to give something to Gail Resnik next door, Matt's older sister, and that she'd return shortly. She didn't return, and the winds began to rise, and I could hear the hissing sound of the trees intensify and then level off in equal proportions to the wind's power.

The first few drops of rain on the windows were light and sporadic, but several minutes later a deluge of liquid walloped the house. I could barely make out any colors outside through the sheet of light gray. The first flash of lightning was bright white and punctuated by the unfolding crackle of thunder several seconds later. My father had taught me that every second between lightning and thunder equaled one mile in distance from the eye of the storm and that if the count declined, the storm was closing in.

After the second flash, four seconds later the low rumble of thunder rolled in and finished with a monstrous crash, and I knew the storm was moving closer. The next flash of lightning was followed by a sharp clap of thunder, so loud and powerful that it shook the cupboards and rattled the dishes in the kitchen. I'd never heard thunder so loud, and I felt alone and susceptible. Intuitively, I knew that the sound of thunder couldn't harm me, and being indoors, I was safe from lightning. Still, the storm had descended upon my house and was trying to bust down the walls. I kept praying that someone would walk through the front door.

The storm was intent on hovering over my street and shaking my house right off its foundation. Amber stood in the center of the living room and howled like a wild coyote, escalating my fears. I curled up on the sofa in a fetal position and cranked the volume on the television, covering my ears every time the thunder boomed. The area around the crack in the plaster above our fireplace was soaked, and the first drop of water fell to the floor, followed soon after by more drops. I was certain this was a sign of doom, and that the roof would cave in and I'd be buried under an avalanche of water, wood, and plaster. Finally, miraculously, the phone rang. I told my mother that Rachel had left me all alone, and within a few minutes she plowed through the front door, dripping wet and panting from her sprint home. She knew I was frightened, yet she didn't call attention to my fear. She immediately dialed a number on the phone and told Rachel to come home that instant. Coincidentally, when my mother returned home, the storm started to drift away, and I felt a little embarrassed for letting it frighten me so.

# Chapter Twenty-Six

*I never suspected the most significant event in my life would* happen only days after my fifteenth birthday. I wondered what was going through Shelly's mind; if the experience had been important to her as well. There must be some sort of protocol to follow after the big event, but I had no idea what it could be. 'I just called to say thanks for the good time and let's do it again...right now?' A phone call seemed too impersonal and routine. I was tempted to ride out to the nearest bookstore and search the shelves for something in the self-help section, anything that might offer a suggestion or two. Yet I was fairly certain they wouldn't have a book entitled, *What to Say to Your Girlfriend After You've Had Sex For the First Time.* Nevertheless, the idea had merit; something more personal, more important, seemed appropriate here, like a gift. I knew the next time we stood face to face would be critical, and I needed something to break the ice. A gift would effectively remove any tension between us and draw her attention to what was inside the neatly wrapped box. It was perfect.

⚜

The Rossmoor mall opened earlier this year under a publicly aired storm of controversy. Some nutcases were convinced that a mall would destroy the very fabric of the American family, while others were concerned that it would drive the smaller mom and pop retail shops right out of business. The management of the thoroughbred racetrack right next door believed the increased traffic to the area might bring in more gamblers. In my estimation the opposite was true: The track brought more customers to the mall, especially if those customers happened to cash in a few winning tickets. Hinshaw's, the city's first major department store down the street and the perennial favorite among long-time residents, saw no compelling reason to take residency in the new, trendy mall. Now, my mother always returned from Hinshaw's and remarked, "My goodness, there's just no one in that store anymore." The mall changed everything for kids, too. It was the first real indoor playground that offered—in abundance—one of America's most cherished pastimes: window shopping. For kids it was like an oasis in the desert; a little piece of the Las Vegas glitz in our own backyard. Everything was bright and shiny and new, the air was cool, and the products were the latest and most fashionable on the market.

Since it was only a few days before the start of school, the mall was jam-packed with moms and their kids shuffling through the stores and scrounging through every rack of clothing. Some of the mothers were tenacious, like hungry alley dogs sniffing through garbage. I only had ten dollars to spend, but it was enough to buy Shelly a decent gift, if selected carefully. I immediately ruled out clothing, which was much too risky given my lack of experience, and was leaning toward something in the area of a trinket or costume jewelry. I perused the Hallmark store and visited the jewelry sections in the major department stores, although nothing really jumped out at me, and when it did, the price tag was far beyond my budget. I was probably trying too hard. This would be the first gift I would bestow upon my first real girlfriend, and I wanted it to be something unique and special.

I strolled down the wide center walkway, passed the circular fountain with yellow lights in the floor of the pool, and turned my head side to side to find a store worth entering. I found a store named B. Dalton Booksellers, and I paused, waiting for my mind to process some information. Then it finally hit me: Shelly loved to read, especially mysteries. Books were in my price range, and if I got something she really liked, it would demonstrate that I paid close attention to her words. I went inside and asked the woman at the counter where the mysteries were stocked. She pointed me in the right direction, and I headed for the aisle.

I decided to select a hardback since it was more like a real gift and something she might keep. I realized her tastes had probably evolved since Nancy Drew, so I searched for something more suited to adults. I didn't recognize any of the authors in the first part of the mystery section until I came upon the authors whose last names started with D. There it was, *The Adventures of Sherlock Holmes,* by Arthur Conan Doyle. The ultimate mystery, at least from what little I knew about mystery books. Besides, it was the only book that sounded familiar. I pulled the book from the shelf and examined it for defects. It was a new reprint edition published this year and had a sturdy black binding with a beautifully decorated paper jacket. I opened the book in anticipation of finding the price on the flap and was excited to see the title listed for $7.95. I calculated the tax and realized that I'd be able to cover the cost with some spare change for candy and soda. I was quite pleased with my selection and carried the book to the front counter, where the clerk rang me up and slipped the book into a plastic bag.

Much to my horror, at the moment I stepped outside the store and turned into the walkway, Shelly emerged from a store nearby. She walked alongside Pete, David, Robin, and another girl I vaguely recognized. Shelly didn't notice me at first, engrossed in conversation with her friends. I quickly contemplated an escape route. I didn't want to meet like this, in front of them, with this bag in my hand. Then she looked up.

"Kevin," she said surprisingly, stopping. They all set eyes on me. I felt on display, almost naked, with nowhere to hide. I actually caught myself checking the fly on my shorts. Shelly was ill at-ease, and I was certain that our expressions were similar: dread, pure and simple.

"Hey Kevy," said Pete. "What's up, man?"

"Nothing," I replied.

"You a bookworm?" asked David mockingly.

"Uh, well, it's a sports book."

"Far out, on what?" asked David.

"Uh, baseball, actually." For some inexplicable reason, it was the first sport that came to my mind, but it proved to be a disastrous error.

"Really, let me see it," said Pete. He approached and held out his hand as though expecting me to hand him the book. I forgot that Pete was a baseball player.

"Come on, dude, give it up," he said.

"It's nothing you'd like."

"What's the big deal, just let me see it."

"I have to get goin'."

I tried to step around him, but he snatched the bag from my hand. I was paralyzed. He withdrew the book and his eyebrows furrowed with confusion. Then he burst into laughter.

"*The Adventures of Sherlock Holmes*?" he said, showing the book to his friends. Robin covered her mouth from chuckling, while David and Pete held nothing back, busting into laughter. Shelly found no humor in the moment, just soaked with embarrassment.

"Say, my good fellow, Watson, why do you suppose this young chap lied to us about the book? Could he be hiding something?" said Pete, speaking with a shoddy English accent and pretending to have a pipe in his mouth.

"Why yes, Holmes, it's elementary, I believe. He didn't want us to know that he actually *is* a bookworm," said David, playing along.

"Ah yes, precisely Watson. By God, you've done it again," said Pete.

"I'm good, ain't I?" said David.

"Hey, I'm a football player, too!" I blurted. Both guys paused and stared oddly at me, then broke into laughter.

"What position, the Hunchback of Notre Dame?" said Pete, making David laugh harder. Pete stuffed the book into the bag and jammed it back into my chest, slapping me on the back like I was a poor sap of a chump.

"Hey, I have an idea, maybe we should buy a book so we can be bookworms, too," said David.

"Splendid idea, let's hurry," said Pete, still using the bad accent.

"Let's," replied David.

The guys entered the bookstore while Robin tilted her head and tossed me a sympathetic look, pulling the other girl inside the store. I was totally humiliated, and since they caught me in a lie, I couldn't really defend myself. I had to stand there and take my beating. Shelly skirted her gaze aside, darting around to anything except my face. Then she stepped closer, her arms folded, and our eyes still nowhere near contact. We stood face-to-face, painfully silent, and this became the exact opposite of everything I hoped for in our first meeting after the rocket launch. It was excruciating.

"The book's not for you, is it?" she said. I shook my head, and our eyes finally met. I wasn't sure if I saw pity or just contempt in her eyes, but at this moment it didn't matter. I was screwed. There was so much I wanted to say and do that it all became just a huge wad of angst stuck in the back of my throat. I simply held out the bag toward her, and she hesitated. I could tell she was reluctant to accept the gift right now, in this place, with her friends nearby.

"Aren't you even gonna wrap it for me?" she said, avoiding the real issue.

"Yeah, sure," I said hopelessly.

"No one's ever bought me a book before, except my parents. I'll let you know if it's any good."

"When?" I said.

"After I read it."

"No, I meant, when can I give it to you?"

She hesitated, and I pictured myself falling and swirling through a black bottomless pit of doom.

"I don't know," she said.

"Hey, are you coming?" said Robin from the store entrance.

I didn't move a muscle and locked eyes with Shelly in a way that begged her to stay. Indecision and anxiety riddled her face.

"I'll see you later, okay?" she said apologetically. I half-nodded and glanced away. Then she turned and entered the store, disappearing into the tall rows of books. I started to walk away from the store, my heart ripped out and hanging from my chest, dragging pathetically on the tiled floor behind me.

# Chapter Twenty-Seven

*I rode home in a slow and thoughtful manner that late* afternoon, reviewing each moment of the horrible event in my mind. There were a million variations I played out and they all sounded better than the one I played for real. I was bothered that Shelly treated me like an acquaintance when just a couple of nights before in the park we shared the most intimate of human experiences. I realized it was time to press the issue and figure out what was going on inside her head, and I wasn't prepared to wait long to hear it.

When I arrived home, I parked my bike inside the garage and picked up the basketball from underneath the front bush. Shooting baskets always helped clear my head. Today, I wanted to shoot alone, but several minutes after I began, Matt and Ronnie wandered over, followed shortly thereafter by Kyle. I usually don't mind when my neighborhood friends came over to shoot, although today wasn't for sport; today was for pondering and planning while I heaved the ball into the metal ring.

"Let's play two on two," said Kyle.

"Me and Kevin, since you're the biggest," said Matt to Kyle.

"Fine with me," said Kyle. "I'll take Ronnie, he plays tough. I like that."

"We get the ball first," said Ronnie.

"No way, we'll shoot for it," said Matt, who took the ball and stepped just beyond the free throw line. He fired up a shot that clanked off the front rim.

"I knew you'd miss," said Ronnie.

"Shut up, and take the ball out," said Matt.

I paired up against Kyle, and Matt guarded his little brother. We often chose these teams because they seemed the most even. Matt and I would usually win unless Kyle had a hot shooting day, and then it was a closer game.

Matt and I jumped out to an early lead and generally controlled the flow of the game. It was an excellent diversion. I could blow off some steam by working up a sweat and trying to dominate the game. Somehow, beating Kyle and Ronnie made part of the humiliation go away. I scrambled for every loose ball, and I went up strong for every rebound. I think Kyle sensed my heightened level of play and tried to match my intensity. As usual, Matt and Ronnie spent the better part of the game mouthing off at each other, continuing a rivalry that had existed between brothers for centuries. Matt and I were ahead ten to eight, one point away from victory, when I drove hard to the basket and was picked up on a double team by Ronnie. I saw Matt drop down low into the far corner underneath the basket, as he should, and I dished him the ball. Kyle turned away, and just as Matt went up for a shot, he extended his arms high and whacked Matt real hard across the wrists, sending the ball bounding toward Ronnie.

"Foul!" shouted Matt.

"Bullshit," said Kyle, spit flying from his lips.

"You hit my arm," said Matt.

"I got your hand, and the hand is part of the ball," claimed Kyle. "I called a foul, so it's our ball. Give me the ball, Ronnie."

"Forget it, he stuffed you like a turkey," said Ronnie.

"That was a foul, right Kevin?" asked Matt. Kyle turned his dead set eyes to me, daring me to confirm Matt's call.

"I heard a lot of flesh," I said.

"That was his hand. Don't cry like a baby because I hit your hand," said Kyle.

"I'm not crying. I'm calling a foul. Foul!" shouted Matt right in Kyle's face.

"Fuck you, it was no foul, our ball," said Kyle.

"If I don't get the foul, then I quit," said Matt, turning away.

"Don't be a fuckin' pussy, man," said Kyle, his face turning red. "You're always pussin' out on us."

"That's because you're always fouling," countered Matt.

Kyle pushed Matt's chest hard with both hands. Matt stumbled backwards, and his face went white from fear.

"Are you gonna be a little pussy all your life?" said Kyle.

Matt sliced a vicious glare at Kyle, though he had no intentions of retaliating physically, realizing he had no chance to win. Dejected, Matt turned and started to plod away. One step before he reached my lawn, Kyle lunged and tackled him to the grass. Matt grunted in pain when he hit the lawn, and then Kyle tried to roll him over and pin him down. Matt struggled but Kyle was too strong for him. Kyle started to pepper Matt's chest with light punches, just enough to hurt but not seriously injure. This was Kyle's form of torture.

"Get off me, Goddamn it!" shouted Matt.

Ronnie stood there helplessly, almost fascinated by the scene. As I watched this situation develop, I began to visualize my image in Matt's place, a younger boy with Kyle on top of me, pounding my arms and chest with punches, his spit splattering my skin while he degraded me with taunts and obscenities.

"You're a pussy-girl," taunted Kyle. "Say it, I'm a little pussy-girl."

I saw myself absorbing the punches and offering little resistance for fear that Kyle would fire the big bombs and really hurt me. It all seemed so childish now, and I even felt like a child for letting it happen. Matt just kept trying to deflect the blows, while Kyle had a feeding frenzy, as if this brutality made him feel better or superior. It became sickening to watch. Then I blurted out, "Get off me!"

Kyle stopped, turned his head toward me, and all eyes were focused on me, puzzled by my strange outburst.

"Does it look like I'm on you, dumb shit?" said Kyle.

"I meant…get off *him*," I said slower and with resolve.

"Oh really, what are you gonna do about it?" said Kyle.

I stepped over and stood with a straight and hard stance above Kyle. I wasn't going to take any more of his bullying, and I was certain my expression reflected my intent.

"Let him go," I said with all the conviction in my body.

I clenched my fists by my side and stared Kyle down, trying hard not to blink. I wanted him to see the unwavering confidence in my eyes, even though my insides were churning and my knees were wobbling. Kyle tried to assess my commitment and whether or not he could take me. Never before had I stood my ground against Kyle, and this display of strength made him hesitate and carefully measure the moment. Thank God for rational thought, even though I wasn't sure Kyle was capable of any.

"Pussy," said Kyle, shoving Matt's arm into his chest almost as the means to eject himself from his body.

Kyle stood and rose an inch above me. I was prepared for him to swing a fist at my head. Instead he scratched his curly head of hair, a little bewildered, and appeared wounded in a way I didn't anticipate. I could see the resentment of betrayal in his injured eyes, a mistrust that only came from choosing sides, and he was on the opposing side. He'd been overruled and finally rejected, for all to witness and record, and the result was a young man unsure of himself and his standing within the group. Someone had finally called his bluff and he knew it.

"Who cares about you dipshits anyway?" he said bitterly. "I've got better things to do."

His head lowered, his arms dangling loosely by his side like his father's, Kyle plodded down my driveway and into the street, bitterly alone.

"Thanks," said Matt, rising to his feet and brushing off the grass from his skin.

"No problem," I said.

"Why is he always so angry?" asked Ronnie. We all turned to watch Kyle make his way toward his house, his shoulders slumped, his steps tired and aimless, glancing around the neighborhood, probably thinking of ways to avoid going home.

"Wish I knew," I said, knowing more than I let on.

"Well anyway, I owe you one," said Matt.

"Mind if I cash in right now?" I said.

"Sure, what do you want?"

"Can I borrow those boxing gloves? I'd like to show my dad. He likes boxing. He'd get a real kick outta them."

Matt bolted toward his yard while I took one last look at Kyle before he entered his house. Kyle raised his eyes to the street and, presumably, toward us, perhaps wondering what he'd left behind, then vanished inside.

# Chapter Twenty-Eight

*Although I hadn't mastered the art of gift-wrapping, after three* tries and about five yards of wrapping paper, I managed to make the book look presentable. I wanted to make up for the disaster at the mall, and the book was my best shot. I rode over to Shelly's house with my left hand gripped firmly on the handlebars and the book tucked securely underneath my right arm. There was a strong wind that blew in my face, and it made the peddling and steering much harder than usual. A funnel of thick clouds had gathered and was pushing in over the mountains. I was determined to make this next encounter with Shelly the one I originally envisioned, one that would bring us closer together and solidify our relationship going into the first day of high school.

When I arrived at Shelly's house, I noticed a car in the driveway. I had to assume that one or both parents were home. Normally this would've sent me riding away, but I had to see her, no matter what stood in my way. I parked my bike and charged straight up to the front door. I knocked three times and then rang the doorbell, waiting anxiously. When the door opened a man answered, tall and proportionately built for his height, middle forties, a thick but sharply-trimmed dirty blond beard to match his hair color, wearing wire-rimmed glasses. He was holding a cocktail glass with ice and a caramel colored liquid inside, something that resembled whiskey or rum.

"Yes?" said the man in a deep voice.

"Um, yeah, is Shelly home?" I said.

"I believe she's over at a friend's house."

I was deeply disappointed and never even thought to say goodbye and leave. We just stood there for a few awkward seconds.

"What's your name, son?" he said.

"Kevin."

"Ah, right," he said, nodding gently with recognition. "Looks like you have something for my daughter."

"Yeah, it's a gift."

"Come in, you can leave her a note with it," he said. He backed away from the door and gestured for me to enter.

"Maybe I should come back," I offered.

"I insist, please, come in," he said, not accepting no for an answer.

I was nervous that Mrs. Vaughn might be inside, but when I entered the house I couldn't find her. Mr. Vaughn trailed me while I stood in the familiar living room and glanced around; nothing ever changed in this living room, no signs of life or a mess.

"Take a seat, Kevin, I'll grab some paper and a pen," said Mr. Vaughn.

I dropped onto the sofa while Mr. Vaughn entered the kitchen and opened a drawer. He kept a curious eye on me while moving about. He likely knew my identity and was intrigued by my visit to his house. I'd noticed that men appreciated acts of courage and bravado even though they might not agree with the reasons.

"There you go," he said, handing me the paper and sinking into his leather sofa chair. I tried to conjure something to write, except sitting there on display, knowing Mr. Vaughn was observing me and realizing these words would be so crucial, made the task literally impossible. "Writer's block, huh?" he said, taking a gulp from his drink. I nodded gently. "Best to start with a greeting like…hello, Shelly."

I wrote those exact words, but again my mind went blank. Mr. Vaughn broke into a playful grin.

"You like my daughter, don't you, son?" I thought my ears had deceived me, and then I replayed the words in my head.

"Uh…yeah, I think she's great."

"I think so, too. A little stubborn. She gets that from her mother. But a woman with no fight in her is no woman at all. Don't you agree?"

"I like a little fight, I mean, I don't like to fight, definitely not with girls anyway. Not with Shelly."

He smirked and examined me, to the point I became uneasy and fidgeted. "Do you mind if I ask what the gift is?" he said, eyeing the wrapped package.

"It's a book."

"Very good. What's the title? Promise I won't tell her."

"*The Adventures of Sherlock Holmes.*"

"Wonderful. She'll enjoy that a great deal. I certainly did."

"She told me that you read a lot... old books."

"She speaks the truth, most of the time." He grinned ironically.

"I'm starting to read more, but I still watch more television than anything else," I said with a hint of shame.

"Let's get this note written, shall we?" he finally responded. "Let's start with... I came by to see you today, but was disappointed to learn you weren't home. Write that."

It sounded real good, so I wrote it. Mr. Vaughn gave me a few seconds while he contemplated the next line.

"Your gracious father invited me in to write this note and leave it with a gift for you. Write that down," he said.

"Think I should use the word 'gracious'? She'll probably know that wasn't me."

"Doesn't matter, it's a nice touch. Makes you look smarter, so just write it."

So I did, and again he waited. He became more animated and used his hands when he spoke. I could tell he was enjoying this exercise.

"I wanted so much to be here when you opened it, to see your eyes light up with joy, only it wasn't meant to be. Did you get that?"

"Uh, only..."

"Only it wasn't meant to be."

"Yeah, got it," I said, scribbling the words frantically.

"I hope you enjoy this gift as much as I enjoyed buying it for you."

"Ooh, that's good," I said admiringly.

He gave me some time to write the line.

"And end it with this... parting is such sweet sorrow, but we must part and say goodbye. I will never forget you, and then sign your name."

I felt the skin on my forehead crinkle. I was confused and brought my focus from the page to Mr. Vaughn. His return gaze was stern and unbendable. Something had changed in his demeanor.

"Um… I didn't quite get that," I said gingerly.

"Yes you did, Kevin. But we must part and say goodbye."

"You mean, for now?"

"I mean forever."

I swallowed hard while he chugged the remainder of his drink. His voice had turned cold and serious, and there was absolutely no give or charity in his stone-like face. He stood from the sofa chair and ambled toward the kitchen. He reached inside the refrigerator and grabbed some ice clubs, then dropped them inside his glass. He opened a cabinet above the countertop, withdrew a liquor bottle of something dark brown, and poured another generous helping.

"Can I offer you a soda, something to drink?" he asked.

"No, thanks," I replied.

Mr. Vaughn briefly stirred his drink with his index finger, the ice cubes rattling against the glass. He returned to the living room and placed the liquor bottle on the coffee table. It was far too quiet and motionless now in this room, and I prayed for the phone to ring or Shelly to come home.

"Do you have any idea what it's like around here for me? Huh?" he said. I sharply shook my head, now on high alert.

"The son of the jerk who's sleeping with my wife is inside my home, courting my daughter," he said, huffing at the irony and hoisting the glass, taking a swig. "Do you know how completely insane that sounds? What is wrong with people today? No boundaries, no manners, no... common decency. My father would roll over in his grave, God rest his puritan soul," he said, more to himself. "Well I'll tell you one thing," he began again, connecting eyes with me, "it's making this house Goddamn unbearable. It's tearing my family apart. My work is suffering. I'm suffering. I don't need this shit."

His voice became edgier and louder, and blood rushed to his face. "I let all this garbage go too far and it came back to bite me in the ass. I'm not making that same mistake with my daughter."

He finished his drink and then poured some more. He stood and moved across the living room, standing against the sliding glass door. He rested one hand on his hip while the other propped up his cocktail, his elbow resting just above his stomach. He gazed out to the backyard with a blank stare. Terrified as I'd become of this excruciating moment, I decided to fill the thick, silent air with words.

"I... I didn't mean to make things more difficult, Mr. Vaughn," I offered. "I just... I don't know, I think she's pretty cool."

There was another long pause while he gathered his thoughts. I was hoping my words had softened his rapidly deteriorating mood.

"I'm not putting all the blame on you. Believe me, my daughter has become quite gifted in the art of manipulation. She's more like her mother that way, though neither one would care to admit it. Those two have been waging a war that defies description, and I'm the one caught in between. Now you are, too."

"What kind of war?" I tossed out.

He turned, about to say something, seemingly encouraged by

my question, and then held his breath, thinking better of it.

"War is war, whether it's fought with guns or words, it doesn't matter. They all leave scars." He paused and took another gulp from his drink. "You…you're lucky. You just get the good parts of my daughter. You don't see what really goes on around here. It's miserable, Goddamn stinking miserable. I'm in the prime of my life. I have a great job, I'm making good money. I should be enjoying myself."

He finished his drink and set the empty glass down firmly on the television cabinet, as if to make a point. In a matter of minutes he'd consumed two cocktail glasses half-full of liquor like they were iced teas on a sweltering summer day. I wondered how many drinks he had before I arrived and how the alcohol would affect him. Then he groaned in a heartsick way, glancing around, somehow disturbed by his domestic surroundings. Just moments before he seemed on the verge of lashing out or maybe dropkicking me out the door, and now he seemed more on the verge of tears.

"I worked really hard to give my family a good home, a stable home. I thought I was doing everything right. But you just can't account for some things, you know?" he said. I nodded only as a way of showing I was paying attention. "Take your parents, for example. You were blindsided by all this nonsense, right?"

"Uh, yeah… completely," I answered, without really understanding the context of the question.

"You never knew your parents were out there experimenting with other couples, trying these…radical new approaches to enhance a marriage… hell, just living it up. You just thought they were good old Mom and Dad."

I was stung in a suspended state of confusion, trying to digest and interpret the information he delivered. His head was turned away, gazing outside, unaware of my complete and utter shock. It was almost as if he was having the conversation with himself, working out the details in his head, and I was just another piece of furniture in the room.

"It was all supposed to be fun and games. Break the monotony of everyday life and meet some interesting people along the way. Seemed pretty harmless until…" Now he turned to me, perhaps remembering I was in the room, "until someone started to have feelings. That's when everything went haywire. Never happened to me, I wouldn't let it. Even though, hell, let's face it, there were times when I could've let myself go. Your mother, for instance…" he said, pausing with a satisfied grunt and grin, recalling a pleasant memory. "Well, let's just say I knew when to pull in the reins and step out," he added defensively. "Fun is one thing, marriage is another. Most of those couples never even considered their families in all that swapping and swinging around, for Christ's sake."

I heard voices echo in my head from the night my parents argued, words that failed to connect at the time, although they were painfully clear to me now. It was as if I'd awakened from a coma to discover that my parents were people I didn't recognize, people with secret lifestyles they didn't reveal or bring home. Not Mom and Dad, but Audrey and John.

"Don't push a guilt trip on me, Audrey. We got in this together," my father's voice replayed in my head.

"Yes, but you never got out. You were supposed to get out!" my mother had shouted in return.

The clarity of meaning crushed me, and the familiar tingling sensation of needle pricks erupted in my chest again. I was torched by the flame of truth and burnt to a crisp by the fire of reality. I sat anchored to the sofa with the crushing weight of awareness, my mouth agape. I tried to keep breathing for the simple sake of staying coherent, but I felt woozy. It must've appeared to Mr. Vaughn as though someone had pulled the plug on my heart. I just couldn't handle his arsenal of words anymore. I had to move my body and do something, go somewhere else, anywhere. I ejected from the sofa and turned to leave.

"Did I say something to upset you?" he asked, with a noticeable sarcasm.

"Um… I gotta go," I replied.

"Kevin," he said as I paused, "remember something. You can never find yourself as a man, until you stand up and face the truth."

What did he just say? Was this guy for real? I couldn't believe this chump was slamming a moral lesson in my face after dropping a nuclear bomb on my head. I was frothing at the mouth with resentment for the so-called truth he was hawking, and I couldn't hold it inside for one second longer.

"Hey man, I'm just a fifteen year old guy who can't stop thinking about a girl!" I shouted, seething. "And just my luck, she lives in *this* house," I pointed angrily.

I turned and marched right to the front door, never looking back, and pulled it shut with force behind me. Once outside I made a beeline straight for my bike. My parents' voices kept reverberating in my head, haunting me, chasing me, with every turn of a corner, every brake and acceleration of my wheels. I kept focused straight ahead and made the most efficient work of the roads possible. The air pressed warm and heavy against my skin, the pale gray clouds now drifting above and in the same direction as mine, and I leaned up high off the seat for maximum leverage and speed, as if running in place. And I *was* running, from everything I knew—from the truth, from something I couldn't comprehend, and yet it trailed me, mocked me, was a part of me, like a regrettable memory that never goes away. As I kept riding hard and pumping my wheels faster and faster, believing I could outrun this thief of hearts chasing me, this criminal of innocence, I heard the sickening crunch and then the hiss of air escaping beneath me. I looked behind to find my wheels had just passed through a patch of broken glass. My front tire began to deflate, the rubber started to flatten out on the road, and the metal rim made contact with the pavement and started to rumble.

I swung my right leg over and dropped both feet down to the road, checking the flat tire. "Fuck!" I yelled with all the rage in my aching body, angrily throwing my bike to the pavement. I'd had it; I was done. I wanted the whole damn world, and everyone and everything in it, to just blow up and die.

Just then a young girl, around six, ventured to the edge of her front yard, a curious wonder in her expression. She was pleasantly licking an ice cream cone. It looked like a drumstick, one of my favorites. As a reflex, I licked my lips.

"Are you okay?" she asked sweetly, somewhat nervous about my response and taking another lick from her cone, probably to calm her nerves.

"Blew my tire," I said dejectedly, motioning with my hand at the wheel.

She pondered my situation for a few moments, and then said, "Get an ice cream cone, you'll feel better." She beamed and turned with a proud hitch in her step, walking away as though she'd handed me the secret to life. Maybe she had. I remembered the days when the world felt a lot nicer and sweeter with an ice cream cone in my hand. They weren't so long ago, yet I knew they'd never return. I lifted my bike upright and started to trudge the long walk home.

# Chapter Twenty-Nine

*Only a few blocks from my house, I started to cut through the* corner gas station. I considered filling my tire with air except I knew that in a matter of seconds it would deflate again. I noticed a brawny man filling up the tank to his new, model white Ford truck, and from the side he appeared familiar. His face was mostly hidden although something in the way he hunched over and pumped the gas, his jet-black hair neatly combed and his leather work boots crusted with dirt, triggered a creepy uneasiness. His hands were enormous and wrapped around the gas pump like he was holding a handgun, and his shoulders were unusually wide. He wore a long sleeve flannel shirt and denim jeans, and his body, while thick, didn't look heavy by an ounce. He turned to replace the gas pump, and I realized he was the mysterious neighbor who lived directly behind our house, the one-eyed half-man, half-monster of my nightmares. I quivered and kept moving, but as he returned the pump to the holder he noticed me. Something he saw gave him pause, and at that moment I was deathly afraid he'd come after me. I kept my head forward although my eyes were cornered at him.

"Hey, boy," he said. I tried to ignore him and kept on walking. I was nearly to the other side of the station when he spoke again. "Hey, aren't you the kid who lives behind me?"

I pivoted for fear that running away would brandish me a coward and only serve to infuriate the monster-man. The burly man approached with a slow and deliberate walk. Like a shadow that grows, he grew larger with each thundering step in my direction, and by the time he stood one full stride away he loomed over me. Although his size and stature were intimidating, up close he was a ruggedly handsome man in his late forties; the kind of man with character and wisdom etched into his face. His deep-set brown eyes were intense and yet receptive, and the diagonal lines that separated his cheeks from his mouth were deep and distinct. His square chin had a half-inch horizontal scar at the base, and his black five o'clock beard gave him a certain earthiness, a sense of calm. There was a pack of cigarettes in the front pocket of his shirt and what resembled a lighter pushing against the edges of the material.

"I've seen you pop your head over my fence, looking into my yard," he said in a low, throaty voice. I wasn't sure if he was making an accusation or simply stating of fact.

"Uh…me?"

"You got a peach tree out back, right? A dog that barks a lot?"

"Uh, yeah, right."

He glanced at my flat tire, and then gestured with his massive right hand, "Blew your tire, huh?" I nodded quickly. "Let's throw your bike in the back. I'll drive you home," he said, tipping his head toward his truck.

With the same deliberate walk, a sort of confident glide, he approached the back of his truck, flipped the latch, and dropped the rear panel with a loud clank. Every movement he made was decisive and natural, and everything about him was connected and real. Reluctantly, like a timid dog, I rolled my bike in his direction. He clutched the metal frame at either end and hoisted the bike like it weighed less than a shovel, dumping it on the flatbed. He pushed up the panel and slammed it secure and brushed by me to the driver side door. I stood still and observed him with a dumbstruck awe—this mountain of a man, the very same man who haunted my dreams. After he opened the door he paused and stared at me with an odd curiosity.

"Well come on, get in," he said, "I don't have all day."

He leaned his body inside the truck and shut the heavy door. The truck teetered when he sat down. I went over to the passenger side, peered inside the window like a child at the zoo, and saw that he was stuffing something inside his glove compartment. When he closed the compartment hatch he noticed me, and out of hurried exasperation, waved me inside. I opened the door and hopped up on the vinyl-covered bench seat, clinging as close to the door as possible. Oh shit, I thought, I was trapped inside the monster-man's truck. What was I doing in here? Why didn't I just keep walking? He started the beefed-up engine, shifted the gear into drive, and pulled away from the station and onto the boulevard.

🚲

Only a little light streaked through the thick canopy of branches on this cloudy day, which made the street a long tunnel of cool, spooky darkness. The wind swirled and leaves pasted against the truck's windshield and then slid away in a flash. A storm was blowing in. The man stared straight ahead with his left wrist propped on top of the steering wheel and his right arm resting in his lap. The inside of his truck was clean and had a black dashboard with polished silver chrome, although the interior reeked of tobacco. I noticed a picture of a brunette woman inside a clear plastic photo holder, dangling from a Harley Davidson chain strapped around the stereo knob. She was attractive, exotic, and earthy, a person from South America, I thought. Her long brown hair was straight and shiny, and her expression was sweetly content. As the man reached inside his front pocket for his pack of cigarettes, he glanced sideways and caught my stare at the photo. He tapped the pack twice against his left forearm, and then brought the pack to his mouth, snapping up a cigarette with his lips. He stuffed the pack into his pocket and withdrew his lighter, an elegant pearl white piece with gold decorative trimming near the top. He lit his cigarette and inhaled deeply, then glanced once more my direction and exhaled a big blast of smoke.

"My wife, Angela," he said, "great lady."

I felt obligated to add something to the conversation. "I've never seen her before. I mean, I've seen you in the backyard, but not her."

"That's because she's dead." I nearly choked. I stopped breathing for a few moments, and when my chest started to tighten, I sucked in a huge gasp of air and coughed. "Smoke getting to ya?" he added. I shook my head and cleared my throat.

"I'm fine," I said.

"Yup, going on… oh… almost seven years now," he added, matter of fact. I wanted to know the details of her demise, though I didn't have the courage to ask. Did he kill her? Did he lop off her head with an axe? No, not this man, I thought. Despite my initial fears, there was something compassionate in the way he moved and talked; something generous in his nature. I think he tuned into my heightened curiosity and decided to put my mind at ease. "Crazy thing, died of a brain tumor. Doctors said it was the size of a golf ball."

I breathed a sigh of relief even though I already concluded there had to be a reasonable explanation.

"They couldn't help?" I pried gently.

"You know doctors, they only do somethin' when it's too late." I nodded and let my eyes drop sorrowfully. "I told her that her brain was too big, too much activity goin' on in there. She'd always smile and say, I need a big brain to make up for yours." He chuckled, drifting into the past and soaking up the bittersweet memories. "Damn, the old man upstairs broke the mold with my Angela," he said with one, sharp shake of his head.

"I'm sorry," I said, figuring it was the appropriate time for condolences. He barely acknowledged my words and for a moment I thought I'd said something wrong. Then he shot out his right hand toward me so fast I flinched.

"Name's George, what's yours?"

"Kevin," I said, relaxing and meeting his hand in a shake. My hand felt like a child's inside his fleshy glove. He whipped out the ashtray in the dashboard and tipped the end of his cigarette inside.

"Now we won't be strangers anymore, huh, Kevin?"

"No," I said.

It was quiet the rest of the way, and when he turned onto Lyncrest Road and drove around the bend, I pointed to our house. He pulled in front of the driveway instead of turning in. "Can you handle that bike on your own?" he asked.

"No problem. Thanks for the ride, George."

"You bet, Kevin."

I exited the truck and unlocked the panel latch. I raised my bike up on the wheels, careful not to scratch his truck, and lowered the bike to the ground. I pushed the panel shut and brought my gaze to the rear window. George's head was turned to his right and angled down, his right arm outstretched for something near the center of the dashboard. Although I couldn't be certain, I wanted to believe he was holding and peering fondly at the photo of his beloved Angela. I wanted to believe he was still so deeply in love with his deceased wife that he couldn't bear the idea of sharing his home with another woman. I wanted to believe that love lasted forever.

George glanced in the rear view mirror, checking my status, and began to pull away. As he rounded the circular end of my street and accelerated, he flipped me a relaxed military salute and I promptly flipped one in return. I thought I caught the start of a smile as he rumbled by and around the bend.

# Chapter Thirty

*When I rolled my bike into the driveway, my father was in the* garage and several pieces of junk were littered just outside the door. I recognized the velvety voice of Vin Scully on the radio, announcing a Dodgers game. While I parked my bike, he pivoted and tossed our old and beaten ocean raft onto the pile of junk. I don't think he ever saw me exit George's truck.

"Glad you're home, you can help me now," he said. "I'm finally cleaning out this garage. This is going to be a whole new garage by the time we're done."

For a few moments with George, I'd forgotten about Mr. Vaughn, Shelly, my family, but everything came flooding back in screaming fashion with the sound of my father's voice.

"I don't feel like doing any work today," I said.

"You said you'd help me, remember?" he said.

"Not today, I'm wiped out."

"Come on, Kevin, give me an hour, that's all I ask."

"You picked the wrong day, Dad," I said. "I'm not doing it."

I started to leave the scene.

"Now wait a minute," he said, approaching me, his clothes streaked with dirt and his hair messy. "I don't ask that much of you. You mow the lawn, pull some weeds now and then, pick up the dead peaches during the summer... I think you could show a little more effort around here."

"Effort, for what? Oh yeah, right, for that huge allowance you give me. If you want me doing something beyond my regular chores then you'll have to pay me for it."

"Oh, I see." He paused. "Well, since you brought up your allowance, then I think you should earn it. You can start by picking up Amber's crap in the backyard and mowing the lawn back there. It's way too long."

"I'll do it tomorrow."

"Today, Kevin," he said sternly.

"I don't feel like picking up crap today, Dad!" I shouted uncontrollably. "I'm sick of picking up crap. I've had it up to here with crap! Everywhere I step there's crap!" I yelled.

My father, while shaken by my outburst, tried to remain calm even though I knew he was ready to bust. He was in no better of a mood than I was, for some reason.

"You still have responsibilities around here. Just because you've had a bad day or you don't feel like doing something doesn't mean you get to dodge your responsibilities. I still get up and go to work every day."

"I don't give a fuck what you do," I snapped and stormed away.

316

I'd never once taken that tone and language with my father. It felt like a sacred vow had been violated, but I didn't care.

"Kevin!" he shouted back.

I marched inside the house and could feel his presence behind me. I stormed past my mother, fired a stinging glare, much to her confusion, and went straight to my bedroom and closed the door. I wanted nothing more than to shut out the entire world and bury myself inside a cocoon. Everyone could just disappear for all I cared. I heard footsteps coming down the hallway.

"Kevin, I want you to come out here right now and talk to me," my father said urgently.

"Get lost."

"Something's obviously bothering you," he said.

"We should talk about it, get it out in the open," I heard my mother chime in.

"Just leave me alone."

As I plopped down on my bed I noticed the boxing gloves on the floor at the base of my closet. They called to me, but I didn't really know why.

"Kevin, come on, open up," my father said.

Then the reason hit me. I sprang from my bed and swept up all four boxing gloves into my arms. I turned, opened my door, and shoved a pair into my father's gut.

"I'll help you with the garage if you go a few rounds with me," I said in all seriousness.

"Where'd you get these?" he said, looking them over.

"From Matt Resnik."

"They look like sixteen-ounce gloves," he said, studying them.

"Can you handle them, or are they too heavy for you?" He let loose a grin and eyeballed me in a way that defended his honor as an athlete.

"I think I can handle them," he said.

"Super, let's go."

"John," my mother protested.

I started to move by them, but he held me up with his left hand.

"We're not boxing until you calm down," said my father.

"I'm calm, I'm very calm," I said. I sucked in a deep, relaxing breath. "See?"

"What were you so upset about a minute ago?"

"I popped a tire on the way home. It made me really mad. Now I have to fix it and I hate doing that." My story sounded reasonable, and conveniently, it was the truth. "Let's go."

I brushed by my parents and plowed into the hallway. I could hear some hushed but intense words between my parents. No doubt they were debating the wisdom of this activity. I reached for the sliding glass door to enter the backyard and slid it back forcefully. My father emerged from the hallway and stepped into the center of the living room. My mother trailed a few steps behind, her arms crossed, making sure we noticed her displeasure. She lost that argument, I thought.

"You know what? I've lived in this household long enough to know you two are gonna do whatever the hell you want anyway," she said. "Just don't expect *me* to watch." In a huff, my mother walked behind my father and entered the kitchen.

"We're just gonna horse around a little, right Kevin?" my father said. My mother clanked a pan into the kitchen sink to punctuate her dissatisfaction.

"Right, horse and a round," I replied. My father shot me a

disapproving glance for my sarcastic remark. He was probably hoping for something that sounded more sympathetic to my mother, anything to cool her down.

I stepped outside the sliding glass door and onto the lawn. I removed my shoes and shirt, surveyed the lawn for the largest space of shit-free territory, found a sizable chunk of land just right of the peach tree, and slid the gloves over my hands. It was gloomy and breezy outside, nearing sunset, and the air had cooled considerably. It didn't feel much like summer anymore, and in a way I was glad about it. I was ready for summer to end. I wanted to move on to something new. My father came outside a few moments later and removed his shoes, then slipped on his gloves. Amber barked wildly from inside the house, wanting to join us, but we knew she'd only interfere. Once the gloves were on and secure, I was the first to raise them into fighting position.

"The boxers always touch gloves before the first round," said my father, extending his gloves. I moved forward and punched his gloves a bit harder than I wanted to, pushing back my father's arms toward his chest. I think he found the whole situation amusing.

"All right, let's just warm up a little," he said, bending at the knees and raising his gloves.

He flickered a few aimless punches that never came close, and I dodged and bounced, moving much too fast for a warm-up punch. It didn't seem as if he intended to make contact with his punches. I fired a jab and hit his right glove, making the *whoosh* sound of air. He grinned, and his eyes focused tighter and his shoulders and arms rose a little. We moved around within our own semi-circles and let loose some punches that never made skin contact. Amber barked from inside the house—high-pitched, frenzied barks—

although they were nothing more than background noise. My father threw some more half-hearted punches, toying with me. Then, as if someone had pushed my back, I leapt forward and let fly a roundhouse right that caught his cheek squarely and bent his head sideways. I saw his eyes glaze over for a moment, and then he blinked hard and steadied. He leaned back and stood straight, wearing an expression that was part surprise and part resolve.

"Tagged you there," I said confidently.

"Not bad, not bad," he said with more respect in his tone.

He brought his gloves higher toward his chin, and the muscle tendons in his arms flexed, as if preparing for a strike. He moved closer and ejected some jabs that forced my gloves back into my face, and I knew immediately, even with these misdirected blows, that his power was far beyond my neighbor Matt's. I kept my gloves high and danced around him, side to side. He had the size and strength advantage, so I had to be tactical about my movements. He was leaving his body wide open, so I made a few undercuts to his belly, and he deflected each punch with his gloves or arms. He wasn't retaliating with many punches and instead, examined me with a strange and distant determination.

"Come on, throw some punches," I said, dancing around him. He simply clenched his jaw.

Feeling cocky, I pretended to be Muhammad Ali and made a shuffle step, unleashing a combination double jab and uppercut that made little contact, if any. It was more for show. My father half-grinned, and oddly, seeing his reaction angered me. As I settled back into my stance and let my gloves drop a notch, pow, he popped me real hard in the chin. My neck bent straight back and I wobbled, although I stayed on my feet. I repositioned myself in a split and staggered stance that felt solid and unmovable. I tried to stay light on my feet, bouncing on the balls of my toes, the tall and thick grass tickling my bare ankles (and yes, the lawn had been neglected for too many days). I didn't believe my father would release a punch harder than the one he'd just thrown, so I stepped in confidently and let loose a wild combination of heated punches that mostly just grazed his head and gloves. He stood there and accepted them all, as if allowing me to vent my frustrations, and kept his gloves tight against his face. His belly was exposed once again, so I jabbed him just above his shorts and he grunted. He backed away and tried to regain his breath.

"That's a big target down there, don't leave it open," I said.

"You won't get very far down there," he said. "Solid as a rock."

While we exchanged these words I felt a drop of rain on my shoulder. I thought my father felt the drops too because he glanced upward to check the sky. I saw my opening, so I shuffled forward and landed a stinging punch right on his cheekbone. He staggered backwards but promptly returned to a ready position. It was my best punch so far and probably the only one that could've knocked him down, yet he was nowhere near ready to fall; this alarmed me. I wasn't certain I wanted to knock down my father anyway, even if I could. As betrayed and angry as I felt about his secret lifestyle, I didn't know how a knockout would change our relationship. Would we ever see each other the same way again? Would I have to move out of the house? Where would I live, how would I survive? I fired another flurry of wild punches, and some of my animosity and pent-up frustration had begun to evaporate into the thick and abnormally humid air. After a few minutes of boxing it felt more like Dad and me in the backyard, throwing a few harmless punches, not really intent on knocking the other down. I wasn't sure my father felt the same way, though. Just a few seconds after I landed the jab, he shuffled closer and struck me hard in the stomach, then swung a roundhouse right that connected on the left side of my head. I doubled over and stumbled to my right, nearly losing my footing. My father stepped in for more while I tried to steady. I raised my hands, and he punched me in the ribs, then higher in my chest. At this point I was simply trying to deflect his blows. He was relentless, coming at me like Joe Frazier when he smells blood and has his opponent on the ropes. I knew I had to mount some defense, so I began to counter. During this assault of punches, I felt more raindrops on my skin and thought I heard the low and surging rumble of thunder over the mountains. Amber barked furiously from the house. It was clear this match had begun to lose any and all semblance of control. There was no banter or half grins, nor any signs of a father and son relationship; just two boxers in a grassy field with a ring of smelly dog shit piles around them and the rain beginning to fall in pea-sized droplets.

I tried to juke from his jabs and throw more punches, whether they had the chance to connect or not. The pace quickened, and everything was happening so fast. I didn't know how far this would go—how many more times my father would hit me, how much longer he'd display that ruthless rage in his eyes. I thought I heard a voice from somewhere near the house. Neither one of us dared turn away, for fear of being hit with the knockout punch. We kept fighting, and his punches kept grazing my face and smacking my gloves. My legs felt weak and my arms were nearly exhausted. My father began to grumble when he punched, which frightened me, like he'd transformed into a ferocious beast. And yet I wasn't willing to stop this fight. I matched him grunt for grunt and just kept unloading punches like a man possessed. His body lunged forward, faking down low. He flared a fast right uppercut that I was too slow in deflecting, and the glove landed squarely on my chin and lifted my body right off the ground. Tiny white stars circled in my head. I was dizzy, stumbling to steady my feet, and the rain fell heavier, and the nearby voice rang out again, but I just kept punching and swinging. I knew that another solid punch to my head and I might be down and out. I didn't want to lose consciousness, and yet I'd never give in, not now, and not to my father. If he wanted a fight to the finish, then I'd give him one. I tried to muster one final blistering charge of punches before my strength gave out. He just guarded his head, and then when I paused he snapped a jab to my forehead. My head bent backwards and I almost fell over. He shuffled closer and I threw out a wild, aimless punch, more for protection than harm. The flush of rainwater made the impact of our gloves sound like heavy thuds of thick leather instead of a sharp, airy whoosh, and bursts of liquid splashed in the air with each punch. I was delirious, I was depleted, and yes, I was beaten. More than anything else, I was bewildered. Who was this tenacious fighter standing across from me? Who was this grunting, snarling, fuming bear of a man trying to knock me down? Surely it wasn't my father, my passive and mild-mannered father; a man who wanted nothing more than to keep the peace in his family? It couldn't possibly be my father, the man I tried to please and make proud, the man I admired for his patience and kindness, knocking me into submission, his staggering and overmatched son.

Suddenly a shriek so loud and shattering filled the backyard

323

that we both froze in place and jerked our heads to the origin. It came from my mother, standing on the edge of the porch, more frantic and distressed than I'd ever seen her.

"Stop, damn it!" she shouted again, drenched with anguish.

Still hunched in our boxing stances and ready to exchange blows, gasping for air, rainwater splattering our skin, we gradually turned our heads to meet each other's gaze. I'll never forget the expression on my father's face, one of restraint and total disbelief, as if he'd awakened from a daydream so real in his mind that his body was helpless not to simulate it. He blinked a few times and looked down at his boxing gloves. He couldn't seem to recall his reasons for wearing them. When he raised his eyes again, he did so with a profound and genuine regret. He appeared so distraught I thought he might break down and weep right in front of me. He stepped forward, reached up to my shoulders with both gloved hands and examined my eyes for any signs of pain or sorrow. I gave him a slight, if not weary nod of my head, just enough to reassure him. He squeezed my shoulders and clutched me with a forceful hug, as if he'd never see me again. I allowed my listless body to fall into his arms, content to be held up by someone stronger.

For the first time in my life, my father had completely lost contact with his wits. I reasoned that maybe this match had become a way for him to work out his own frustrations and problems as well. I just never suspected that he'd work them out on me, his youngest child. I was grateful that my mother had come outside and yelled at us. The extension of this battle, and most likely, the disastrous ending to it, would've surely and irrevocably changed the course of history in my family.

"John!" I heard my mother shout. My father and I split apart, now feeling more awkward about the long embrace, and turned our attention to her. "I just got off the phone with the hospital," she said with an urgent tone, her face expanding with blood and her eyes red and teary. "Rachel's in the emergency room."

# Chapter Thirty-One

*I sat in the back seat of the station wagon while my father drove* us to Rossmoor Methodist Hospital, where I was delivered into the world. My parents only spoke in reserved, brief exchanges, meant to confirm the available facts and nothing else. I peered out the blurry window, water splattering our car like bacon sizzling in a frying pan, still groggy from the boxing match and trying to listen to their conversation. The only information that made any sense was something they mumbled about drugs. My parents wouldn't divulge any more than that. I sat quietly and stared out the window at all the familiar stores and buildings, waiting for the hospital to appear and wondering what kind of heartbreak awaited us.

We hurried down the brightly lit hallways and came upon a white Formica counter with a nurse stationed there. She pointed up the hallway and my parents immediately peeled away in that direction, so I followed right behind on their heels. I was terrified of what we might find. Would Rachel be on her deathbed? Had she been disfigured? Naturally I feared the worst, since the last few weeks had conditioned me to do so. We finally came upon a door at the end of the hallway and my parents paused, tried to compose themselves, and pushed through. A pudgy and balding doctor was leaning over Rachel, checking her eyes with a small, silver flashlight.

"Doctor," my father said, his voice cracking with fear.

The doctor leaned up and turned from Rachel. All the color had drained from her face, and she had IVs running from both of her arms, one for blood and the other for some type of clear liquid. They taped the IVs to her forearms; her ankles and wrists had been restrained with leather straps. There was no movement in her face or limbs that indicated she was even alive.

"Oh my God... Rachel," gasped my mother, covering her mouth and beginning to sob.

"How is she, doctor?" asked my father, trying to bury his emotions.

"I think for the time being she'll be fine, but I'd like to talk to you, privately, if I could." The doctor's eyes slashed uneasily at me and then away. My father got the message.

"Kevin, wait outside for us, okay?" said my father.

I nodded absently and let my eyes linger on Rachel a while longer. I wanted to wake her, to hear her voice and to see that sweet smile. I wanted to make her laugh in her rambunctious way, except her form remained still and lifeless, no signs of revival.

I pushed outside the door and waited in the hallway, falling back against the wall. I felt a surge of emotions rise up from my chest and lodge into my throat. My eyes began to swell but I choked back the waterworks, not wanting to sob in the public and well-traveled hallways of this white-walled building. I slowly ambled down the hallway, believing that movement would keep my mind preoccupied, and turned into the waiting room. I was relieved to find an empty waiting room. There were numerous magazines on the table so I picked up a copy of *Life*. I sat down on the cheap cushioned bench and opened the magazine. I stared at the pictures without any interest at all. I was absolutely spent. I closed my eyes and titled my head back against the wall, trying to drift away to somewhere else, anywhere else. The first image that emerged was the rocket, and I allowed myself to be swept away into the memory of being with Shelly on that glorious night. I tried to concentrate on her image, on her sweet, luscious lips, on her voluptuous body, on being passionately intertwined, except the image of my sister lying deathly still kept breaking through. I couldn't shake it. I heard some nurses, walking closer, talking while their rubber shoes squeaked against the linoleum floor. As they approached the opening in the waiting room their words became more comprehensible.

"It's a horrible shame about the other girl," said one.

"What was her name?" said the other.

"Jamie."

My eyes popped open, and I rose abruptly, lunging toward the hallway opening.

"Excuse me," I said, sticking the upper half of my body outside the doorframe. They both paused and turned. One was short, older, and somewhat thick around the waist, while the other was taller and more youthful. "Did I hear you say the name Jamie?" They exchanged troubled glances and hesitated.

"Are you her brother, honey?" the older one said.

"No, I'm Rachel's brother... Rachel Copeland. Jamie was a friend."

The older one turned to the taller one and said, "I'll handle this."

"Thanks," said the taller one, who walked away, not without tossing a concerned glance at me. The older nurse stepped closer with an expression of warning and trepidation. She reached out and grabbed my arm, squeezing it gently.

"Jamie died of a drug overdose, honey. I'm so sorry. Your sister was very fortunate. She made it through the worst part."

"Jamie's... dead?" I said, immersed in a complete state of shock.

"I'm afraid so. We did everything we could. They'd taken way too much."

"But... how? Where were they?" I asked, still struggling with the news.

She averted her eyes momentarily and appeared reluctant to speak. My question had jostled her, and I could tell she was trying to formulate the appropriate response.

"I think you should discuss that with your parents. The circumstances are not something we get involved in, especially in this case. I'm really sorry, but I have to attend to another patient now, okay?" I wondered why she dodged my question with such diplomacy. "Will you be all right?" she asked kindly. I nodded absently, and she left.

I returned to the bench in the waiting room and plunged down, devastated and wrestling with the agony of Jamie's death. I wondered how close Rachel came to joining Jamie in the afterlife. Why was Rachel spared and not Jamie? After several dreadful minutes in the waiting room, my father finally appeared in the doorway, listless and disturbed, and gestured for me to follow him. When we entered the room, the doctor was gone and Rachel remained in the exact same position I'd left her. My father reassured me that Rachel would be fine, although she'd have to stay overnight in the hospital. I asked him what had happened, but he wouldn't reveal much more than I already knew. Drugs nearly took her life. Someone had informed my parents about Jamie, presumably the doctor, and even though I gently pried for more details, they would not or could not offer any.

My mother sat quietly next to Rachel's bed and stroked the hair just above her forehead, over and over, without ever moving her tear-swollen eyes from her face. My father stood glumly next to Rachel's side and clutched her right hand, tenderly rubbing her skin with his thumb. I stood at the base of the bed and stared at my sister's pale face, her paralyzed form, and again wondered how close she'd come to leaving this earth; one more pill, one more shot, or perhaps one more drink. She looked so frail and helpless. I reflected on my own despicable behavior lately with drugs and berated myself for so easily being influenced by the crowd. I remembered Craig, the pot dealer, and his offer to drive me to another party, and then soon after, his bone-crushing crash. I made a vow that I'd never let this happen to me, that I wouldn't end up there, looking like that, a slab of sallow flesh that was much closer to death than life; I wouldn't become just another casualty of drugs. I observed my parents, so utterly spent and shattered to pieces, trying to comfort their daughter and probably experiencing pangs of guilt and regret for letting their family—and marriage— slip away from their grasp. I silently vowed that if I ever married, I wouldn't treat my marriage like some kind of lab experiment, where after many years of commitment, intimacy, and love, my wife and I would decide to exchange our priceless bonds for something debauched with strangers; something dangerous. I'd find my one true love—like George did—and marry for life, hoping and praying that fate would never take her away from me.

Times had changed, certainly my parents had changed, and yet despite everything, I knew they loved their children with the greatest depth of the heart. They were still my parents, no matter how they decided to conduct their marriage outside the sometimes suffocating confines of our family. There was no shortage of love or caring or affection in that hospital room, nor inside the stucco home on Lyncrest Road, just the misguided and ill-conceived strategies of parenting and personal relationships. It was a strange and turbulent time, this year, these past few years. From what I understood of recent American history and the more conservative ways that families lived, there'd been a loosening of morals, a shift in priorities, a sudden self-awareness not realized before. Perhaps we were all learning together how to manage these changes. People had begun a phase of experimentation from which some would emerge unscathed, relatively unaffected, while others would dive from too high and fall too far, inhaling too much for the heart and soul to digest, arising the next morning to find someone unrecognizable, never to see themselves, their loved ones, or the world around them in the same way again.

I thought back to the boxing match and the way my father had pummeled me. While it was disturbing on some level, I'd convinced myself that he never intended to hurt his youngest child. I no longer felt so emotionally injured by his onslaught of punches, and instead felt proud that he stood toe-to-toe with me, like real men, and tested my strength of will and courage. Even though I'll probably never understand why he launched such an aggressive attack, I'd like to believe he was preparing his son for something important; maybe for the patches of broken glass along the road of life. I'd like to believe that my father knew exactly what he was doing, and if not, that he loved me anyway.

# Chapter Thirty-Two

*The number of students filing into the high school from every* conceivable direction was overwhelming. Amidst the mob of bodies I felt lost and insignificant. I tried to search for people I knew, but with the exception of a few familiar faces, the perimeter of the school was inundated with strangers. I'd heard that seniors sometimes ambushed sophomores in painful and humiliating ways on the first day of school, so I watched for any type of suspicious behavior lurking nearby. More than anything, I was searching for Shelly. I wanted desperately to see and talk to her, but so much had elapsed during the last few days that I never had the chance. We hadn't spoken since the day I met her father and learned of my parents' experimental marriage.

Rachel was recovering fairly well and seemed content to stay home, almost confined to her room, while my parents waited on her hand and foot. Their tortured agony over the possibility of losing a child had evolved into a deeply implanted guilt. They were lavishing enough love and attention on Rachel to sustain an entire orphanage of neglected children. In the process, my parents found a fragment of the love and commitment they'd lost. I noticed a glimmer of hope in my mother's eyes and a more caring and sympathetic tone in my father's voice, although it was far too early to predict an outcome. Love, I had discovered, was a precarious thing.

My parents and Rachel had several hushed, closed-door conversations. I reasoned they were probably learning more about their youngest daughter than they ever imagined. Not unlike my parents, Rachel had been conducting her own type of experiment into personal relationships and sexuality. I couldn't grasp that my sister had ventured into something so contrary to everything I knew and thought she was. Yet I was well aware that above all else, she was simply searching for acceptance, for unconditional love, from anywhere she could find it. Finding that person and giving her that kind of power must be intoxicating and irresistible, on multiple levels.

Sarah had arrived at the hospital with the Doctor about an hour after we did, much to the dismay of my brother, who showed up a little later. It was obvious that Jay was flustered when Sarah informed everyone that the Doctor had moved into her apartment. Jay's expression sunk into a sour, pale droop, as if he'd contracted food poisoning. I suspected this would happen and was actually pleased by the news. Sarah was a happier person with a man in her life, and now the Doctor actually had a place to live. Jay, on the other hand, wanted no part of their relationship. I reasoned that he'd been aware of it and was struggling to cope with his best friend and sister being lovers, much like he was struggling with my parents' open lifestyle. The most important people in his life had betrayed him somehow, disappointed him, including me when I'd stolen that photo. Now I understood why he kept his distance, both emotionally and physically, from the family. The flame of truth was scorching white hot, so why touch it? Why even get near it? Jay had decided to follow his own advice: sometimes the only way to win is not to play.

I rolled my front tire into one of the few empty bike racks still available and leaned over to lock the wheel to the metal guards. I straightened and flipped my canvas bag of school supplies over my shoulder and started up the sidewalk. One right after the other, cars funneled into the driveway of the main parking lot. Engines idled to a stop, car doors opened and closed, and students gathered and became reacquainted. There was a kind of static electricity in the air. I noticed a blonde girl shutting the driver side door to a brand new Japanese compact car with only a dealership plate. I kept walking closer to the parking lot until I realized it was Shelly. She was brimming with pride and exuberance. Her friend, Robin, exited the passenger side while Shelly swept her hand admiringly across the hood of her shiny, new red car. Curious, I watched them stroll over to another car where two guys had their backs turned to me. The guys pivoted when Shelly and Robin arrived, and I recognized them as Pete and David. Shelly didn't hesitate a moment in nestling herself right into Pete's chest, planting a wide, open-mouthed kiss on his face. Robin did virtually the same with David. My heart plunged into the pit of my stomach. I couldn't wrestle my eyes from this horrid scene despite the outbreak of war inside my head and chest. I stood in a stupefied shock, all the events of the last few weeks flashing in my mind as though everything had been some dramatic movie in which I simply played a leading role. It happened so fast, I couldn't be entirely certain that any of it actually occurred. Yet my aching body and thick scabs were proof it did. While I kept my stunned gaze fixed on the happy foursome, a hand slapped my shoulder and startled me.

"She dumped ya, huh?" said Kyle, standing near me and observing the foursome, his hand comfortably resting on my shoulder. I was still heavy in shock and didn't even recognize Kyle at first. Somehow, it wasn't right or logical that he was here, talking in the space near me, while my supposed girlfriend attended the first day of school with another guy's mouth attached to her lips. They should've been my lips.

"You were right, she's totally uncool. Not your type. Should've gone with your first instinct."

"Yeah," I responded.

"Don't sweat it, man. This school is crawling with chicks. You'll get another one."

"Right," I said, steeped in doubt.

"Where's your first class? I'll show you the room," said Kyle.

"History, room nineteen," I said, trying to figure out why Kyle was talking to me, and with such sincerity in his voice.

"Mr. Parker?" said Kyle.

"Yeah."

"He's pretty cool, you'll like him."

Kyle nudged my shoulder forward and we began to walk together into Rossmoor High School. This was not how I imagined my first day of high school.

"He gives a lot of tests, but they aren't that tough. You should be able to pull a B with no problem at all."

While I took my first steps into high school, my heart clinging to life support and trying to handle the notion that I'd been unceremoniously dumped by my first girlfriend, I realized I had two options: shed my tired summer skin, bruised and scarred, and plaster a smile on my face, or carry my wounds like a cynical soldier into every class, into every chance encounter with a new friend, and wallow in self-pity until I sank into a deep well of despair. It was during this moment of indecision, deciding which road to travel, that I had what could be called my first true epiphany: I, Kevin Copeland, the youngest of four children at fifteen, officially got laid this summer. I was entering high school a fully experienced man. Okay, so it wasn't an epiphany of epic proportions, nor did it mean that my life would change in wonderful ways. But it gave me something firm and solid to hold on to, something to inspire me, and this I urgently needed.

Breaking me from this cheerful thought, Kyle said, "Come here," and grabbed my arm, guiding me toward two foxy girls standing and chatting near the front entry gate, holding books. "Kristi, Sharon, this is Kevin, he lives on my street."

"Hey Kevin," said the petite blonde, real cute and bubbling with friendliness.

"Hi," said the other, a striking brunette with a smooth, olive complexion.

I glanced sideways to catch a glimpse of Shelly, but she was lost among the crowd; no doubt lost forever, right along with summer. Returning my gaze, I released a hopeful grin at the brunette and decided that despair, though well-deserved and easier to adopt, couldn't possibly take me where I wanted to go. And I had many places left to explore.

# ABOUT THE AUTHOR

**Michael Stringer** has written numerous media articles, short stories, screenplays, and nonprofit grant proposals. Through his grant writing and fundraising efforts, he continues to help secure needed resources and services for underprivileged children and adults. He resides in Long Beach, California with his lovely wife and two wonderful daughters. Michael recalls the 1970s as a decade of extraordinary discoveries, awesome music, nonstop athletics, and endless infatuations. *Training Wheels* is his first novel.

Visit his author website at:

*https://sites.google.com/site/michaelstringerbooks/*